MASQUERADE

By Rivka Spicer

Copyright © 2012 Rivka Spicer

ISBN: 978-1-4717-0074-3

All rights reserved. This book, or parts thereof, may not be reproduced in any form without permission from the author. Exceptions are made for brief excerpts used in published reviews.

*For those that were there in my darkest night
And reminded me that day will always dawn
You know who you are.
I love you now and always.
R xxx*

*I thought once how Theocritus had sung
Of the sweet years, the dear and wished-for years,
Who each one in a gracious hand appears
To bear a gift for mortals, old or young:
And, as I mused it in his antique tongue,
I saw, in gradual vision through my tears,
The sweet, sad years, the melancholy years,
Those of my own life, who by turns had flung
A shadow across me. Straightway I was 'ware,
So weeping, how a mystic Shape did move
Behind me, and drew me backward by the hair;
And a voice said in mastery, while I strove, ---
'Guess now who holds thee?' --- 'Death,' I said. But, there,
The silver answer rang, --- 'Not Death, but Love.'*

Elizabeth Barrett Browning (1806 – 1861)
From her book: Sonnets from the Portuguese

Prologue

...The first thing you leave behind when you become a vampire is your sense of morality. All life becomes a game, a twisted masquerade where everyone is a pawn to be used to suit your own ends. I used you mercilessly and I will confess all but you should know that it is the hardest thing I have ever done. The remorse I feel is the only thing keeping me upright and loving you and I hope that one day you will forgive me...

CHAPTER ONE

"Don't you think this is all just a little too...19th century?" Oceana complained, curving a piece of wire across her friend Jo's nose to make a template.

"No." Jo grinned at her. "Come on! It's a masquerade ball! It's romantic and fun and an opportunity for you to make bucketloads of money in the name of a good cause. You know everyone will buy their masks from you when it's announced."

"But what if I can't make them?" Oceana pointed out. "That one for the local drama group might have been a fluke. They're complicated."

"I know. But I've seen the drawings and I know the theory works and that one you made for the play is awesome so stop complaining and do what it is you do best."

"Fine. Whatever." She worked in silence for a while, curving several pieces and writing measurements on a piece of paper. "What colour are we going here?" She asked when she had everything she needed. "Have you picked a dress? Is there a theme other than masquerade?"

"I haven't picked anything and the charity doesn't really have a theme outside of work which we do every day so I don't know. I want something striking."

Oceana thought about it. "Traditionally I think most masquerade masks are either animal shaped or plain black, red and white. I'm not sure what I've got." Rolling her chair to the other side of the workshop she lifted down her two largest bead trays and set them on her desk, flipping the lids to look through them.

"These are gorgeous!" Jo immediately selected a handful of deep cerise fire polished beads that shimmered in the light. "Have you got anything that would go with these?"

"Probably." Oceana took them and smiled. "Give me a couple of days to draw up a design and I'll bring it to work on Tuesday."

***

"That's an extraordinary mask." A voice as rich as chocolate slid into her ear.

"Thanks. It's one of mine." Oceana turned round to see who had spoken and, despite the mask he was wearing making it hard to tell, she was pretty sure she didn't know him. A plain black leather band covered the upper half of his face but it couldn't hide an unruly mop of thick black hair and startlingly blue eyes, or a jaw line you could injure yourself on it was so chiselled.

"One of yours as in you made it?" He seemed amused and she self-consciously touched the beads to make sure they were all still in place.

"Yes. I made a few of them that people are wearing." She pointed to a couple nearby and he looked obediently.

"But yours is the most beautiful." He replied when his attention returned to her. It was said with just enough humour to be charming instead of sleazy and she laughed, flattered.

"Thank you." There wasn't much else she could say without sounding ungracious.

"Is it sea glass?" He lifted a hand to her face and touched gentle fingers to some of the free hanging beads at her temple.

"Yes. I collected it myself on a holiday to Scotland last year. I bought the pearls though."

"And where is home?" He enquired, still pouring on the charm. "I assume it's not Scotland? This is rather a long way to come for a party."

"West country." She'd been in her job too long to give out too much information to strangers she'd just met. "What about you? I'm pretty sure we've never met before. Where do you live?"

"Here and there." He laughed easily. "I split my time between here and London but I travel abroad a lot too. What do you do...?"

"Oceana." She held out a hand but instead of shaking it he raised it to his lips and kissed it gently.

"It's a pleasure to meet you Oceana. What a beautiful name and of course the mask now makes sense. I am Tristan. So, what do you do?"

"I'm a data indexer." She was so flustered she struggled to get the words out

"It's a little more complicated than that." Jo interrupted, obviously deciding Oceana needed help. "She's part of an investigative team."

He didn't take his eyes from Oceana's. "So you don't make jewellery for a living?" He queried and Oceana shook her head.

"It's just a hobby." Feeling a little unnerved by the way he was gazing at her, those ice blue eyes in the middle of all that black leather, she turned to Jo. "How is the party going? Are we raising a lot of money?"

"A fair amount. That's why I came over." Her eyes turned pleading behind the cerise and gold chequered mask Oceana had made for her. "So many people have been talking about the masks I was wondering if you'd consider offering one as a prize for the auction? I know they're expensive to make – I'll give you the costs back." She took Oceana's hand. "Please? Pretty please?"

Laughingly, Oceana agreed. "Sure. They were kind of fun to do."

"Excellent! I'll come back for a business card for the winner." Jo hugged her and rushed off to add the prize to the expanding list on the board by the raffle table. Oceana turned back to Tristan but he was gone. Puzzled, she craned her neck to look around but she couldn't see him anywhere. That was weird. He'd been so charming and she hadn't even heard him leave.

"That guy seemed kinda cute." Jo commented later as they waited for the dessert plates to be cleared from the huge dinner they had just eaten.

"Most of his face was covered with a mask." Oceana replied drily. "Having nice eyes doesn't mean he doesn't look like a horse."

"Ah, but you thought he had nice eyes." Jo grinned and swatted her playfully on the arm. "Where did he go?"

"No idea. I think you scared him off." Oceana deadpanned. "He ran away when we weren't looking."

"I'm sure he'll find you later. The dancing hasn't even started yet."

"Whatever." They hushed as the coffee was served and then before they could speak again the raffles started. The first few went quickly with a couple of speeches in between and then the auction started. There were almost twenty items to get through and because everybody was well-oiled with champagne they were going for crazy prices. By the time they got round to the masquerade mask they had raised almost three thousand pounds for the charity not including the entry tickets and the atmosphere was electric.

When the prize was called everyone wearing one of Oceana's masks stood up to display them as instructed by Jo and people started clapping when the auctioneer commented that they had been designed and made by one of the organisers of the event. Blushing, Oceana abruptly sat down and if anything the cheers got louder.

The bidding started and quickly went up to three hundred pounds but it petered out at three twenty-five. The auctioneer called for three thirty and searched the crowd but the people driving it up all shook their heads. The auctioneer raised the hammer to close it and then a voice rang out clearly from the back of the room.

"Five thousand pounds."

The room went silent as everyone spun round to see who had spoken, Oceana among them. She got to her feet to see who had made such an insane bid and didn't know whether to be amused or astonished when the stranger in the black leather mask stepped forward.

"Five thousand pounds for the mask." He repeated again.

"Are you sure?" The auctioneer was just as astonished as everyone else and Tristan grinned, revealing a perfect row of shining white teeth.

"Yes I'm sure. Five thousand pounds."

"Well...uh...ok." Clearing his throat the auctioneer looked around and composed himself. "Anyone bidding higher than that?" Silence greeted his question and he shrugged. "Five thousand pounds it is." The hammer came down and the room went wild.

Tristan's eyes met Oceana's across the room and slowly, so she couldn't mistake it for anything else, he winked at her.

"Oh my God!" Breathlessly Jo leapt to her feet and crushed Oceana in a hug squealing ecstatically. "That's doubled the amount for the charity!! Oh my God!"

"What the hell?" Oceana was just too stunned to take it in.

"I told you he liked you!!" Jo was still squealing. "Oh my God! Five thousand pounds! Just think of all the people that will help!!" That was true and Oceana shook off enough of her astonishment to be overwhelmed with gratitude. It was a charity close to her heart – the Police Dependents Trust was there to care for her friends and colleagues and those they left behind. They fundraised for it every year but this year...with that extra five thousand on top of the biggest and most lavish ball they had organised yet, they were looking at almost doubling any previous totals. It was incredibly humbling. God only knew how they'd top it next year. She didn't know what on earth Tristan had been thinking. He must be crazy. Rich and crazy.

When the furore died down and the auctioneer continued with the rest of the auction Oceana left the hall and went to the ladies to calm down. Her cheeks were flaming and she was finding it hard to breathe in the crowd. It was all too much.

Crashing through the doors she tore at the ribbons holding her mask on and pulled it away from her face, the pieces of tumbled glass tinkling against the porcelain as she set it on the edge of the sink. Cooling her trembling hands under the cold tap she held them to her cheeks and forehead, gulping in great heaving lungfuls of air until her heart finally settled.

"Are you okay?" His voice startled her into a yelp and she spun round, catching a heel on the tiled floor and tumbling right into his arms.

"What are you doing in here?" She demanded, cheeks flaming from embarrassment now as he set her back on her feet. "This is the ladies room."

"I saw you run out. Thought I should check that you were okay." He shrugged. "I waited in the hall but you've been in here almost ten minutes."

"So you just decided to come right on in?"

He held his hands up in defence. "I was pretty sure there was no-one else in here and I could hear the taps running."

"Oh." Turning away she paced the few steps to the wall and back. "What were you thinking?" She blurted suddenly. "Five thousand pounds?! That's insane! Most of these masks retailed for a couple of hundred."

"I was curious." He stepped towards her and tucked a loose curl that had fallen forward onto her forehead back into her up-do. "My, aren't you a pretty little thing?"

"Could you be any more patronising?" She demanded but he didn't back off, laying gentle hands on her bare shoulders.

"What are you Oceana?" He pressed his cheek to hers as he whispered in her ear and the hairs on the back of her neck stood up as he inhaled the fragrance of her hair.

"I told you. I'm a data indexer." She hated that her voice sounded breathless.

"I didn't ask what you did." His breath was warm against the shell of her ear and the leather was almost sensual against her skin. "I asked what you are."

"What do you mean what I am?" Bewildered she pulled away from him and he searched her face, frowning.

"You-" He was interrupted by Jo's entrance and they sprang apart.

"Oh! I'm sorry!" Jo didn't look sorry at all – her smirk clearly said she thought they had been kissing. "I was looking for Oceana. The dancing has started."

"You found me." Her cheeks were burning again. "I was just coming back." She reached for her mask but Tristan beat her to it, deftly sweeping it from beneath her fingertips.

"Here, allow me." He waited for her to turn to the mirror and lifted the mask to her face, brazenly meeting her eyes in the glass, piercing blue in all that inky black. She bizarrely found herself thinking that he had spectacular eyelashes. "Is that too tight?" He murmured, deft fingers arranging her curls over the ribbons.

"No. It's good, thanks." He turned her towards him and untwisted a small dangling pearl that was sticking out so it could hang free again.

"Beautiful." He smiled dazzlingly at her and she wondered what was under his mask...if he was as gorgeous as the bits she could see promised. "Well, since I have just promised an obscene amount of money in return for one of these..." he flicked a crystal sending it spinning in the light "...the least you could do is honour me with a dance."

"Too right." Jo stuck in her tuppence worth and Oceana sighed inwardly.

"Of course." She smiled graciously and accepted the arm he offered her, allowing herself to be swept past Jo and back out into the party.

In line with the theme of Masquerade they were dancing in large groups following a caller so they didn't get much of a chance to speak but he didn't take his eyes off her as they swung and passed and met up with each other. He held her confidently and with a practised ease that spoke of many hours spent dancing with women. Oceana didn't know what to make of it all. She knew she had a pretty face and a figure some women would kill for but men found her intimidating. The few blind dates she'd allowed her friends to set her up on had been disastrous. She was too blunt, too articulate and not at all free and easy with her body. It had been a lonely few years.

They danced for most of the hour, sipping drinks in between sets, until finally the caller stepped down and the string octet launched into an unscripted piece. Without asking Tristan drew her into his arms and swept her into a slow and stately waltz.

"Stop fighting me." He told her mildly as she tried to minimise body contact and concentrate on not stepping on his toes both at once. "Relax and flow with the music. I know you have rhythm."

"Sorry. I don't know how to do this." She blushed under her mask and he laughed, flashing again those pearly white teeth.

"You don't have to. Relax into me. Come closer." Realising that ignoring him would be a disaster and possibly cause her to be a laughing stock, Oceana gave up and relaxed into his arms, allowing him to press the full length of her to his body. "And now move with me." He dropped his cheek to hers and counted softly with the music as they stepped as one. The sensation of whirling about in perfect harmony was so amazing that Oceana totally lost sight of her discomfort about being so up close and personal with a stranger. She spun when he pushed her out and leaned when he swayed her body. They stepped and whirled and spun and stepped again until Oceana was laughing and it felt like they had covered acres of dance floor, totally lost in the music and the rhythm, the melody of his voice counting in her ear and the warm masculine scent of this charming and perplexing man.

When the music stopped there was a round of applause and Oceana flushed beetroot red behind her mask as she realised everyone around them had stopped to watch and they were dancing alone in the wide space.

"Take a bow." Tristan told her mischievously and she realised he had known all along they were causing a scene. Mortified, she dropped a quick curtsy and went to leave the dance floor. "Not so fast!" He pulled her into his arms again, his muscles feeling like corded iron beneath his tux. "Now that we have the hang of it perhaps we can talk this time?"

The strings struck up another tune and the dance floor filled around them with other people happily waltzing about.

"What would you like to talk about?" She asked, unsure whether to lean her head against his chest or try and look up at him.

Amused, he pressed her head back to his chest with the arm that was around her back. "When can I come and claim my prize?" He asked and she shrugged, letting her head rest against the hard planes of his chest.

"I'm off on leave until Wednesday and then after that it'll be the weekend as long as I don't get any call outs."

"Call outs?" He asked and she realised she'd have to give away some detail.

"I work in a specialist unit that deals with serious complex crime and murders. They're managed on a different database to regular crime so if one of these major crimes happens my team all gets called in to work on it. We can do up to 16 hour days in the first rush of the investigation."

"And the rest of the time?" He seemed genuinely interested and Oceana didn't realise she had tensed until she relaxed into him again.

"I'm a full time indexer so I work nine to five on all the current cases we still have ongoing at a smaller station closer to home...the unsolved cases or the ones where information is coming in slowly. If there's nothing coming in at all, which is rare but sometimes happens, I form part of a team that reviews other force's cases. Fresh eyes sometimes spot leads that the original team missed. We do that two or three times a year."

"That sounds fascinating. So do you get to travel much?" He spun her out so she waited to answer until she was back in his arms.

"Not usually. Sometimes I'll travel for murders if the area it happened in doesn't have an indexer and they need to establish a forward control but it's always within the force and Avon and Somerset isn't a massive area."

They were silent for a few moments while he absorbed that information and then he chuckled. "So as long as no-one gets murdered between Wednesday and Friday you'll be off next weekend?"

"Yes. But it's only Saturday." She pointed out, lifting her head to look at him. "You can come any time between now and Tuesday if that suits you better."

"True." He flashed her another dazzling grin as his eyes focused on her own. "Perhaps I'll come Monday. Is your address on the business card?"

She nodded, feeling a little dazed at the force of the megawatt smile-gaze combination. "Can you stop with the eye thing?" She said awkwardly and he blinked.

"What eye thing?"

"That look that says you're trying to drown parts of my soul before you imagine me naked." She quirked her lips in a grin. "You focus your gaze absolutely and then your right eye narrows slightly in something that's halfway between a suggestion and a wink."

"I didn't realise I was doing it." He was still grinning though and now she didn't want to know what was going through his mind. "Are you sure you won't tell me what you are?"

"I have no idea what you mean by that." She replied helplessly. "I'm just a regular person with a slightly macabre job."

He stepped back as the music finished and studied her carefully with none of his earlier teasing before leaning in to whisper in her ear once more. "Then why aren't you afraid of me?" Before she could answer he spun on his heel and walked away, moving quickly through the crowd, and Oceana didn't know whether to follow him to ask what he meant or be astonished into motionlessness. She opted for astonishment and was staring after him when Jo caught up with her.

"It's just like a fairy tale!" She gushed excitedly. "Except he's Cinderella – the stranger at the ball who has to go before the stroke of midnight. Where's he going?"

"I think he's leaving." She could just see that mop of black curls at the payments table, obviously laying out the five large he'd bid for one of her masks. Then, without looking back, he made for the door and left.

***

Oceana stayed in a hotel overnight on Saturday and travelled home to her house in Gillingham on Sunday afternoon after helping with the clear up at the venue in Bath. The staff had worked miracles so there wasn't much to do. She and Jo between them settled bills, collected found items of property and packed up the remaining merchandise and adverts that were still left lying about. She got home about four o'clock in the afternoon and roasted herself a small chicken. It seemed excessive for one person living alone but she could have it in sandwiches and salads for a couple of days afterwards and the extra potatoes and vegetables would make a fine bubble and squeak. It had been so long since she'd had to cook for anyone else that she had stretched meals out to a fine art.

She went to bed early, still exhausted from the ball, and awoke on Monday morning to find it was a beautiful day. The sun was shining across her terraced garden but it wasn't quite warm enough to sit outside so she made a pot of tea and a couple of slices of toast and went through to her workshop to start on a commission she was supposed to be making for a guy at the station. She was busy cutting jump rings with her jewellers saw when the doorbell rang and she was so engrossed in her work she didn't hear it the first time.

It wasn't until it rang the second time that she remembered Tristan might be stopping by to get his measurements done. "Damn it!" She rushed her plate through to the kitchen, checked she didn't have any smears of jam on her face and then opened the door. There he was, standing in the porch looking like a male model. That jaw line was balanced out by gorgeous cheekbones, accentuated by the dark streaks of his brows over those startling cornflower eyes. "My," she said drily "aren't you a pretty little thing?"

He grinned. "I guess I deserved that."

"Come on in." Stepping aside she let him into the house and took his jacket, refusing the impulse to breathe in the fragrance from it as she hung it up in the hall. "Can I get you a drink?" She offered. "Tea, coffee, soda, juice, squash, beer...the list is endless. It's maybe a little early for beer."

"I'll have whatever you're having." He replied easily, following her through to the kitchen, and for one crazy moment she was tempted to pour herself a stiff vodka. Luckily she reined it in and went for the fridge.

"I'm going to have iced tea. It's warm in the workshop today."

"That wasn't on the list." He poked fun at her. "Sounds lovely though." He examined the kitchen as she fetched down tall glasses and poured from a jug she already had made up. "You have a beautiful home. Do you live here alone?"

"Yes. And thank you. It was my grandparent's house. They left it to me." She handed him a glass. "The workshop is through here." She walked past him and stepped through the archway into the huge sunny oak frame conservatory her grandparents had added onto the house just a couple of years before they died. The light was so clear and bright in there it made the perfect workshop and Oceana loved it. She'd made sun catchers to hang from the rafters that swung gently in the breeze from the open windows, painting the simple white-washed wall a myriad rainbow colours.

"Wow." Like most people he was drawn to the racks of beads at the far wall, poking around in them with a gentle finger. "You have a lot of stuff."

"I make a lot of stuff." She smiled. "Did you have any idea what you wanted? I was going to say, considering the amount of money you bid you don't have to have a mask if you don't want to. I'm happy to make you a piece of jewellery instead."

"Actually yes." He turned those hypnotic eyes on her. "I was hoping you would give me your mask."

"My mask?" She blinked. "The sea glass one? You want that one?"

"Yes." He seemed amused. "I thought I might hang it on my wall as a memento of an excellent evening."

"Oh. Then yes. Of course you can have it." Slightly flustered, Oceana retrieved it from the drying racks by her ultrasonic cleaner and reattached the ribbons. There had been a couple of smears of face powder on the inside so she'd put it straight in to clean when she got back. "Are you sure you don't want something else? I can make you something else just for you."

"You can if you want to." He shrugged. "I'm happy with just the mask but I'd be honoured to have an original I can wear."

"Okay." Feeling slightly happier she studied what he was wearing. There was no jewellery to go on and his clothes were casual but trendy. She couldn't see any logos which probably meant they cost more than she earned in a year. Frowning slightly she asked him what kind of jewellery he normally wore.

"I'm curious to see what you would choose if you didn't have my input." He told her with a small quirk of his lips and she frowned again.

"Okay." She thought about it for a moment and then went to her fabric shelves. Rummaging through the boxes she finally produced a sheet of soft leather tanned a gorgeous mahogany brown. She'd been saving it for a rainy day project but it had never really seemed to fit anything until now. Tossing it onto her work table she moved on to the trays of findings, selecting several bags of stainless steel and bronze jump rings in different sizes, adding them to the leather. Finally she selected two tiny buckles and put them on the pile. "Right." Settling in with a pen and pad of paper she quickly sketched up a design. It was going to be a cuff with a wide leather base and a raised layer of leather on top of that which the buckle would attach to. Over that upper layer she was going to make a flat narrow strip of decorative chainmail in large steel links with bronze detailing to add some flair to the design. She drew the top view and the side view and then handed him the pad. "I've got a picture somewhere here of what that particular weave looks like." She flicked through a portfolio and finally showed him a picture. "This is the same weave done in sterling silver and gold but it'll look good in steel and bronze. Especially in contrast to the leather."

"I'm impressed." He actually seemed surprised. "That looks exactly like something I'd buy."

"So would you like me to make it for you?" She prompted and he nodded like he didn't realise he was doing it.

"Yes, please. That would be great."

"Cool." Feeling immensely pleased with herself, Oceana propped the pad on her display stand and returned the portfolio to the shelf. She tried to ignore the closeness of him as she measured his wrist and wrote down the numbers. "It'll take several hours to make. Are you back down this way at any time to pick it up or would you like me to post it to you?"

"How many hours?" He checked his watch and Oceana shrugged, trying to work it out in her head.

"Maybe three or four. That weave is fiddly but it won't need soldering."

"Then I'll happily park my ass in a chair and wait. I'll even treat you to lunch." With a face that brooked no argument, he sat down with his iced tea in her comfy armchair under the window where she liked to sit and sew and watched her with an intent expression.

"Oh. Okay." Slightly nonplussed Oceana just got on with it. There wasn't much else she could do.

With practised hands she started connecting up jump rings, referring to her manual occasionally for instructions on the weave. It was a design she didn't make very often and there were so many hundreds of weaves she just couldn't remember them all. An hour later she had her strip of chainmail and after she'd tested each closure again she put it into her tumbler to bring up the shine and remove any burrs from the saw. While that was going she cut the leather and stitched it on her heavy duty machine. It was one of the most expensive items of machinery in the workshop and it shot through the soft leather as though it was no harder than butter. Once that was done she stitched the buckles onto one side and then made handmade rivets for the straps. He mostly watched her in silence but when she started fixing the chainmail to the leather with tiny handmade wire staples he cleared his throat.

"How did you get into this? Isn't it kind of a weird hobby for a data indexer?"

"Not really." She was too focused on the piece to look up at him. "They're actually very similar disciplines, especially with the graphical indexing. It's all about the attention to detail and how things link together – fact to fact, bead to bead, link to link, wire to wire. They're both time consuming." Fixing the last staple she flexed the cuff several times to make sure it moved and nothing fell off and then she grinned. "All done. Now the moment of truth..."

She went to him and fixed it to his wrist, fitting it snugly. "That's pretty awesome." He held his arm up to admire it and Oceana grinned.

"It's a pretty kickass cuff, even if I do say so myself. Can I take some pictures for my portfolio?"

"Of course." He let her snap a couple of shots and then he sat back in the chair. "I find you something of an enigma, Oceana." He declared suddenly. "I believe you when you say you don't know what you are but I don't know how that's possible. Do you know what I am?"

"I'm guessing you own your own business because you travel a lot?" Oceana suggested and he frowned.

"I didn't ask what I did for a living, I asked if you know what I am."

"Not a clue." She said cheerfully. If he wanted to ask these questions all over again she might as well just let him get on with it.

"What do you feel when you look directly into my eyes?" He questioned intently and she looked at him.

"Maybe a little flustered. They are very blue."

"Flustered? That's it?" He seemed startled and Oceana blushed, nodding. It wasn't like she could admit that just looking at him turned her on. It wasn't the sort of thing one said in polite company. Getting to his feet he came closer to her and his voice dropped to a soft purr. "Are you afraid of me Oceana?"

"No." Confused by...certainly. Turned on by...definitely. But scared? No. "Should I be?"

"Yes. You should." Taking the camera from her hands he tossed it onto her desk and took her shoulders in strong hands. "You should be very afraid of me and I don't understand why you aren't. I'll ask you one last time, do you know what I am?"

"You're kinda weird." She pointed out but that clearly wasn't what he was after.

He bared his teeth and faster than she could blink four tiny little fangs snicked out of his canines with an almost audible whisper. "Now is it any clearer?" He asked and Oceana gaped, leaning in for a closer look.

"Oh man! That is some incredible dentistry! These must have cost you a fortune!" Reaching up she went to touch one and he jerked his face away incredulously.

"They're real." He growled, half horrified and half in disbelief. "Are you crazy?"

"Well what did you want me to say?" She demanded defensively. "Back off or I'll stake you Mothersucker?"

"What?" He blinked, taking in her last few words again and then he started howling with laughter. He had to let her go and bend double, he was laughing so hard he couldn't stand straight.

"I'm sorry but I don't believe in vampires." She held up her hands. "There's no such thing."

"I beg to differ." He wheezed, finally getting his breath back as the laughter trailed off. "I'm right here."

"Yeah well you may well just be crazy." She pointed out. "Did you think of that?"

"I can prove it." Slowly and deliberately he unbuttoned his shirt and bared his chest, Oceana's eyes following his every move as she swallowed. "Come here." He pulled her to him, brushed her hair out of the way and pressed her ear to his chest. "Listen very carefully." He commanded.

For several moments they stood in silence and then Oceana realised what he was trying to show her. "Oh my god." The blood drained out of her face. "You don't have a heartbeat."

"That's because I'm dead." He said it as though he was agreeing the sky was blue. "But in case it wasn't enough, watch this." He reached for a pair of scissors from a nearby toolbox and drew them across that perfect expanse of chest, leaving a bloody gash behind and then, right before her eyes, the skin began knitting itself together, sealing up the cut in moments and after a minute or two there was nothing there to say it had ever been injured except a bright crimson smear of blood on the surface.

"Oh my god…"

CHAPTER TWO

Oceana woke up in her bedroom and blinked at the ceiling, totally disorientated. "Welcome back." Tristan sounded amused and Oceana flinched, realising he was sat in the chair under the window, his shirt still gaping open.

"I'm guessing that crazy stunt you pulled downstairs wasn't a dream then?" She muttered and he laughed out loud.

"No it was real. I can do it again if you want?"

"No that's quite alright." She pushed herself upright. "How did I end up in here?"

"You fainted." He smirked. "I didn't want to leave you on the floor. This seemed like the logical place to bring you."

She frowned at him. "The polite part of me wants to thank you for your consideration but the rest of me thinks it's totally your fault for freaking me out like that."

He shrugged. "You can hold it against me. I'm an amoral bastard. I couldn't care less."

"Why did you tell me?" She asked curiously as she swung her legs over the edge of the bed and faced him. "Aren't you worried I'll tell someone?"

"Who would believe you?" He pointed out calmly. "Besides, I could kill you faster than you could open your mouth to scream so it's not worth you even thinking about."

That was chilling. Oceana absorbed this for a few moments and then got to her feet. "I think I need a cup of tea before we have this discussion." She walked out without waiting to see if he would follow and went down to the kitchen, grateful that her wobbling legs didn't give way beneath her. She boiled the kettle in silence as her brain tried to process what she had just seen. It had to be an illusion. Vampires didn't exist and that was all there was to it. She was sure a good dentist could explain the teeth and he may just have a very slow, very quiet heart beat. It was the cut that floored her. She had seen it with her own eyes slowly knitting up into unblemished skin. She just couldn't see how it was done.

Ignoring Tristan she went back through to the workshop and picked up the scissors he had used, examining the blade. It was smeared with viscous red liquid and when she held it to her nose it smelled metallic. It smelled like blood.

"I'm telling you the truth." He said quietly from the archway to the kitchen. "I know it seems insane but it's real."

"I'm sorry but it's going to take me a while to accept that." She told him honestly. "My brain is trying very hard to explain what it thinks is an elaborate hoax. I don't even know what to ask first." She returned to the kitchen to finish making the tea and he gave her space to pass, watching her warily in case she freaked out again.

"Try with the obvious." He said eventually and she sighed.

"How old are you?" Her hands shook as she fished the teabag out of the mug and set it in her little dish.

"Old enough to remember Hadrian's Wall going up." He replied calmly and Oceana shook her head in disbelief. That was almost two thousand years ago.

"Do you drink blood?"

"Yes." He grinned again but the fangs were nowhere in sight.

"But how? You can't just go round biting people. We'd know."

He shrugged nonchalantly. "I keep pets."

"Pets?" Oceana was bewildered. He drank animal blood?

"Yes pets." He stretched out in his chair. "I have six women at the house who regularly donate but I don't actually bite them all that often."

"Women?!" Oceana was horrified. "You called women pets?!"

"Well what else do you want me to call them?" That twisted quirky smile was back. "Mobile blood banks? Sentient protein shakes? I house them, I feed them...I don't socialise with them. They're pets."

"That is so fucked up." Oceana was utterly repelled by the idea.

"I need to eat." He wasn't defensive about it, more determined to make her understand. "What else can I do? Raid the hospitals? Hunt people in the streets? They have a nice life. I keep them well."

He had a point but it was still a horrible concept. "So...what? You don't bite them?"

"No, one of them was a phlebotomist. They fill blood bags."

"Why?" Oceana was dumbfounded. "Isn't that why you have fangs?"

"It's part of how we hunt in the wild. Our fangs are very like snakes – they inject a viral venom. I'm the world's deadliest predator. Ordinarily if I was hunting I'd snare someone with my eyes and bite them and they'd wake up two or three days later feeling like they'd had the flu with a vague memory of blue eyes and nothing else."

"What do you mean snare them with your eyes?" She'd managed to suspend her disbelief enough to develop a morbid fascination with the process.

"It's the predator-prey fear reaction." He leaned forward and gazed at her. "That's what makes you so unusual. When I gaze at anyone else they freeze like a rabbit in the headlights. It's involuntary. You on the other hand gave me attitude. I don't know why that is and therefore it's dangerous."

"I'm no danger to you." She promised but he shrugged.

"I'm a pragmatic man Oceana." The name rolled smoothly off his tongue. "If I can't control you someone else might and I can't allow that."

"That's crazy." A ripple of fear slithered down her spine. "If you hadn't liked my mask you'd never have approached me at the ball. You'd never have known I was different. I'm not even convinced I am different. I'm just a regular person."

"What's done is done." He dismissed her protest. "I need to know what you are and why my gaze doesn't work on you."

"And if you can't figure it out?" She was proud that her voice didn't shake.

"I haven't decided yet. The simplest thing would be to kill you but it's been a really long time since I was with anyone that didn't turn into a mannequin the moment I looked at them."

"What do you mean *with* anyone?" Her heart sank into her boots. "I'm not going anywhere with you. Have you forgotten who I work for?"

"That wasn't what I meant." His eyes twinkled and despite her fear something warmed low in Oceana's core. She could imagine that several hundred years of relations with unconscious women would make a man...vampire needy for some reciprocation.

"So you kill me or seduce me?" She demanded. "What kind of choice is that?"

"An easy one." He winked. "There is a third choice...we work out what you are."

"I'm a regular person!" She insisted and before she could blink he was up and leaning over her, a steady hand placed firmly on the worktop on each side of her.

"No, you're not." He slowly and deliberately inhaled the fragrance of her hair. "Personally I prefer the option that involves fucking like bunnies so if you want to maintain the argument that you're a regular woman be my guest."

She tried to push him away but it was like trying to move a megalith. "What are the possibilities?" She asked, giving up on pushing his chest and trying to move sideways instead. "What could I be?"

He easily scooped her into his chest and held her there with both arms. "Stop fighting me. I don't intend to kill you yet." Yeah...yet. "I suspect you're some sort of witch."

"A witch?" That was almost as bizarre as the existence of vampires.

"That or you've been given some charm or amulet." Strong fingers trailed down the back of her neck searching for a necklace and making her shiver all over. "Do you have an item of jewellery that you were wearing the night of the ball that you're wearing today?"

"No." She had been wearing a sea glass bracelet at the ball but her mask had been so spectacular her neck and ears had been unadorned. She wasn't wearing that bracelet now.

"Any tattoos?"

"No."

"Are you sure?" His hand slipped under the back of her top and caressed the bare skin beneath. "Can I check?"

"No you can't." She flushed crimson and he laughed, his breath rustling her hair.

"Are you wearing any jewellery now?"

"A bracelet but it's nothing like the one I was wearing on Saturday. Different stones, different wire too."

He frowned. "But you made them both?" She nodded and he shrugged. "Perhaps that's it. Perhaps it's any piece of jewellery you make that's charmed. Take it off."

"I can't. You're squashing me." He released her but she didn't take the bracelet off. "What will you do to me if this means you can snare me?" She asked quietly, fingering the links of the bracelet in shaking hands, and he studied her.

"I'll put it back on. If you can make magical jewellery it might be a useful skill."

"Do you promise?" He might be an amoral bastard but his behaviour so far had been relatively honourable. Relatively being the operative word.

"You have my word." He took the cuff that she had made him off as well and waited as she removed her bracelet, setting it carefully on the counter. "Now...look at me."

She turned her face to his and her breath caught in her throat. His eyes really were extraordinary...that clear, perfect cornflower blue that shone like the silvered touch of moonlight. They were so beautiful they made her throat ache. They seemed luminous and otherworldly and Oceana finally had to accept, even as she felt like she was suffocating in them, that he was something other than human. She didn't feel fear. She felt full of awe and wonder, like someone had opened her eyes to the mysteries of the universe. They were so beautiful she almost felt like crying.

"Oceana?" Someone was calling her name from a distance but she ignored it, trying to hold onto the spell for as long as she could, like a dream she didn't want to emerge from. "Oceana?" It was closer now and she blinked, looking down as something tickled at her wrist. Just like that the spell was broken and the air and sound rushed back in.

"Oh my God!" She gasped, stumbling backwards and catching herself on the work top. She turned her back to him and tried to pull herself together but her legs were shaking and she had to lean on the counter to hold herself up.

"Are you okay?" He sounded cautious and Oceana took a shaky breath.

"You were so wrong." She muttered, touching her bracelet to reassure herself it was back where it belonged. "So wrong."

"About what?"

She was about to tell him and then realised it was a foolish thing to do. If he thought she was afraid of him it might come in handy later when she needed to do something he didn't expect. The sad truth of it was that the memory of the extraordinary beauty of his eyes still ached in her consciousness...it was like spending a single day with an incredibly handsome and charming man and knowing that nobody else would ever compare. It might pass and she hoped it would but right now she felt like he'd ruined her for any other man.

"It wasn't long enough." She protested weakly. "I didn't have a chance to try and move."

"Oceana you were under for several minutes." The amusement was back but she sensed he knew she was lying. "I had time to kiss you thoroughly and then put my bracelet and yours back on before you blinked."

"You kissed me?" Her hand flew to her mouth but she couldn't recall the slightest sensation of lips moving against hers.

"Well it was that or bite you and I didn't want you incapacitated for a few days." His calm attitude was so chilling...like a fundamental violation of her person and rights was completely acceptable to him. "Putting mine back on didn't break the snare...it was putting yours back on that did which makes me believe that they're designed to protect the wearer, not prevent anything."

"Then I'll make you some things to take away and you can have any woman you want." She told him angrily, still too shaken to turn round and face him down.

There was a silence and then his hands came around her shoulders. "I can't figure out if you're upset that I snared you or upset that I kissed you."

"I'm upset that I ever bloody met you." Her heart had gone into freefall realising that now he had proof he was never going to let her just continue with her life. "I wish you would leave me alone."

"Well now my feelings are hurt." He didn't sound hurt. There was an amused arrogance to it. "Too late princess. I'm here and I'm staying around. I am just *dying* to know what else you can make."

"Right now I'm going to make lunch." She tried to shake his hands off her shoulders but they tightened and he swung her around to face him.

"Don't you understand that this is an opportunity for you to learn about yourself?" He asked irritably. "You have a gift. I can help you learn how to use it."

"For what purpose?" She shot back. "I was doing just fine with my life without knowing what my jewellery does. You want me to learn so that you can use me so forgive me if that doesn't exactly sound like a great deal on my part."

"There are worse people out there than me." He told her. "Sooner or later somebody would have put two and two together when they came across someone they couldn't snare."

There were more of them out there? Oceana guessed it stood to reason but it was still a frightening thought. "And what happens when I'm no longer useful to you huh?" She demanded. "You just kill me?"

"It's a possibility." He responded calmly and Oceana's jaw dropped. He was serious. "Look, this is a pointless conversation to have. You may be useful to me all your days."

"Well that's just great. I spend the rest of my life as a slave to your needs or I die." She'd never felt so helpless in her life. "You know what Tristan? I'd rather die free. You may as well kill me now. I'd rather have no life than spend the rest of it beholden to you."

His jaw twitched. "You want to die now?"

"Yes." She gazed at him steadily and her voice didn't shake. "I only ask that you make it quick."

For the longest time he stared at her and then he shook his head. "I won't do it Oceana. You're too valuable an asset." Relief almost made her knees buckle but she was filled with a bleak despair. "And don't try to kill yourself." He said softly, searching her face with something akin to concern on his own. "I'll just bring you back. Working for me isn't as bad as you think it will be."

She gritted her teeth. "Yeah, I heard you treat your pets well."

He chuckled, rich and melodious. "Oh Oceana, you'll never be just a pet. I might bite you once in a while when you are disobedient but I want you for much, *much* more than that..."

Something in her thrilled low and dark at the word disobedient as it flowed off his silver tongue and she squashed the sensation ruthlessly. "Well whatever it is you want, you're not going to get it willingly."

"Oh I will." He smiled at her, not his usual dazzling beam...this was something darker, twisted and mischievous. "Half the fun is making you want me."

"I'm just some game to you?" She demanded incredulously.

"Existence is a game." He replied lightly, chucking her under the chin. "And I always win. Now make your food. I have to fetch something from the car."

Something turned out to be a blood bag and he sat there drinking it through the tubing while Oceana ate her chicken salad. It wasn't as disturbing as she thought it would be, even when he tried to wind her up by making slurping noises.

"You'd think you'd have learned some manners in the centuries you've been alive." She remarked acidly. "For an old guy you're surprisingly childish."

"I've really missed someone being rude to me." He sounded surprised. "Who'd have thought? I don't even want to kill you right now." He smirked. "Bite you yes, but kill you no."

"Why do we never see bite victims?" If she couldn't get rid of him then she needed to learn what she could. It might come in useful later. Part of her was thinking that her colleagues at the station would turn over every stone on earth looking for her if she just vanished and she needed to be as armed with knowledge as possible to leave them clues. "I know you said you don't bite people all that often but they take a while to heal up."

"It's to do with the venom." He took another slurp from his baggie. "How up are you on your science?"

"I studied biology at A-level. Try me."

"Do you know what a retrovirus is?"

"Yes." Vaguely. She could look it up later to remind herself of the specifics but she knew it was a virus that altered the DNA of the host's cells.

"Vampirism is a retrovirus. It alters the host DNA to force massively accelerated regeneration in response to trauma. When we bite someone enough venom is injected to force the regeneration of the damaged area so it heals up before the fever fades."

"And the fever?" It was fascinating.

"Classic immune response – the body naturally fights the virus. It's like having the flu."

That made a weird kind of sense. "So how do you become a vampire if the body naturally fights off the infection?"

"You have to overwhelm the immune system – multiple bites all over the body over a sustained period of time until the body gives up and the heart stops."

"That sounds…" she swallowed. "Brutal?"

"It is." He grinned.

"What about those myths that you can make it pleasurable?" There had to be some basis for them.

"It is pleasurable for me." That dark smirk was back teasing his lips. "For the victim it depends on their pleasure-pain response. For some people when they are together sexually a little pain just gives the pleasure that special edge and a vampire's venom can be milked much like a snake's to make the bite harmless for a brief while. Of course that means the bite doesn't heal but then a lot of subs enjoy being marked."

"You're doing the eye thing again." She told him drily, ignoring the fluttering of her libido. "It's not going to work Tristan. So what else isn't true? Daylight clearly doesn't bother you. Is garlic an issue?"

"I don't eat solids. The smell bothers me but I'm not allergic to it." His eyes twinkled. "Well, I say I don't eat solids but that doesn't mean I don't like sinking my teeth into solids."

"What about stakes through the heart?" She asked, ignoring the suggestion.

"Doesn't work. My heart doesn't beat. Stabbing it won't make any difference. Crosses don't bother me either."

She wanted to ask how you kill a vampire but figured that would probably give it away. "Do you have a soul?"

For the first time he looked a little disconcerted but he quickly recovered. "If I have then it's as black as pitch and probably beyond redemption."

"See here's the thing Tristan." She said boldly. "I don't think you're as dark and twisted as you like to make out. Yes, you're a predator and yes you're used to getting what you want but you're not lost. You're not lost."

"What makes you think that?" He asked coldly and Oceana gave him a level look.

"There's too much humour and charm in you. Yes, there's a black backdrop to it but it's there. And you've learned restraint. If you had lost every shred of your morality you would have abducted and raped me the minute you realised you couldn't snare me. It wouldn't matter whether I wanted it or not, it's the fact that I was moving while you did it that's the novelty."

"And are you so sure I won't do that if you continue to refuse me?" His voice was still cold but Oceana was sure her intuition was right.

"I don't think you will." She took a deep breath. "I think you're lonely."

"Lonely." He said flatly. His jaw twitched and then before she had time to blink he was up and had yanked her out of her chair and pressed her up against the wall. "Let's get one thing straight princess. I can have you and then discard you any time I want."

She gasped as a firm hand slid up her rib cage under her top and his thumb caressed the cup of her bra. "You can. But you won't." She repeated breathlessly.

"Are you trying to provoke me woman?" He growled, pulling her head to one side and dipping his, lowering warm lips to her neck.

"No. Just speaking the truth." She felt the barest scrape of teeth against skin and then he backed off. She didn't realise she was shaking until she realised she'd heard his fangs snicking out and had come within seconds of being bitten.

"Fuck." She wasn't sure which of them had said it first but they were both breathing heavily.

"I see vampires breathe then?" She tried to regain control of the situation and he nodded slowly.

"We don't have to but it's a useful habit to maintain the illusion of humanity."

"I see." For lack of anything better to do she retrieved her plate and carried it to the sink, scraping the last few lettuce leaves into the compost bin. "I have things to do this afternoon." She managed a little more calmly when her hands had stopped shaking. "I need to go to the supermarket and I have commissions to make."

"It's been a while since I last went to a supermarket." He declared mildly and she stared at him.

"Tristan, you can't follow me around all the time. Eventually you're going to have to go and deal with your women. I certainly don't need you coming food shopping with me."

"I don't trust you not to run."

She sighed. "What are you going to do when I have to go back to work the day after tomorrow? You can't follow me in the station. It's a secure building. And you can't stay here. You're going to have to leave eventually." He levelled an amused look at her and her heart sank. "Oh no...you are NOT staying over!"

He broke out into a full blown grin. "I am just *dying* to see you try and throw me out."

"Tristan, this is my home. I'm not going to run. I have nowhere else to go." She pleaded. "You don't have to stay."

"Maybe I want to." With infuriating casualness he returned to his chair and leaned back in it. Sensing he was getting a perverse satisfaction from her distress, she refused to play along.

"Very well. I shall make up a guest room." She walked to the hallway she slipped on her sandals and fetched her bag. "See you at the supermarket." Without a backward glance she stepped out the front door and headed for the car. She heard the door slam behind her and then there was a rush of air as a dark-clad figure sped past her. By the time she arrived at the car Tristan was standing next to the driver's door smirking at her. "As you wish." She tossed him the car keys and went round to the passenger side. His jaw twitched but she wasn't sure if it was with amusement or confusion.

Settling herself in the chair she stared serenely out of the window as he climbed in the driver's seat and started the engine. There was an awkward silence in which she couldn't help grinning and then he turned to her. "So where's the supermarket?"

"Well now, you were so keen to drive I thought you knew where we were going."

His jaw twitched again. "Fine." He backed out of the driveway and drove to the end of the cul de sac where it met the main road, looking back and forth, left and right. Finally, with clearly no idea at all where he was going he turned right and tried to find somewhere they could buy food. After a good half hour of pointless driving he pulled over and turned to her. "Okay. You've had your fun. Where the hell are we going?"

"Turn left at the next set of lights." She could have played all day but she knew they were running low on petrol and being stranded with him might have taken some of the shine off her amusement at his helplessness. She directed him to the shops and even allowed him to open her car door, despite thinking it was terribly old-fashioned. He drew the line at pushing the trolley and instead followed her around the shop, observing with a perverse fascination the whole process, poking at packages of raw meat with morbid curiosity.

He followed wordlessly through the checkout, dropping items into carrier bags and loading them into the car after ensuring she was safely in the passenger seat. For a brief, disconcerting moment Oceana found herself thinking she could get used to it. Then he got in and smirked at her.

"Where to now?" He asked and she fixed the smile back on her face.

"Home please chauffer. I have projects to be getting on with."

"As you wish." Definitely amused now he drove her home and carried the bags in while she unpacked.

"You know, you're terribly domesticated for someone that likes to think of themselves as a dangerous predator." She couldn't resist teasing. He was entirely too full of himself.

"I find this all rather intriguing if I am honest." He gestured all around him at the house and the food. "I haven't needed to pretend to have a normal life for many centuries. Last time I had need of actual cooked food it was of the kind that we hunted with bows and arrows and roasted on spits over open fires."

"Yes." She smirked this time. "You do have a touch of caveman about you..."

He did a good impression of affronted but she sensed he saw the funny side of it. "I'm sure it adds to my charm."

When she was done unpacking, she made herself a cup of tea and then returned to the workshop to work on the projects she'd started before he had knocked on her door that morning. Tristan spent a while touring the house, perusing books and looking at pictures before he finally followed her through to the workshop and sat back in the chair he had first sat in that morning.

"What are you doing?" He asked and she blinked.

"Micromaille." She was connecting tiny jump rings under a magnifying glass with her finest pliers.

"Micro what?"

"Micromaille." She held up what she was working on for him to see. "It's chainmaille in miniature. These unit weaves are for charms on a charm bracelet."

"May I?" She nodded and he examined them in detail as she continued the one she was working on. They were extraordinary and he found himself staring at her, wondering if she had any idea at all how good she actually was. "So what are you thinking as you make them?" He questioned and she shrugged.

"Nothing. They're so intricate and fiddly that you have to focus totally on what you're doing. With tiny charms like this the minute my mind starts wandering I get them wrong or drop them."

"That's odd." He sounded troubled. "Most magic comes from the will or intent. If you aren't exerting any will or intent then it must come from something else but I don't know what."

Oceana set her tools down on the work bench. "What do you mean 'most magic'? Are you saying there are other people like me out there?"

"There are many of them but most keep well hidden. We don't have much interaction with them – they can be dangerous to vampires and most are well trained in protecting themselves." He set down the charm he was looking at and picked up another one to study. "In a lot of cases the magic streak runs in the family...witches grow up knowing exactly what they are. Do you have anyone in your family that is of the occult persuasion?"

"No." Oceana shook her head. "But my grandma died when my dad was just a kid. He doesn't remember her and I certainly never knew her."

"I'll look into it." He returned the charm to the desk and went to sit back in the chair. "Sorry, I'm interrupting you. Carry on."

He watched curiously for the rest of the afternoon and she ignored him absolutely, focusing on her work with single-minded dedication. By the time her stomach rumbled loudly she had finished enough charms for 2 bracelets and had made up enough chain for 3. Looking at the clock she realised it was early evening so she went through to the kitchen and made up the bubble and squeak she'd planned the day before. Tristan watched with bizarre fascination as she mashed up leftover vegetables and fried the cake in butter but he didn't comment and sucked his way through another blood bag while she ate. When the washing up was done she was tired so she showed him how to use the tv and where the guest room was and then went for a long bath.

Emerging an hour later she wasn't really surprised to find him lying on her bed but it did present something of an issue. If she played the game straight she just wouldn't comment and climb in beside him but that might give him totally the wrong idea. If she went and slept in the guest room herself he'd know he made her uncomfortable. After a second's hesitation she sighed inwardly and climbed under the covers. Eventually he'd give up trying to get a reaction from her. Tomorrow night she'd wear her onesie.

"You are just no fun." He declared as she turned her back to him and turned the bedside light off. "Can we spoon?"

"Whatever." She managed not to flinch when his arms came around her and he was surprisingly warm. "Goodnight Tristan." She mumbled sleepily, snuggling into his warmth, and he sighed.

"Goodnight Oceana."

CHAPTER THREE

He woke her up by shaking her gently. As her eyes focused blearily Oceana looked at the clock and saw it was just after 4am. "Phone." He told her. "It's for you."

She blinked and realised he was holding her mobile out to her. It had been on silent on the bedside table so it hadn't woken her when it rang. "Hello?" She answered sleepily, sandwiching it between her head and the pillow. "Uhuh. Uhuh. When?" She rubbed her eyes. "No I'm still on leave until Wednesday. Oh I see. Sure. Do we have a suspect? Right. I'm on my way." She sighed and pulled the phone out, ending the call and chucking it on top of the covers.

"You have to go somewhere?" Tristan asked and she nodded.

"There's been a multiple homicide. I have to go in."

"Oh. Here, I'll help." He got up and went to make coffee while she got dressed and threw a few things in an overnight bag. When he returned with the hot mug she was almost done and he got dressed himself. "You look exhausted." He commented, noting with concern the dark rings under her eyes. "Where do you have to go?"

"Bristol. They'll put me up in a B&B until they have enough of a case to arrest the guy."

"Then I'll drive."

Too grateful to argue she forced herself to eat a bowl of cereal with her coffee and packed several snacks into her handbag while he loaded her overnight bag into his car. She knew from previous experience that meal breaks were few and far between when a case was just taking off and hunger was distracting. She slept most of the way into the city and woke up as he was pulling up outside Police HQ.

"Thanks for the lift." She told him quietly when he opened her door and he semi-smiled in the pre-dawn light.

"My pleasure. Don't assume this means we're done for now. I'm coming to collect you at the end of the day. You don't have a car after all."

"Oh." She wasn't sure what to make of that.

"My number is in your phone. Text me when you're almost done and I'll come fetch you."

"Okay." He squeezed her arm and watched her walk into the station. It was going to be a long day.

***

He collected her just after 8pm and she looked absolutely shattered. She stared grim-faced out of the window as they drove through the city, not saying anything except to give directions to the hotel they had booked her into. All the B&Bs were full but she didn't really care. It was just a bed to sleep in – she'd be back in the office at 7am the following morning.

"Have you eaten?" Tristan asked after they had checked in and she shook her head listlessly.

"I'm not really hungry. I just want a shower."

"You have to eat." He told her stubbornly. "Go shower. I'll order room service so it'll be here when you get back."

"Okay." It was like the fire had gone out of her. Pale and drained she turned from him and sloped into the bathroom. Moments later he heard the shower start up and then the unmistakeable sound of sobbing. Torn, he didn't know what to do. She was desperately vulnerable in her naked state and wouldn't appreciate his presence but then she was clearly hurting and he needed her to be on her game. In the end he left her to it and ordered a steak sandwich with a side of chips so that at least she could sleep on a full stomach. While he waited he switched the tv on and scrolled until he found a news channel. The murder was the headline story on the local news – 3 kids found dead in their home, all stabbed multiple times with a kitchen knife. No wonder she was so distraught. Murder was never a clinical business but this was particularly gruesome, especially with the victims being children.

He switched it off when he heard the water cease and a few minutes later she came out dressed in her pyjamas just as there was a knock on the door. Tristan took the tray, tipped the staff and carried it to her in bed.

"You have to eat." He said firmly and so she took the plate and chewed through the food, not really tasting it but using it as a distraction. "You want to talk about it?" He asked, taking the now empty plate from her lap and she shook her head.

"I can't. Data protection."

He hid a smile. "I've seen some of it on the news. I know it was kids. I just want to know that you're okay."

"I'm fine." For a second it looked like her face might crumple but then she collected herself. "It's a bad one but it's as much frustration at the system as it is sadness for the victims." Her eyes turned distant. "It could so easily have been prevented." She murmured. "If only the system wasn't so goddamn lenient. Makes you think they should never have done away with the death penalty." Sighing, she dry-scrubbed her face with her hands. "Sorry. In the day when you're there you just get on with the job and detach yourself from the details. It catches up with you later. I'm fine. Really."

He didn't believe her but having an argument would just make it worse and she'd been at the office for more than 12 hours. "Okay. Let's just sleep. What time do you want waking?"

"6am please."

He climbed in beside her as she stretched out flat and folded her into his arms. "Consider it done."

***

For the next 3 days they followed the same pattern. Oceana was in the office by 7am every morning and didn't leave until after 8pm. Tristan picked her up, drove her to the hotel, listened to her sob in the shower and then fed her dinner, watching her sleep in disturbed exhaustion. He knew this wasn't an ordinary case, that she didn't get this distraught over 'regular' murders. Finally he persuaded her to let slip a few details and then he understood why.

The kids had been killed by their stepfather. He'd had an unnatural interest in the daughter and when she had told him about some boy she'd been in the playground with at school he had flown into a jealous rage and butchered them all with a kitchen knife. The mother's statement and the statement from the doctor that had done the post mortems had been harrowing. What was worse was that the stepfather had been in and out of jail for various violent offences and the mother had left him several times, seeking help through women's refuges, but like a drug addict she had returned to him time and time again until eventually he had snapped. The social work system had failed those kids, the mother had failed them, the justice system had failed them...and now they were dead. It was guilt as much as a desire for justice that was driving the investigation team. They had to do right by those kids because everyone else had let them down and they'd paid the ultimate price for it.

On the fifth day Oceana finished early and Tristan picked her up outside Police HQ just after six.

"You broke the case?" He asked her as she climbed into the passenger seat and she nodded.

"They have enough now to get him remanded indefinitely until trial. I can help from my regular office from now on. They're keeping on staff who live closer to here in the major incident room so they don't need me any more."

"Then I'll take you home. Let's go pack your bag."

"No." She took a deep breath. "I need to stay in the city tonight. I have this...ritual." She couldn't look at him. "We all do...everyone has things they do at the end of a really bad investigation...you know...to remind ourselves we're still alive when it's been a really brutal case. For me I go out...I drink and dance a lot and..." She didn't seem able to finish and Tristan nodded understandingly.

"You pick up some guy and have wild anonymous cathartic sex until you've let it all out." He finished for her. She turned away to look out the window and he could sense the rush of blood beneath her skin as she flushed, ashamed of her need to be alive and free. "It's okay." He told her gently. "I get it. You need to feel alive."

"I hate it afterwards." She said in a tiny voice, still staring out the window. "I've only done it a couple of times and I'm always safe but I hate it and I feel dirty in the morning."

He studied her for a long time. "Would you hate yourself if it was me?" He ventured carefully when the silence became too much to bear and her shoulders slumped.

"I don't know. Why would you even offer that?" Exhaustion was creeping into her tone. "It won't make you feel like you won Tristan. It isn't you I'll want...it's the physical act. It's the peace I can get from being a mindless bundle of pleasure. Somehow I don't think that's going to be enough for you."

"You're right." He started the engine and eased the car out of the parking space. "It isn't enough and I won't feel like I've won but I really need you to pull yourself together and after spending six days with you I feel possessive enough that I might be forced to rip the throat out of anyone that comes within a mile of being in your pants."

"Hey, don't be so stingy on the honesty..." She cracked a brief smile and he grinned, reaching across and squeezing her arm.

"Don't ever make the mistake of thinking that I'm human Oceana." Despite the smile his tone was serious. "I don't have the same motives or morals."

"Like I hadn't figured that out..." She finally turned to look at him. "You just about referred to me as a possession just then, like I'm some sort of pet or tool. Humans don't keep other humans as pets."

"Don't ever forget it." He focused on the road as they drove back to the hotel and they didn't talk much more until they got back to the room. Oceana rummaged through her back, pulling out a small bundle of soft black fabric that she shook out into a small spaghetti strap dress. Her defensive look dared him to judge her for coming prepared but he held his hands up and went to the cupboard to fetch a fresh shirt instead, ignoring the sounds of swishing fabric and splashing in the bathroom as she stripped to get in the shower.

They went to a restaurant first and he watched as she ate a hearty meal, playing with his glass of wine and watching with some amusement. "Why blood?" She asked as her dessert was served. "I get the whole virus thing but I can't understand why it makes you need to ingest blood."

"We can only consume liquids." He explained. "Peristalsis stops with death, much like the heartbeat. If I tried to eat something solid it would get stuck halfway down my throat." He made a face. "It's not pretty. The regeneration process takes a lot of nutrients, most of which are found in blood. That's why our physiology is adapted to it."

"Do you miss food?" She asked curiously and he shrugged.

"I didn't used to. It's been so many centuries I've forgotten what it tastes like. But now...watching you demolish that dessert I'm wishing I could understand what it was that gave you such pleasure."

"Food was a big part of my childhood." She wasn't ashamed of her appetite. "I love to cook and I eat out a lot at home. I don't mind travelling to good restaurants." She grinned as she polished off the last of her ice cream. "I always said that if I got rich I was going to treat myself and my brother to dinner at the world's best restaurant."

"Which is?"

"El Bulli." She sighed, pushing the remaining sticky toffee pudding around the bowl. "Unfortunately it has a six year waiting list and it just closed for an indeterminate length of time so I guess if I got rich we'd have to settle for the second best restaurant in the world."

"Which is?"

She grinned. "El Celler de Can Roca."

"I've never heard of it." He admitted and she laughed.

"Why would you have? Food isn't your thing and in any case it's in Spain. I don't suppose you ever take holidays out there to check out the local gastronomic scene..."

"True." He gestured to her bowl. "Are you going to eat that?"

She looked at the squidgy mess she'd made of the remains of her dessert and shook her head. "No."

"Then let's go dance." Despite her protests he paid the bill and they went in search of a club.

Finally they found one playing dark, heavy rock beats that thrummed through the street and sang in Oceana's blood. "This one." She murmured and he took her hand, pulling her to the head of the line and snaring the doorkeeper with his eyes to let them past. "Neat trick." She muttered and he grinned.

"Being undead has its advantages. What do you want to drink?"

"Something with a lot of alcohol in it but no whisky. And nothing fizzy please."

"Your wish is my command." He kissed her hand and let her dance away into the pulsing gyrating crowd on the dance floor.

They danced for a couple of hours, sliding up against each other in the semi dark, the touch and rhythm a promise of something primal to follow. They were moving, lost in their own world, hips touching, fingers stroking, eyes closed, breathing together with the music flowing through them limb to limb. He sensed it, the moment she finally let go of the death and destruction, the sadness and horror. She was pressed against him and she looked up into his eyes, her pupils dilated with a heady blend of alcohol and desire.

"I'm ready." She murmured under the music and he nodded.

"Okay." He took her hand and led her to the door and they rushed up the street in search of a taxi. They sat in silence all the way back to the hotel but she was tracing circles on his arm with lazy delicate fingers. It was maddeningly sensual, especially given the way her dress clung to her body, sliding against the curve of her breast every time her arm moved.

They rushed through the lobby and up the stairs, too impatient to wait for the lift and Tristan let them into the room with a crash as they almost tumbled through the door. Their lips crushed together as he kicked the door closed behind them and he pressed her up against the wall as her fingers deftly undid the buttons of his shirt.

"Slowly...slowly." He whispered, catching her hands. "We don't have to rush." He kissed her again, more gently this time but she was hungry for more, her hands twining around his neck to hold him close. Scooping his hands behind her thighs he lifted her up and she wrapped her legs around him as he ground into her, their hips sliding together almost as though they were dancing to silent music.

"Yes..." She whispered as his lips marched south along her jaw line and down the side of her neck. "Oh god that feels good."

She pushed his shirt off his shoulders and he carried her across to the bed, shrugging out of his shirt sleeves as he knelt over her. She lifted her hips as he slid her dress up and over her head and tossed it over his shoulder somewhere into the dark room behind him. She lifted her hands to the button of his jeans as he kissed her again and he lifted his head to look down at her. Her face seemed almost haunted with hunger and he closed his eyes.

"Forgive me." He whispered, releasing the catch on her bracelet and flinging it away across the room.

"Wha-" She blinked and he opened his eyes, gazing down at her and she was snared instantly by him. "So beautiful..." She murmured, reaching up to touch his face with trembling hands and he sat back.

"Go to sleep Oceana." He stroked her hair back from her face and got up, pulling the covers over her. "Go to sleep."

***

She woke the following morning as he was putting their bags by the door ready to load the car. He'd laid out an outfit for her and she blinked around in disorientation as the previous night's events came flooding back to her. "Tristan?" She rubbed her eyes and sat up.

"I'm just going to put these in the car. Your wash kit is in the bathroom." He didn't look at her as he shouldered the bags and reached for the door.

"Tristan why did you stop?" She sounded confused and he paused for a moment. She could see his jaw twitch.

"Because it wasn't me you wanted." Before she could say anything he was gone and out the door and she was left wondering what had happened.

When she returned from her shower breakfast was waiting for her and he had paid for his share of the room. Hers had been paid for by her work so all she had to do was eat while he made another trip down to the car with her toiletries and then they left the hotel to head back to her home in Gillingham.

"Are we going to talk about this?" She asked after they had driven in silence to the outskirts of the city and he shook his head.

"No." He glanced across at her. "Are you hungover? Do we need to stop for aspirin?"

"No I'm fine." They drove in silence for several more minutes and then she swallowed thickly. "Thank you. For stopping. I'm confused but I don't feel...dirty."

He made a non-committal hmm sound and carried on driving.

Eventually she snapped. "Tristan we have to talk. I don't know what you're doing or where the hell we go from here. I have to be back in the office on Tuesday. When are you going to run out of blood? When are you going home? What is it that you want me for? I already told you I'd make you whatever you wanted."

"I'm not going to discuss it with you while I'm driving." He told her bluntly. "We'll talk about it when we get to yours. Our meeting was no accident Oceana. I was looking for you. I have a proposition for you."

"But..." She didn't understand. How could he have been looking for her if he didn't know what she was or what her jewellery did? He had seemed surprised when he couldn't snare her and she'd spent enough time with him to realise that his surprise had been genuine. It didn't make any sense and she stewed over it in silence all the long way back to her home.

He carried the bags in while she made a cup of tea and then they sat in the living room, looking out across the garden.

"So speak." She gestured as he settled down. "Why were you looking for me?"

"Because you are the best at what you do." He replied simply. "I had need of an indexer with a specialism in investigation. I asked around and everywhere I went I came up with the same name...yours. The fact that you happen to be gifted with magic was entirely coincidental."

"Why didn't you tell me? We've spent six days together. And what on earth do you need an indexer for?" She stared at him. "I don't understand."

"I didn't tell you because I needed to know I could trust you. And I need an indexer because something is going on. I'm being used and I can't see why or for what purpose." He flexed his shoulders and leaned back in his chair. "I hunt vampires for a living Oceana. I am the long hand of the law...the Executioner for the Vampire Council and believe me, I am *very* good at my job. Every now and then I get a kill list – vampires that have broken the rules or threatened to expose our kind – and I go out and kill them." He gave her a grin that was all tooth and fang but it soon faded. "Lately I've been getting names on my list that don't make sense. Vampires I know, people that would never break the law or expose us. I don't know why they are being placed on the kill list and every time I try to ask questions I get shut down. I don't like it."

"So why can't you investigate yourself?" She asked and he shrugged.

"I don't have time. If my kill rate goes down or my actions start looking suspicious I may well find myself on someone else's kill list and that would be...inconvenient."

"So hire a private investigator. Indexers aren't cops. We don't actually investigate." She pointed out but he shook his head.

"I know your job. I know you are the ones that write the actions that the cops obey. I know you know how to investigate but that's not the main reason. When I started getting more names that didn't make sense I started collecting journals from the vampires I killed. I need you to index them, find the links. There has to be one somewhere."

"Vampires write journals?" She didn't know why that sounded so weird but it did.

"Most of us do after the first century or so." His eyes turned a shade wistful. "That's when you realise that your memories fade just as they did when you were a person. After a while you can't remember anything in detail so most of us write down the main events in our lives for future reference." He sipped his tea. "I've written journals containing first-hand accounts of every major event since I was turned...the rise and fall of the Roman Empire, the discovery of the New World, the black death, the great fire of London, two world wars...I was there at all of them."

She shuddered at the thought of all that time stretching incomprehensibly away from her. "That's fucked up."

"And yet part of you is curious." He pointed out, his self-confident smirk firmly back in place. "You want to read them."

"Of course I do." She didn't see any point in lying. "Anyone would but that's not the point. You want me to index the journals of your victims to try and find the link between them?"

"Can you do it? I will pay you extremely well."

She shrugged. "That depends. How many are we talking about here and over what time period? I need to know what software you have – I like to index graphically. And I'll need to take some time off work. That might take a while to organise."

"That's not an issue." He dismissed her concern about leave. "So far I've collected 12 sets of journals dating back to the dates they were turned but I have a feeling you'll only need to dig back a couple of years at most. If it was an issue from further back than that I'm certain they'd have been on my kill list long before now."

She gaped at him. 2 years worth of 12 sets of journals. "Do you have any idea how much work that is?" She demanded. "Depending on the detail in the journals it could take me months!"

"Then quit your job. Work for me full time. I said I would pay you handsomely."

"I can't." She looked troubled. "What happens after I've found your link? When you don't need me anymore? I can't burn my bridges here Tristan – I may well need a job to come back to."

"I'm pretty certain I can find you employment for the rest of your natural life." He insisted calmly but she was shaking her head.

"No. Tristan I can't do it. I won't immerse myself in your world. My job is my lifeline to the outside world...if I didn't have that I would never see anyone or spend any time with other people. I have dreams...dreams that involve getting married and having kids. How would I explain you or your kind in that?"

"You are already in my world whether you like it or not." He pointed out. "Sooner or later one of us would have started following the chain of people they couldn't snare back to you. If you work for me at least I am a generous employer. Others would simply enslave you."

"I can't Tristan. I'm sorry."

"Okay...let me put it like this. If you come and work for me I will do my damndest to ensure you get your dreams. You can go out, meet someone, get knocked up for all I care and I will make sure you never want for anything. If you stay here then I cannot and will not protect you. I have too many other things to be concerned with. But I feel it is only fair to point out that my time here will not go unnoticed. Others will come to investigate and you will be ripe for the plucking. You are already in danger Oceana. You are already in my world."

"You bastard." The seriousness of her situation was slowly sinking in and her hands started to shake. "You knew coming here would put me in danger."

"I came here because I needed you." He said simply. "That's all there is to it."

"Then I'll take my chances." She announced boldly, her cheeks high with colour. "I'm not coming with you."

"Fine." For the first time he looked angry. "Don't say I didn't warn you." And with that he got up and left, slamming the door behind him.

***

For the next two days nothing happened but in the early hours of Tuesday morning Oceana came awake in the night, alerted by some small sound. Seconds later her mobile rang and she picked it up.

Jo didn't bother with small talk. "Your neighbour just called in suspicious persons trying to break into your house. I've got a unit en route but I needed to know you were okay."

Fuck. Her stomach quivered as her heart turned to ice. Tristan had been right. They were coming for her. She heard a small rustle at the back of the house. "I'll go check it out and call you back." She disconnected the call without waiting for argument and sent a rushed text to Tristan – 'They're here, please help'.

Without turning any lights on she crept down to the workshop hoping that they hadn't realised she was awake. She couldn't be sure how many of them there were but she could hear tiny noises that said they were trying every door and window. Picking up some leather cord she began knotting it, sliding charms on here and there until she had a decent length of it and then she waited, her heart in her throat, for something to happen. At first she couldn't make sense of what she was hearing and then she panicked. They were lifting roof tiles. Giving up any hope of pretending to be asleep she grabbed a hammer and nails from where she had discarded them on the kitchen table earlier that day and hurtled headlong up the stairs. Balancing on the banister she frantically hammered the leather cord across the roof hatch opening to the attic and dropped back out of reach as the trapdoor was yanked upwards.

"What magic is this?" Howled a strange voice in frustration and Oceana caught a glimpse of a pale man with dark hair as she fled down the stairs. Realising it wouldn't take them long to start dismantling the ceilings she headed back to the workshop, scattering beads everywhere in her haste to find more leather. She heard the unmistakeable sound of footsteps landing in the bedroom above and heading for the stairs and she was just about to hammer another charm bracelet across the doorway to the workshop when the night outside lit up with blue lights and sirens began to wail. Sobbing with relief she waited for the footsteps upstairs to recede and ran through the kitchen, across the hallway and out through the front door onto the lawn, straight into the arms of the first officer to appear.

"What happened Oceana?" He asked, holding her reassuringly. "Did someone try to break in?"

"They came through the roof." She was shaking all over. "I think they knocked a hole in one of the ceilings. I was hiding in the workshop."

"Okay." Another two units pulled up to the house and her neighbour's lights started coming on as curious people stared out of windows at the scene unfolding in the street. Letting go of her, the officer spoke into his radio requesting CID assistance for a scenes of crime examination and then headed into the house. "Wait here."

"What happened?" Tristan was striding across the lawn looking furious and her shaking intensified.

"I don't know how many of them there were." She told him, her teeth chattering. "They came through the roof."

He pulled his coat off and wrapped it around her shoulders. It was a cool night and she was standing in her pyjamas with bare feet. "It's okay, you're safe now." He pulled her into his arms and they stood and waited for someone to give them the okay to head into the house.

When they were certain the house was clear and no intruders lurked anywhere within the officers called out to tell her it was safe to return. "You'll have to let me go first." Oceana whispered to Tristan, slightly more assertive now she had her fear under control. "Otherwise you won't be able to get in." Curious he let her step through the front door and she unobtrusively removed the bead and wire creations hung on either side of the door. "Try now." She murmured and he stepped through the door unhindered.

"That's why they came through the roof?" He asked, gathering the situation at once, and she nodded.

"I've been practising. I did all the doors and windows but I forgot the hatch to the attic."

"Clever." He smiled at her but she didn't have a chance to say anything else as they were called through to the kitchen.

It took the officers almost three hours to take statements and carry out the scenes of crime. Tristan went up to secure the roof with a tarpaulin as they were leaving and the last of the officers stopped at the door. "You going to be okay here?" He asked Oceana and she nodded.

"Tristan will stay."

"Good." He checked his watch and she realised it was almost 6am. "The DI says not to bother coming in today or tomorrow. Get your house to rights and we'll let you know what we come up with."

"Thanks." She waited until he was out the door before she let the tears start sliding down her face.

"Are you okay?" Tristan was coming down the stairs looking angry but concern had softened the lines on his face.

"It could have been so different." She tried to swipe the tears away but they just kept coming. "If it had been any operator other than Jo on the night shift tonight they wouldn't have called me and I wouldn't have been able to block the roof in time for everyone to get here. I didn't know if the wards were going to work. I had no way to test them."

"You were lucky." He agreed. "Lucky that you are who you are so they sent so many units as well. These were old ones...they could have taken out just two cops without too much trouble."

"You recognised them?"

He nodded grimly. "I saw them take off across the rooftops but I didn't know if you were alive or dead so I came here first."

"Thank you. I didn't know who else to call. How did you get here so quickly?"

A rueful smile flitted across his lips. "I didn't go far. I figured you'd change your mind after they came for you."

That stung slightly but she couldn't help feeling grateful. "Well thank you."

"You're welcome. Go get in the shower. It's pointless going back to bed now. We'll talk when you're a little warmer and calmer."

"Okay." She allowed herself to be shooed upstairs and obediently took a long hot shower, washing away the last of her fright in the tumbling warmth. She felt a lot calmer by the time she returned to her bedroom and even managed to crack a smile when a text came through from Jo – 'The boys tell me tall dark and sexy turned up. Spill now!!' Grinning she ignored the text and pulled on her favourite jeans and sweater, returning to the kitchen where she could smell fresh coffee.

"I would have made you breakfast but this is all alien to me." Tristan said without turning round as he examined the toaster.

"That's okay. I appreciate the coffee." He poured her a fresh mug from the cafetiere and sat opposite her at the kitchen table as she poured a bowl of cereal.

"So...the wards. How did you make them?" He asked curiously and she blushed.

"You told me that magic was about the will and intent so I fixed in my mind that I wanted them to keep vampires out as I was making them. It seemed to work."

"But only for the portals they were warding." He frowned and it made him look brooding. "There must be a way of protecting the entire house. I've seen it done before...centuries ago. There were temples we couldn't enter, wardings laid into the foundations of buildings."

"It never occurred to me that they'd come through the roof." Oceana pointed out, slightly embarrassed. "Perhaps the intent has to be slightly less specific. I was thinking of keeping them from coming in, in relation to the doors and windows...perhaps I should have been thinking that I didn't want them in the house full stop."

"It's not an exact science." He admitted. "I was intending to raid my library when we get back to the house, see what texts I had on the subject." She made a face at the use of the word 'we' and he levelled a steady look at her. "You do understand now that you must come with me?" He told her. "They will not stop. They'll come again and next time they'll be prepared. What would you have done tonight if they'd had humans with them?"

"I get it Tristan." She snapped. "Just don't expect me to like it or be happy about it."

"Well now you've hurt my feelings." He was too smug to mean it and she resisted the urge to throw her bowl at his head.

"Suck it up fang boy." She said acidly. "What the hell am I going to tell my boss? I can't just request a career break with immediate effect. I have to give notice."

"I'll deal with it." He flashed her one of his dazzling grins. "I know people who know people. It's not a problem."

"Even if you can deal with my boss I'm still going to need a cover story." She persisted. "It's a Police station. There are bound to be questions if I just vanish without a word."

"I said I'll deal with it." He told her. "You just do whatever it is you have to do today and I'll take care of everything. And don't worry about the mess upstairs. I'll get someone in to fix it."

"Thanks." She finished the last of her cereal and stood to take her bowl to the sink.

"One last thing." Without warning he blurred across to her and held her in a vice-like grip in his arms, jerking her head so that her neck was exposed to his mouth. "Don't ever call me boy again. I've lived more than fifty times your life span." He scraped his fangs lightly across the skin above her jugular.

To her credit she didn't shake or flinch, she just went very still and very limp in his arms. "But the fang part was okay?" She questioned meekly. "I can tell you to suck it up fang man?"

For a split second he was torn between ripping her throat out for her impertinence or being amused at her courage and then he roared with laughter, letting her go. "You play a dangerous game woman!" He warned her, amusement written into every line in his face. "One of these days you'll cross a line and I'll kill you."

"Then you would be cutting off your nose to spite your face." She pointed out. "You would be without witch or indexer."

"There are others." He reminded her mildly. "Not as good maybe but they're out there."

"I'll bear that in mind." She carried her bowl to the sink and rinsed it out, leaving it to drain on the side. "I have no idea what to do now. I was supposed to be going back to work today."

"Why don't you go into the workshop and work on your wards? I have calls to make."

"I've run out of wire." She admitted. "I wasn't expecting to have to bejewel my entire house. I've put in an order but it won't arrive until tomorrow."

"It maybe doesn't have to be expensive wire." He speculated. "Perhaps we could go to one of those DIY shops humans are so fond of and purchase some fencing wire."

"Maybe but I'd have to get some tools while we're there. I'm not using my jewellery tools on coarser wire."

"That's fine. I'm sure my budget can stretch to it." He grinned and she sighed.

"I'm not letting you buy me things I'm going to keep. Besides, while we're there I can get whatever I need to fix the hole in the ceiling up there."

"I said I would take care of that. And if I want to purchase you tools that you'll be using to work for me then you can consider it an expense. It's like having a uniform and a computer at your desk. They are the tools you need to do the job." His eyes twinkled fiendishly. "Would you wear a uniform for me?"

"Describe what you're after and I'll consider it."

"Well...uh..." Slightly taken aback it took him a second to regain his composure. "I'm thinking there'd be thigh high boots involved. And maybe a closely tailored dress...satin or velvet, I haven't decided yet."

"So far so cliché." She smirked. "I'm assuming it would be low cut and either black or red?"

"Actually no. I'm thinking forest green or sapphire blue...colours that would bring out the warmth of your skin. Maybe a warm autumn damson."

"Classy."

"But you were dead on about the low cut." He broke out into a full grin and Oceana laughed out loud.

"Of course. Well, get it made and I'll try it on but I'm not promising anything."

"Are you serious?" His jaw had actually dropped and Oceana nodded, trying to keep a straight face.

"Yes I'm serious. I just didn't realise you were that masochistic...watching me walk around in that all day and knowing you'll never get to lay hands on it, never get to take it off and find out what's underneath. It's going to drive you crazy. So yeah, I'm serious. Get it and I'll wear it. I'll consider it payback for you royally fucking up my life."

She could almost hear his teeth grinding. "I could have had you already, or was I mistaking your intent in Bristol on Saturday?"

"You could have. But you didn't. And I'm grateful."

Just like that his grin was back. "How grateful?"

"Not that grateful." She laughed. It was beyond her how anyone could be so mercurial. "I'll go get my shoes on. There's bound to be somewhere open this early."

"You will come to me willingly." He promised her quietly as she headed for the hallway. "One day in the not too distant future you'll come to my bed because you want to."

"Don't hold your breath." She muttered but he heard her and laughed.

"Why not? I'm dead. It's not as though I need the oxygen..."

CHAPTER FOUR

They returned from the hardware shop with 50 metres of aluminium fencing wire and 50 metres of steel wire along with several industrial tools. Oceana took them through to the work shop and it wasn't long before Tristan heard her power saw start up so he guessed she was cutting jump rings. It would be interesting to see what she made.

He made all the calls he had to and by the time he was done it was almost lunch time so he wandered through to the workshop with a cup of tea. "It's time for you to eat." He told her and she startled, dropping the piece she was working on.

"Damn it." She looked at the jumble of jump rings on the bench and her shoulders slumped. Once you lost the shape before you fixed it you might as well just give up and start again.

"Sorry, didn't mean to startle you." He set the tea down on the bench next to her.

"It's okay. I was concentrating. I didn't hear you come in." She smiled gratefully for the cup of tea and stretched her back out, twisting her neck to loosen it up. "What time is it?"

"Almost one. You've been in here for hours."

"One? Really?" He nodded and she blinked. "Wow...I must have been concentrating harder than I thought. Here, give me your hands." She took him by the wrists and bound them around tightly with a length of basic European 4 in 1 maille weave. "Try and snap that." He pulled his wrists apart seemingly without effort and twisted jump rings scattered everywhere. "Good. Now try and snap this." She wrapped them round again with another length that looked exactly the same and then watched his face carefully. At first he appeared untroubled and then he looked determined. Eventually he strained all out at the chain but it didn't seem to matter how hard he pulled, he couldn't get it to break.

"That's excellent." He studied them. "What was the intent? To tie a vampire up or simply to be unbreakable?"

She looked at him oddly. "To be unbreakable. Why on earth would I want to tie a vampire up?"

He raised an eyebrow. "Do you really want me to answer that question?"

"Knowing your filthy mind, probably not." Despite the obvious temptation to leave him like that she unwound his wrists and dropped the chain into a drawstring bag, already bulging with aluminium links. "I made a lot...figured it would come in handy at some point and it's easy to make."

"And lightweight. Aluminium is far lighter than steel."

"Yup." Setting the bag aside she selected a loose looking unit weave. "Um...this might hurt." She weighed it in her hand, indecision warring on her features.

"Will it kill me?" He asked bluntly.

"I don't think so. Not from your hand."

"You don't think so?" He gave her a long, level look and then sighed. "Okay, hit me with it."

She dropped the weave onto his upturned palm and instantly the flesh beneath it blackened and smoked, peeling back in raw red welts. "Fuck!" She snatched it away leaving behind a smell of roasting flesh. "I'm so sorry." Her stomach heaved and she legged it for the bathroom.

She returned, shaking, a few minutes later and he showed her his hand, unblemished. "All healed, no harm done."

Abruptly tears filled her eyes. "I can't believe I made something so horrible." She choked. "I was just so angry that they came into my home...I wanted to hurt them. I'm sorry."

"Don't be." He picked up a pair of pliers and poked idly at the weave. "You have every right to defend yourself."

"These are weapons Tristan. Not defensive mechanisms. They're designed to wrap around whatever you throw them at."

"Clever." Fascinated he teased one out so it lay flat like some sort of futuristic starfish. "I'm impressed."

"Well you shouldn't be." She snatched it from beneath his curious hands and tossed it in the bin under her work bench, grabbing everything similar from her desk and throwing them away too.

"Don't be foolish Oceana." He caught her arms and pulled her to him. "You live in a dangerous world now. I swear to you that you will never have to throw one of these in anger but it makes sense to have them to defend yourself."

"I don't want them." She reluctantly allowed herself to be drawn down onto his lap.

"I know. And that's what makes me believe you are the right person to have them. Listen 'Cean." He pronounced it She-an, like a shortened version of her given name. "I may not always be home to protect you. I have to travel for my job. It would make me feel better if I knew you could defend yourself while I'm not there. And if you will not carry them for your own sake then please make enough of them for the others...if anyone breaks into my home to steal you they will not spare my pets or my staff."

She drew a deep, shuddering breath. "I'll make them for your staff on one condition."

"Name it."

"You bring another vampire to the house so I can try and make wards specific to you...that will only allow you past. Once your house is safe these weapons can be destroyed."

"Done." He didn't even hesitate. "I know someone that owes me a favour."

"But can you trust them?" She pressed. "I thought you didn't want it getting out what I was or what I can do."

"I don't. But everyone knows that if you betray me you die." He grinned and his fangs snicked out. "I have something of a reputation."

"Great. Of all the vampires in all the world I had to meet the bogeyman." She managed a weak smile and he laughed.

"That's rather apt. Come on, drink your tea. I'll take you out to lunch."

***

When they returned there was a van outside her home with two workmen who spent the afternoon clearing up the destruction from the guest room where the vampires had come through the ceiling. They replaced the roof tiles and then came inside to replaster the ceiling. They worked quickly and efficiently but it was still after 6pm by the time they were done and they left promising to come back in a few days to paint the new plaster.

"You'll have to leave a key here." Tristan told Oceana seriously. "We need to head back soon. I'm running low on blood supply. Unless you don't mind me chowing down on you of course. I can try and remove my venom with a glass and some clingfilm."

"Not a hope."

"Shame." He flashed her a lopsided grin. "You look pretty tasty."

"Talking of tasty, I need dinner. Go sit somewhere and look ornamental while I cook."

"Ornamental?" Amused, he let it slide and sat at her breakfast bar while she put some water onto boil for ravioli. When her phone rang she was busy shredding herbs so he put it on speakerphone on the worktop between them.

"Jo!" Oceana smiled at the caller ID. "Aren't you at work tonight? How're you doing?"

"You ask me that?" She sounded furious and upset. "I'd say hurt and betrayed just about covers it."

"What?" Oceana stopped chopping and gaped at the phone. "Jo what happened?"

"What happened is that we got an email saying you were leaving and you didn't even bother to give me a warning. You're supposed to be my best friend Oceana."

"What?" Oceana was totally bewildered. "What email? Who from? What did it say?"

"I think this is where I step in with an explanation." Tristan had the grace to sound a little ashamed.

"Who's that?" Jo demanded.

"It's Tristan. Hey Jo." He cleared his throat. "Oceana didn't know. I went behind her back after her house was raided. I'm her government liaison."

Government liaison? Oceana mouthed at him in confusion but he shot her a glare.

"What do you mean she didn't know?" Jo sounded as confused as Oceana was.

"Yeah Tristan...what did you do?" Confusion made her tone acid.

"I spoke to my boss at the intelligence service. He pulled some strings and got you seconded onto the project with immediate effect. You're coming back to headquarters with me so I can keep you safe."

"But-" Oceana was astonished

"What project?" Jo was bewildered too. "Oceana, how long have you been working with Tristan? Is this why your house got broken into?"

"She can't tell you about the project." Tristan got there before Oceana could. "It's classified. And we haven't been working together yet. I approached Oceana with a consultancy offer after meeting her at the ball." Oceana stared at him, lying so glibly. It was a shocking reminder of his lack of humanity. "Her house got broken into by the operatives we're gathering intelligence on so yes, Oceana's life is in danger for as long as the project is running."

"Fuck." Jo sounded a little dazed. "I had no idea."

"Me either." Oceana levelled a steady glare at Tristan who tried unsuccessfully to swallow a smile.

"Sorry I got so mad Oceana. Will you be okay?" Jo had changed from hurt to concern and Oceana shrugged, forgetting momentarily that Jo couldn't see her.

"I won't let any harm come to her." Tristan promised. "I'll get numbers and email addresses to you as soon as we have encrypted safe lines."

"Oceana, can you take me off speakerphone please."

"Sure, just let me wash my hands." She rinsed the herb juice off her fingers and dried them, picking up the phone. "Okay, I'm here." Tristan gestured that he could still hear but backed off.

"Oceana, is he telling the truth?" She asked quietly. "Is your life really in danger?"

"Yes." That certainly wasn't a lie. Tristan could snuff her life out in a moment and his enemies had already broken into her home.

"Oh my god." Her voice broke. "Can he really keep you safe? Are you going to be okay?"

"He is the best at what he does Jo." Oceana responded quietly just as Tristan's arms encircled her waist. "If anyone can protect me it's him." He squeezed her once in assent.

"I had no idea." Jo sobbed. "How did you get mixed up in this? Why didn't you tell me?"

"Um...apparently I came highly recommended. I have...specialist skills." Tristan squeezed her again and she drew a shuddering breath. "I didn't tell you because I didn't know how...a secret project? Mysterious break-ins? Government agents? Who would have believed me?"

Jo gave a shaky laugh. "Well...when you put it like that..."

"It's all happened so fast Jo." Now Oceana was fighting tears. "I didn't have any choice. Tristan came to me and now I'm in danger and I can't back out of it until it's over."

"When are you leaving?" Jo was snuffling and Oceana tried to dry her own eyes.

"Tomorrow." Tristan whispered and Oceana took a deep breath.

"We're leaving tomorrow." She told her best friend. "I just need to pack some things."

"Where are you going?"

"I don't know." She admitted honestly. "To a safe house."

"Can I come in the morning? On my way home from work?"

Tristan nodded, his cheek brushing against hers, and Oceana smiled through her tears. "Yes, you can come by. I'll do breakfast. It'll be good to see you before I go." She could hear a radio crackling in the background. "You'd better get back to work. See you in the morning."

"Will do. Tell that man that if he lets even one hair of your head get harmed every man and woman in this station, officer and civilian, will hunt him down and break him."

"I'll tell him." She didn't have to. His body had stiffened...he had clearly heard it loud and clear.

"Good. You sleep well." Jo hung up and Oceana put the phone down.

"Government project?" She swung round. "Don't you think you could have given me some goddamn warning?"

"How was I supposed to know your boss would send an email out announcing your departure?" He asked mildly, refusing to relinquish his hold. "Hey, you look kinda good in my arms."

"Get out of the way Tristan. I need to finish cooking dinner and then I need to sort out what the hell I'm going to pack. I assume your house will need warding?"

"Yes." He released her back to the chopping board. "But you don't have to worry about that right away. Right now all I'm concerned about is getting you somewhere safe and the rest of it can follow later. I'll either send a team to pack up what you need or we'll come back in a week or so and collect your kit. I can even buy you new things...whatever. Your safety is my main priority."

"That's bollocks and you know it." Grinding her teeth she gently laid the knife down so she wasn't tempted to hurl it at his head. "If my safety was your main concern you'd never have come here or spoken to me. *You* are the biggest threat to my safety and we both know that."

"Yeah." The look in his eye chilled her to the bone. "And don't you forget it."

***

After dinner she retired to her room to pack some clothes and then headed into the bath for a soak. When she emerged Tristan was standing in her doorway.

"I can't get into your room."

"You're right." She smiled at him. "You are not my lover. You have no right to be in my room."

"Oceana!" He looked wounded but it had mocking undertones. "I'm hurt!"

"You'll live. Guest room is up the hall." Turning her back on him she folded another item of clothing to put in her bag.

"And there was me thinking we were getting along so well." He sighed. "Now I'll have to knock a hole through the wall just to get in."

"You can try but it won't work." She smiled sweetly at him over her shoulder. "I made that ward this morning. You can't come through the wall, you can't come through the ceiling, you can't come through the floor and you can't come through the bathroom. I'm many things Tristan and one of them is a fast learner."

Grudging respect lit his eyes. "That is so harsh."

"Good night Tristan." Walking over, she pushed the door closed in his face and went to climb into bed.

"Well now I'm really hurt." His voice was muffled through the door. "You leave me no choice." She heard him slump to the floor and then he started singing in an off-key voice. "Nine hundred and ninety nine green bottles sitting on the wall, nine hundred and ninety nine green bottles sitting on the wall and if one green bottle should accidentally fall there'll be..."

Grinning Oceana rummaged through the drawers by her bed. Before she'd done her indexer training she had done Jo's job and was well equipped for night shifts with the best silicone ear plugs money could buy. Finding the small box they came in she moulded them into her ears and drifted off to sleep in blissful silence.

***

When she emerged the following morning Tristan was in an absolutely foul mood. "How long did you sing for before you realised I couldn't hear you?" She asked, filling the kettle and switching it on.

"Not long." Judging by the clipped tone of his voice he'd clearly been out there an hour or more.

Hiding her amusement Oceana went to the fridge and started pulling out everything she needed to make pancakes. "Are you going to be grumpy all day?"

"Actually no." He stretched out in one of the chairs by the kitchen table. "I don't need to be. I've won. This afternoon you're coming home with me and after that it's only a matter of time before you're mine in every way. Last night was just a temporary blip."

"What is with the whole spooning thing?" She asked curiously. "Are you so desperate for physical contact?"

For a moment she thought he was going to brush it off lightly but then his shoulders dipped a fraction. "I have been alone a very long time Cean. You remind me of what I was...before."

"I'm surprised you can remember that far back." She didn't mean it in a nasty way and he didn't take it as such.

"There are some things you never forget." He said it so quietly she almost didn't hear it. She wanted to ask more but then the front door opened and Jo came in. Tristan moved so quickly that Oceana didn't realise he had until Jo squeaked in terror and froze in the doorway with a knife pressed firmly to her throat. "Jesus H woman!" Tristan roared, pulling the knife away and tucking it back into a sheath Oceana hadn't even noticed. "Didn't anyone ever teach you to knock? I could have sliced your head clean off right then."

"Jo doesn't need to knock when she comes to my home." Oceana said firmly and Tristan rounded on her.

"When there are people trying to kill you, everyone needs to knock! Do you want to get dead?"

"I'm sorry." Jo sank into the nearest chair when shaking legs wouldn't hold her up. She looked so pale Oceana thought she might faint.

"Don't apologise." Glaring at Tristan, Oceana went to her and hugged her. "You weren't to know. It's okay."

"Fuck." The adrenaline had gone straight to Jo's head and she collapsed in a fit of something halfway between giggles and sobs. "Sorry, night shift heebie-jeebies...I'll be alright with some coffee in me."

"Coming right up." With one last worried look, Oceana let her go and returned to making the breakfast.

***

Jo left to sleep at around nine and Oceana packed the last few things she needed while Tristan loaded the car. By eleven they were on the road.

"Where are we going?" She asked him. "London?"

"No. I have a pad there for when I have business in the city but it's too small to maintain my household so I have a home in Buckinghamshire."

"In the Chilterns?" She had travelled there on holiday frequently as a kid.

"Yeah, it's in the Wendover Forest." He glanced across at her. "You'll love it. Very beautiful and peaceful."

"And your pets? They live there?"

"Yes but they have a separate annexe. You won't be staying with them. You will never see them."

"What if I want to?" She toyed with the frayed hem on her sleeve. "I don't want to be all on my own in a strange house in the middle of a forest." It was like something from a Grimm's fairytale. "I need company Tristan."

"I'll be there." He told her stubbornly. "And it's not as though you'll never see the staff."

"You have staff?" For some reason she found that peculiar.

"Of course I have staff." He sounded offended. "Who else do you think does the cleaning? Me?"

A brief vision of him in a pinny and marigolds scrubbing a toilet flashed through her mind and she snorted with laughter, mentally filing it away for future reference. "Good point. Do you have a cook? Do you even have a kitchen? I mean...since you don't eat food."

"The house was designed with a kitchen in it." On a safer topic he relaxed slightly. "I hired a chef in anticipation of your arrival. He comes for a couple of hours a day three times a week. He's stocking up the freezer for days he's not there."

"Wow." She wondered if it would be ungrateful if she asked if she could bake occasionally but decided not to bother. She had no idea how long she was going to be there so that was a conversation for a later date. "So...the vampires that broke into my house...who are they?"

For a moment she didn't think he was going to tell her and then he sighed. "A very old family that pissed off the council royally. Back in the 20's most of their founding members ended up on my kill lists at one time or another. They're too weak to go up against the council directly but since it was me that carried out the executions it's me they're focusing their hatred on."

Oceana's heart sank. "So even if I can figure out what's going on...what the link is between these people you've killed...that family are not going to stop hunting me?"

"It depends what you find." He reached across and squeezed her hand reassuringly. "If it turns out that the council has been playing me for a fool I will go after them and if that is the case then the Monteverdis may well turn out to be useful allies. I will seek a truce with them under the auspices of a common goal. I can't go it alone against the council...that would be suicide."

"What do you have to do to end up on a kill list?" Oceana asked curiously. "Upset a council member?"

"Actually no. The council rarely uses me for personal vendettas. We as a society have very few rules so we take it seriously when someone breaks them."

"And what are the rules?"

"Not to reveal our existence to the general public. Not to turn someone without a licence. Not to harm the mate of another. There are others but those are the main three."

Oceana had so many questions she didn't know where to start. "You have to apply for a licence to turn someone?"

"Yeah. I'd like to say it's just the usual bureaucratic mumbo jumbo that pervades everything else in society but the truth is that some people just aren't suitable to become vampires. Any candidate that's put forward has to undergo a period of vetting and a range of psychological testing." He grinned at her. "You'd make an excellent vampire."

"No thanks. I quite like being human." She was a little flattered though and his smirk said he knew it. "When you say mate I assume you mean partner? Do vampires marry?"

"Not often. I mean...you can draw up contracts of binding and so on but forever is an incredibly long time to bind yourself to someone legally. It's more of a possession thing."

"Possession?" Oceana winced.

"Yes, possession. Vampire society has a hierarchy based mostly on strength, age and family name. When two vampires come together, the stronger of the two declares the other to be his or hers. Say for example that you were a vampire and we got together, I would publicly declare that you are mine and that would give you special status."

"That sounds a little chauvinistic."

"It's not always a man that's stronger." He told her reproachfully. "There are several matriarchal families. It's not always the man that is the stronger of the two."

"I'm sorry." And she meant it. "I had no right to judge."

"It's okay. It's hard for an outsider to understand." His easy smile reappeared. "That said, I suspect you'd have no trouble at all linking up all the ages and politics to figure out who's who in our world."

"Do people of the same rank ever get together? What happens then?"

"One usually concedes to the other. Usually the one most capable of defending the partnership is declared the stronger. Again, say we were declared mates...no-one could harm you but anyone with a legitimate claim could still challenge me and if I died vampire law dictates that possession of you would pass to them."

"But that's crazy!" Oceana was horrified. "You can't just pass people around like Pokémon cards. What if I didn't like the person that killed you?"

"The stronger of the two can dissolve the partnership. That said, I suspect the only time anyone would be stupid enough to challenge me would be if they wanted you."

"So why does anyone do it?" Oceana was mystified. "If it runs the risk of binding you to someone you want nothing to do with, why does anyone agree to be a mate?"

"There are a lot of reasons. Security. Social mobility. Money. Protection mostly though. If you were turned I would declare you mine for your own safety otherwise your powers would be available to anyone stronger than you. Vampires with gifts are wise to seek out the protection of those further up the social ladder than them and really, it's not as though the sex is a big price to pay."

"I disagree!" She turned in her seat to stare at him. "I can't believe anyone should have to sell their body in return for protection. It's almost prostitution."

"Don't get angry at me!" He held a hand up defensively. "I didn't write the rules. And for your information I have never taken a mate."

"You haven't?" All those hundreds of years he'd been alive and he'd been alone? It didn't bear thinking about. "But you're pretty high up right? You must have been asked?"

"Many times but I'm not interested."

Sensing they were venturing into territory he didn't want to discuss Oceana changed the subject. "Will you get in trouble for telling me what you are? If the rule says you're not supposed to reveal yourself you've kind of broken it spectacularly."

"It's a nebulous law. When it says the general public it actually means several people. I know you won't tell anyone and you are in my employ. Breaking the law would be draining somebody of blood in front of witnesses with video cameras and leaving them somewhere obvious for the law to find and puzzle over. Besides...you're a special case. You're not actually technically human – you're a supernatural. You belong in our world."

She ignored that. It wasn't worth the argument. "So is there a court? If you break a rule do you get a trial?"

"Not in the human sense, no." He frowned slightly. "It's complicated to explain without knowing how our society is made up."

"Oh." She went quiet for a moment trying to think of something else to ask.

"Since we're on the whole 20 questions thing..." He began. "Why is it that vampires in modern literature always go for the limpid teenagers? I've never really understood it. Why would a being that's been alive for hundreds of years have anything in common with someone that hasn't really lived yet and exists in a state of whiny emo angst? Why is it that a 50 year old dating a 17 year old would be totally frowned on as a cradle snatcher but a 150 year old is fine?"

She tried to hide a smile but failed miserably. "If you're talking age gaps then you being with *any* human is a little weird don't you think?"

"It's not about the age gap. It's about the experience." He explained. "A 17 year old is still a kid. You? You're *all* woman. You've lived. You've dealt with death. You've found your place in life and you know your dreams."

"What difference does it make to you that I know my dreams?" She demanded. "Just knowing you has crushed them. You tell me you don't care if I meet someone and get knocked up but in the next breath you're telling me that any man who comes within a mile of my pants will get his throat ripped out. And do you really think I'd bring a child into a world where people want to kill me just because I know you?"

"You are not without the means to protect yourself." He pointed out and she bit out a laugh.

"Sure. I've got a gift I have no idea how to use."

"You are learning fast and I did say there may be something in my library that can help you. I've collected more than one Book of Shadows in my time on this earth."

"What's a book of shadows?" She swallowed her anger and tried to pay attention.

"For real?" He gaped at her briefly before turning his attention back to the road. "You've never heard of a Book of Shadows?"

"Up until 10 days ago I had no idea there was such a thing as a vampire." She reminded him.

"Good point." His teeth flashed in a brief grin. "Well a Book of Shadows is a witch's record of spells. A lot of witches write it like a recipe book...a list of chants and ingredients and diagrams. Others write it almost as a journal of their spiritual path. Depends on the witch and the gift and the path I guess. We should get one for you to document your workings...how you made the wards and the death stars."

"Death stars?" She knew what he meant but it was such a ridiculous name she couldn't help repeating it. That said, it was better than Starfish of Doom. "Whatever." She gazed out of the window at the passing countryside. He was driving fast but handling the car with comfortable ease. She guess with reflexes like his driving at speed was like taking a walk in the park.

After a moment of silence he shifted slightly in his seat. "If you met someone and I thought you truly loved him I probably wouldn't rip his throat out." He admitted quietly and she stared at him.

"Probably?"

"I'm not going to say definitely. I fully intend to possess every part of your body Oceana but if there's something you need that I can't give you I'm sure we'll work it out. If I want you to survive I need you to be at the top of your game."

"You know, the more you tell me you're going to have me the more determined I am not to let it happen." She told him with a touch of irritation in her voice. "I'm just stubborn enough that this whole arrogance thing feels like a challenge."

"It's not arrogance." He brushed gentle fingers swiftly down her thigh before she could protest. "It's confidence. I didn't mistake the desire in your eyes at the ball."

"That was before I knew what you were and what you're capable of." She pointed out. "You might be a good-looking guy Tristan but you said it yourself – you're an amoral and antisocial bastard who kills people for a living."

"I'm not expecting you to get emotionally attached to me." He sounded amused. "I just want you to want me. I want the sight of me walking across a room unbuttoning my shirt to make you squirm in your seat. I want it to turn you on when I grin at you in a certain way. When I touch you I want you to imagine me fucking you until it gets to the point that it all explodes and you give in and open up to me. I want you to voluntarily come to my bed and ask me to take you because it's driving you crazy not to have me inside you."

"Well you don't want much at all do you...?" She quipped sarcastically but he looked at her, a teasing smile playing around the corners of his mouth.

"Admit it, you thought about me taking my shirt off just then? You thought about me touching you?"

"Of course I did." She shrugged. "I'm only human. It's like telling someone not to think about pink frogs."

"And when you thought about it did it excite you?"

She thought about it. "I'm not squirming."

"That wasn't an answer and you know it." He declared triumphantly. "Oh woman...you'll be mine. Sooner rather than later."

"Whatever." Shaking her head but unable to stop the smile on her lips she turned to look back out of the window.

CHAPTER FIVE

"Here it is." She'd dozed off slightly and rubbed her eyes awake as they emerged from under the canopy of trees onto a long, straight driveway bordered with extensive rolling lawns. In front of them was one of the most gorgeous houses she'd ever seen.

"Wow." She blinked at the mock-Tudor oak framed house with the massive picture windows through which high vaulted ceilings were easily visible. "That is totally not what I expected."

He frowned. "What did you expect?"

"I don't know. Something more...gothic I guess." Realising she was stereotyping again she blushed but he just shook his head.

"I've lived enough centuries to know it's sensible to go for comfort and ease of defence over style. It's an excellent house." She pondered that statement as they neared the building. It served again to highlight the difference between vampire and human - a human would have said it was a beautiful home or they loved their home...not that it was an excellent house. Houses were built of bricks and timber. Homes were built from love and memories. She wondered if vampires were capable of love and how many years of memories it took before they stopped being special. It was a sobering thought.

When he opened her car door she breathed in the fresh air and the silence. The house was clearly situated in the middle of nowhere and the driveway had been long enough that they were a fair distance from the road.

"We'll get your bag upstairs and then I'll take you on a tour. Are you hungry?"

"A little." She admitted. It had been a relatively long drive.

"Then I'll ask the housekeeper to make you a sandwich." He shouldered both their bags easily and took her hand, leading her up the front steps to the glass fronted section of the house. Inside was a spacious entrance hallway floored in oak and decorated in autumn colours. It was warm and beautiful in the summer sunshine and, despite his insistence on calling it a house, it actually felt very homely. There was a woman waiting patiently by the sweeping staircase at the far end of the room and Tristan smiled at her as they entered.

"Mrs Wells, it's good to see you."

"And you Master." She smiled warmly at him.

"Oceana this is Mrs Wells." Tristan introduced them. "Mrs Wells, this is Oceana."

"Nice to meet you." Oceana smiled but she was too far away to offer a hand. Mrs Wells smiled warmly at her too.

"Nice to meet you..." Her voice trailed off uncertainly.

"I swear to God if you call me Mistress I'll leave right away." Oceana grasped the problem immediately. "Oceana, please. Or just 'hey you' if you can't remember."

Tristan looked like he was about to protest but Oceana shot him a glare and he wisely kept his mouth shut, turning instead to Mrs Wells. "I'm just going to take our bags upstairs. Would you please prepare lunch for Oceana?"

"Of course. I wasn't sure which rooms you'd want so I made up the one next to yours and the one at the far end by the study. If you'd rather have the red room I can do that instead."

"No, I'm sure Oceana will be happy in either." He shook his head and took Oceana's arm. "We won't be long." She wandered off as he and Oceana started on the stairs.

"This really is a beautiful house." Oceana told him as they ascended onto a mezzanine floor which branched onto a wide landing that traversed the length of the building.

"Thank you." He seemed proud of it. "I'm guessing from your behaviour last night that you wish to have your own room?"

"I think it would be a little weird for me to sleep in yours." She pointed out but he merely shrugged.

"The offer is there if you would like some company."

She frowned at him. "Just out of curiosity...if I opted to stay in your room would you behave in a purely platonic manner?"

"Of course." His eyes flashed with something...hope or nostalgia, she wasn't sure.

"I might consider it eventually." She conceded. "Right now I'm still mad at you for getting me involved in this mess."

"Then can I at least ask that you choose the room next to mine? I feel that the closer you are to me the safer you will be." He had turned left at the top of the stairs and was leading her onto the landing where there were three doors, one to the right, one to the left and one at the end. He opened the door to his right and after a few moments to orient herself Oceana gathered that they were at the back of the building. "This is one of the guest rooms."

"It's beautiful." It was done in warm solid oak and cream linens. The carpet was soft and deep in a homely biscuit colour and at the far side of the room was a massive bay window that looked out across more lawns and some large outbuildings. The bed was a four-poster draped in sheer diaphanous cream chiffon and it should have looked ridiculous but it didn't.

"Excellent." He deposited her bag at the end of her bed on top of a blanket box and gestured to a door to their right. "Your bathroom is through there. It should be well stocked but Mrs Wells will replace anything you use or need." She followed him back out onto the landing at his gesture and he opened the last door at the end. "This is my room." His decor was much darker than hers but still, somehow, not at all what she expected. He had the same oak furniture but the linens were all in rich jewel tones, sapphire and ruby and emerald.

"Also beautiful." She trailed a hand along the red velvet throw at the end of his bed and looked out of his window which faced a short expanse of lawn and then forest. "I hope you paid your interior designer well."

"Of course." With a smirk he dropped his bag on his own blanket box and took her hand, drawing her out of his room and onto the landing. "That's the red room." He pointed at the closed door they had not yet opened.

"What's the red room?" She asked curiously and he tensed slightly as though he thought she wouldn't be happy about the answer.

"If I bring the pets into the house to...feed or whatever we use the red room."

"Oh." She didn't want to see it. She could imagine. "And over the other side?"

"Come and I'll show you." The doors were laid out exactly the same on the opposite end of the landing. The door to the left was another guest room, this time done out in duck egg blue and a muted dove grey. It was incredibly calming and Oceana was half tempted to go there instead but as though he was reading her mind Tristan tightened his grip on her hand and pulled her from the room. At the far end was a large room split half into a study and half into an entertainment centre with a large wall painted white and left blank for a cinematic projector. "I watch films in here sometimes." He explained. Drawing her back onto the landing he opened the final door which led into a library. Apart from the window and door, all four walls were completely covered in books and there were some smaller shelved rails dotted about in between armchairs and a small desk.

"When you said library I didn't realise it was an actual library." Oceana didn't think she'd ever seen so many books in one private collection.

"I've had a long time to collect." He shrugged.

"Fair enough." She followed him back out onto the landing and down the stairs, realising that the house was a lot smaller than she had imagined, given the size of the estate. The rooms were all huge and the ceilings were very high so it felt spacious and airy and light but there weren't actually that many rooms.

Downstairs there was a large living room to the right of the front door that led through to a slightly smaller study containing two desks. "This is where you'll be working." Tristan told her, gesturing to one of the desks with an array of screens and computer equipment on it. "I've cleared a couple of the walls if you need to put stuff up and the shelves with the journals are right here. If you need anything else just give me a list and I'll obtain it for you."

"Just pens and pencils and a notepad." The equipment all looked new but the journals looked anything in age from a month to a century. Some of them were tattered and ancient and others were obviously recent additions.

"Not a problem." He tugged her hand and led her back across the entrance hall. "The kitchen is through here." There was a modest kitchen to the rear and a small dining room to the front of the house. Oceana wondered why he needed a dining room when he had no use of plates or, in fact, any kind of crockery. She was pretty sure blood bags didn't count as crockery. Perhaps he entertained other humans here sometimes. "We'll stop for lunch before we do the rest of the tour." He told her gently, leading her into the kitchen where Mrs Wells was just putting the finishing touches to a plate of sandwiches. They sat at a breakfast bar under a window looking out across the front lawn and Oceana ate everything on the plate that was put in front of her. It was delicious – there was a fresh selection of salads with ham and cheese sandwiches cut neatly into four.

"I'm going to have to watch my waistline while I'm here." She joked. "Keep feeding me like this and I'll be the size of a house in no time."

"I'm sure I can help you find a way to burn off the calories." Tristan smirked at her and she laughed, she couldn't help it. He might be an arrogant and amoral bastard but he was certainly charming with it.

"I think you'd just like to try." Pushing the empty plate away she settled back to look at him with what was left of her drink. "What do you want me to start on first? Making the house safe or the indexing?"

"The indexing. I'm going to be here to protect you for a couple of weeks at least and it's going to take me a few days to get you a workshop set up here. You can draw me up a list of tools in the morning."

"I still think we should have brought my stuff from home." She sighed.

"Just as well it's me making the decisions around here then." He grinned at her. "Are you done? You want to finish the rest of the tour?"

She drained the rest of her glass and got to her feet, carrying her dishes to the sink.

"You didn't have to do that dear." Mrs Wells smiled benignly.

"I know. But I wanted to." Smiling back, Oceana allowed Tristan to take her hand again and he led her from the kitchen. He headed out into the hallway and towards the back of the building where there was a glass sided walkway leading to the outbuildings. Oceana hadn't realised they were all connected but it made sense.

First stop was a large mostly empty room with some gym equipment at the far end. "This is my training room." Tristan explained as she stuck her head through the door. "You're more than welcome to come and use the equipment any time you like. Once you're settled in I'd also like to give you some self-defence classes."

Self defence classes? From an assassin? Now that was something money couldn't buy... "Sure." She grinned and followed him back out into the walkway.

He took keys from his pocket to open the next door. "This is the armoury." He explained, standing back to allow her to enter. She'd been expecting racks of guns but there was more steel than firepower in the room. "I'll get you keys cut." He told her as she studied the rows of blades. "We'll store your death stars and any other weapons you make in here."

"Is that really necessary?" She winced. "I'm not sure that I want access to them."

"As long as you are a human in this house you are in danger." He told her bluntly. "As soon as I can reasonably expect you to handle one without hurting yourself I'll expect you to carry a blade with you at all times too."

"Why not a gun?" She asked, both horrified and curious. "Surely that's safer?"

"Because a bullet won't kill a vampire and it might not even slow it down. A blade on the other hand will inflict damage that takes longer to heal and will buy you time to get to safety or to me. If you take off a hand or a foot it will take your enemy hours to regenerate it. There is one way and only one way to kill a vampire – you take off its head. Even then you're safer burning the body because some of the really old ones could still come back."

"Would you? If someone cut your head off would you come back?"

"Maybe." He shrugged. "I sure as hell wouldn't want to risk it."

"I'm not surprised." Backing away from the steel she left the room. "What's next?" They rounded a corner and she saw the walkways were laid out around a courtyard. Halfway along the walkway running parallel to the house were sliding doors that led outside but Tristan ignored them and turned instead to a door on their left.

"This is a storage space." He opened the door onto a hallway. Oceana stepped through and he closed the door behind them. "Through here is the pantry for stuff that can't be kept in the kitchen and my stocks." He showed her a room lined with shelves and fridges. She figured that by stocks he meant blood supply so she didn't open a fridge to check. They left that room and moved onto the next which he had to unlock and was full of filing cabinets. "These are my documents and case files." He explained. "I keep records of my work for the council amongst other things."

"Are the files for the people I'm indexing in here?" Oceana asked but he shook his head.

"No. I left them with the journals. I figured you might find them useful."

"Thanks." They left that room and headed to the final one in the building which required a series of keys and a security code. Whatever was in there was valuable to him she realised.

"These are some of the things I have collected over the centuries." He told her by way of explanation. She stepped through the door into the midst of a collection that most museums would kill for. Artefacts were carefully stored and preserved in climate controlled cases, the hum of the generators the only sound in the hush. There were weapons, documents, jewellery, crowns...

"This is incredible!" Oceana breathed. Then her eyes lit on a large cabinet at the back of the room. "Oh my god!" Carefully stepping around the items closest to the door she came to a stop on front of a mail shirt on a stand. Abruptly she couldn't breathe. The artistry of it was incredible. "Is this what I think it is?" She whispered and Tristan stepped up behind her.

"What do you think it is?" He sounded faintly amused.

"A Viking haubergeon...probably 7th Century." She studied the links, eyes wide with wonder. "It can't be...it's so well preserved."

"I'm impressed." He sounded it. "You know your stuff. You were right on the money...7th Century Viking mail."

"But..." Her heart was racing at the treasure in front of her. "That's insane. I can't...I can't even...oh my god..."

He laughed and squeezed her shoulder. "I'll get you keys for in here too. Then you can come trawl any time you want."

"I might never come out." She murmured sounding a little dazed and he chuckled again.

"Don't worry, I'll come fetch you." He took her hand and pulled her away from the cabinet. She resisted for a few moments but he was too strong and eventually she reluctantly followed him out of the room. He locked up behind them and reset the alarm before taking her back out into the walkway. "Only one more place to see." The next building along was much smaller and unlocked. Tristan pushed the door open and stepped back to let her look in. "This will be your workshop." He told her. "It's been empty for a while. The girls were using it for storing some of their stuff but they've had a sale recently so it's empty now. I know it's not as nice as your workroom at home but you can have whatever you want or need in here."

"It'll do just fine." It wasn't her workshop back home but the ceilings were high and there were large windows. It clearly had power to it and with a couple of work benches and some decent shelving she'd get on just fine. "I'm not going to be using it that much though I guess. Once the house is warded you won't need me to make anything else."

"If there's one thing that I've learned in my ridiculously long life it's to expect the unexpected." He reminded her. "A lot could happen in the next few months. I'd rather have you set up here to make anything at short notice than get caught short in a crisis."

As if she needed another reminder that he had snared her up in a dangerous tangle. "Aren't we going up there?" She asked, pointing at the huge buildings he had conspicuously missed on his tour as he turned to head back the way they had come. "What are those buildings?"

"The one on this side is the guest annexe. It's just spare bedrooms for when members of my House are visiting. The other is where the pets live." He said shortly.

"Can't we go visit them?" She was curious about these women that gave blood for a living. "I'd really like to say hi."

He seemed to be weighing it up in his mind but then he sighed. "Fine." He walked back past her and headed for the door of the house. He knocked as she caught up with him and they waited together until a woman opened the door.

Whatever Oceana had been expecting it certainly wasn't a plump middle-aged woman with neat hair in a greying bun and home-knitted cardigan.

"Master!" She kept her eyes lowered to the ground but she sounded genuinely pleased to see him. "You're home! Come on in."

"Thank you." Stiffly he stepped past her into the house and Oceana followed him in.

"Master!" Several voices chorused at once and they all sounded pleased.

"And what's this?" The lady who had answered the door asked cheerfully. "Did you bring us a new sister?"

"Uh no." Oceana blushed bright red. "I'm doing some work for Tristan, not...uh...donating." She could see he was fighting not to smile and nudged him reproachfully.

"Oceana is staying in the main house." He stepped out of nudging reach as he explained. "She wanted to meet you since she'll be here for a while. She thought she might need the company."

"Well of course you're welcome here any time." The woman who had answered the door held her hand out. "I'm Lucy."

"Nice to meet you." Oceana shook the proffered hand. "I'm Oceana."

"What a beautiful name." Lucy smiled and turned to gesture at the others, introducing them one by one. Mary was another middle-aged but achingly stylish woman with a brunette bob. Rebecca was slightly younger, in her mid-twenties with arresting blue eyes and a mass of waist length curls. Naomi was a strikingly beautiful girl with gorgeous almond eyes, honey coloured skin and piles of glossy black hair. She could have been anywhere from 20 to 30. Oceana had no idea. Ellen was another older woman with grey streaks in her auburn hair and a kind smile. She had to be in her sixties.

"Where is Mia?" Tristan asked, looking around.

"She's in bed." Naomi looked concerned. "She had an accident the other morning – fell over the back step and broke her leg. It was a bad one but we couldn't take her to the hospital in case they needed to operate so we did the best we could and waited for you to come home."

"You should have called me. I'll go deal with it now. Did you sedate her?"

Ellen nodded. "Mrs Wells brought down some medical supplies. I dosed her up with antibiotics too."

"Good. You'll need to check your paracetamol levels. Once I've fixed it you'll need to keep the fever and swelling down."

"We know what to do." Ellen flashed him a dry look before returning her gaze to the floor. "We've dealt with your bites before."

"Of course." He turned to Oceana. "Are you sure you want to see this?"

No. She wasn't. She wanted to run like hell. "Sure." She forced a grin and followed him as Ellen led them both out of the communal living room and up a narrow flight of stairs to a medium sized bedroom where a girl in her twenties was sleeping fitfully in bed. Her skin was flushed and she was obviously dreaming. Tristan sat on the edge of the bed and brushed the hair out of her face with cool hands.

"Mia?" He murmured, taking her hand and squeezing it. "Mia wake up."

"Master?" She blinked her eyes open groggily and tried to focus on him. "Is that you?"

"Yes, I'm home." All his stiffness and discomfort were gone and for the first time Oceana saw that he really cared about these women. For all his insistence that they were just pets, he clearly wanted to do right by them. Mia smiled like the sunrise and struggled to sit up. "No it's okay." He pushed her back gently. "You stay lying down. I came to fix your leg."

"I'm so sorry." She gasped as pain shot through her. "Such a stupid accident."

"It happens." He waited until she settled again and then he cleared his throat. "Mia, you've been bitten before. Are you sure you want this?"

"It's better than a broken leg." She forced a grin onto her pale face. "I'd rather have a three day fever than six weeks in a cast."

"I'll sedate you and set you up with an IV." Ellen told her gently from the doorway where she was watching. Oceana realised Ellen must be the one that used to be a phlebotomist. She'd obviously had nursing training somewhere along the way. "You won't even feel it until you wake up in a few days."

"Excellent." With another shaky grin, Mia took a deep breath. "I'm ready." She raised her eyes to Tristan's face and he gazed at her for only a few nanoseconds before her body went utterly limp.

"Is she snared?" Oceana's voice sounded strangely strangled as she wondered if she had looked like that the day Tristan did it to her in the kitchen.

"Yup." He waved a hand in front of her eyes to be sure but she was definitely gone, just gazing at him wide-eyed. Quickly he got up and pulled the covers back to reveal a make-shift splint on her right calf. Ellen wordlessly handed him a pair of scissors and he cut the bandages holding it on, gently pulling them away to reveal a bruised and swollen shin. The skin had broken where the bone had snapped and they realised it must have sheared straight through the skin. Naomi hadn't been kidding when she said it was a bad one. "This is deep." He told Ellen. "I'll have to bite deep and probably more than once. You may need to keep her under for more than just 3 days."

"I'll keep an eye on her temperature." She replied. "I'll wait until the fever breaks and keep her under for another day just to be sure. She'll be fine."

"Good." He was almost subconsciously stroking Mia's hair, glancing down to ensure she was still snared. "Then let's do this. Ellen, take her foot. Hold it steady. 'Cean, can you steady her hips –make sure she doesn't twitch when I bite." He waited until they were in place and then gently scooped his hands under Mia's calf, angling her shin bone towards him. "We ready?" He waited until they nodded and then his fangs snicked out. He lowered his mouth to the bruised and swollen skin and slowly, carefully, sank his teeth into it. Mia didn't even move. For a second Oceana thought that Mia was moaning and then she realised the tiny noise was coming from Tristan. His eyes had closed and he was making sounds of involuntary pleasure. Feeling faintly voyeuristic, she looked away and Ellen caught her eye. She was smiling knowingly and Oceana went red, looking away completely so she didn't have to watch.

She felt Mia moving slightly as Tristan withdrew his fangs and shifted position. Unable to stop herself she turned back to watch him sink his fangs in again. It was kind of fascinating the way the skin resisted up until a certain point of depression and then the fangs suddenly punctured it. She watched until he began making the sounds again, his throat moving as he swallowed. Tearing her eyes away she stared at the far wall until she felt him move again.

"Oh wow." He blinked unsteadily as he came upright and almost toppled over backwards. "How much morphine did you give her?" He was grinning and his bloody fangs were still on show.

"Oh my god....are you high?" Oceana burst out laughing at him as she pushed herself upright and he focused unsteadily on her.

"Fuck woman...you are some kinda beautiful. You know that?" He gave his most dazzling grin and fell hard on his ass on the floor. Oceana laughed so hard she almost lost her own balance but she went round the bed to help him while Ellen busied herself with setting up a drip. "You're shining." He whispered, lifting a hand to her face. "Like an angel."

"Put your fangs away you silly sucker." She tried to pull him to his feet but with surprising strength he pulled her down onto him instead.

"I really, *really* want to sleep with you." He told her sincerely, cuddling her to him and inhaling the fragrance of her hair. "You're so warm and sexy and...and mobile."

"Mobile huh?" Amused, she tried to disentangle herself. "Let me up Tris. You're high."

"Yes I am." He was still grinning down at her. "It's a beautiful thing."

Trying to be serious so she didn't dissolve into helpless giggling, Oceana looked up at Ellen. "Have you ever seen him like this before?"

"Not me personally but there are some notes on it in the journals of the sisterhood. He'll be fine in half an hour or so. He has a fast metabolism."

Half an hour? He was going to be like this for half an hour? Right. First things first, she had to get him back to the house. "Look, I'm not going to let you tumble me here on the floor Tristan."

"To the bed then?" He was trying to sound dashing but he came across as being totally goofy.

"If you can get all the way to your room on your own then I'll certainly consider it. Why don't you attempt the journey and I'll help Ellen finish up with Mia here?"

"Don't be long." Kissing her thoroughly with added wandering hands, he shot to his feet and staggered from the room.

"Nicely done." Ellen congratulated.

"I'm hoping he'll either not make it or get there and fall asleep while he's waiting." Oceana confessed wryly and Ellen chuckled.

"It wouldn't be a terrible thing if he didn't. He's somewhat gifted in that department."

Oceana's jaw dropped. "Uh...you and Tristan...?"

Ellen laughed unselfconsciously. "We all have at one time or another. I wasn't always old. I've been in service to him for almost thirty years."

"Oh. Right." Dusting herself off feeling slightly embarrassed, Oceana climbed to her feet. "What are the journals of the Sisterhood?"

"The women who serve as donors for the master maintain records." She explained. "We have for many years. Just names and brief descriptions and anything that seems pertinent to vampire lore. I am the current record keeper so I have studied them."

"Oh right." There were so many questions Oceana wanted to ask but she knew that this was neither the time nor the place for them. "Can I come back here? When I'm not working?"

"Of course you can dear." Ellen smiled at her and returned her attention to Mia. Taking it for the dismissal it was, Oceana left the room and went in search of Tristan.

To her surprise he had actually made it to his room without demolishing anything on the way. She stopped outside the door not wanting to go in but concerned that he hadn't actually made it to bed.

"I can hear your heart beating." He called from the other side of the door. "You'd better get in here."

Cursing softly under her breath Oceana pushed open the door of the bedroom and stepped in. To her relief Tristan had made it to bed but the relief was short-lived when she realised he was mostly naked.

"Oh my God! What are you doing?!" She averted her eyes but she could hear rustling as he stretched out.

"I made it to bed." There was some more rustling as he patted the sheets. "Come to papa."

"I said I would consider it!! Not that I'd get into bed with you. It's the middle of the day!!"

"I can assure you I am in fine working order whatever the hour."

Yeah...she just bet he was. "Trust me, the minute you come down you are going to be so embarrassed by this." She warned him.

"Come to bed beautiful girl." He crooned. "Otherwise I might have to come and get you."

Oceana tried to judge how badly his coordination had been affected in comparison to the distance to the door and decided to make a run for it. "I am not sleeping with you." She told him calmly and then bolted, slamming the door behind her.

She had made it to the head of the stairs by the time the door crashed open behind her and she took the steps three at a time, speeding across the front hall and out the front door. She'd barely made it twenty metres across the lawn before she was tackled from behind and they both went crashing down in a flurry of limbs.

"Hey!" He sounded hurt. "Why did you run?"

"You were going to haul me in like some caveman!" She cleared the hair out of her face. "Of course I ran."

"I caught you." He grinned and at least the fangs and bloodstains were gone. "Oh man...would you look at the colours out here? This is incredible!" He ran his fingers through the grass wonderingly and Oceana couldn't help herself. She burst out laughing. He was just so cute when he was stoned. Cute and mostly naked.

"Look at the clouds." She encouraged and he flopped onto his back, taking her with him so she was now lying on top. He held her close and just watched the sky.

"They're beautiful!" He murmured, mesmerised.

"Yes they are." Resigning herself to remaining where she was for the time being she lay quietly as he watched the sky until eventually he stopped breathing and she realised he'd gone to sleep. Thank God for that.

***

When he awoke he was back to his usual self and a little confused as to how he ended up on the lawn in just his briefs. Oceana tried to contain her laughter as she explained to him about the morphine in Mia's bloodstream but it was hard and eventually he went off to get dressed in a huff. At least there was no permanent harm done, nothing irreparable had happened. She ate a quiet dinner alone in the kitchen with a book she'd borrowed from his library and went for an early night. It had been a rollercoaster day.

CHAPTER SIX

The following morning Oceana was awoken by a huge crashing sound coming from outside. Slightly confused she checked her clock and realised she'd slept in. It was just after 8am and there was the sound of an almighty fight going on outside. Staggering upright she rushed to the window and looked out. Tristan and someone else were fighting in the courtyard and it was clear from the speed they were moving that the other person was a vampire. The crashing sound was explained by the shattered glass lying all over the grass and gravel. They had tumbled clean through the walkway and at least one of them had been bleeding.

They had come for him and possibly for her. Panicking she clawed through her bag looking for the death stars Tristan had insisted she bring with her. Without bothering to put anything over her night dress she grabbed the bag and ran to help him. Flying down the stairs she shot past the kitchen and out into the walkway, running out through the hole they had left and flung almost the entire bag of chainmail starfish at the back of the strange vampire as he was facing away.

The vampire let out an unearthly shriek and dropped instantly.

"What the...?" Tristan stared at his opponent and then gaped at Oceana.

"Are you okay?" She blurted out. "Did I get here in time?"

"A little help here please!!" Demanded the vampire on the ground weakly and Tristan just dissolved into laughter.

"You can take the death stars off." He told her. "He won't hurt me."

"Are you sure?" Confused, Oceana stooped towards the smoking vampire on the ground and gingerly picked the chainmail off his back.

"I'm not going to hurt him." The vampire bit out through gritted teeth, hissing as one of the little mail units pulled some skin away. "We train together. What the hell did you throw at me?"

"She invented them as a weapon." Tristan sounded pleased as punch. "Pretty cool huh? I would show you one but I can't touch them either."

"I'm so sorry." Mortified, Oceana picked off the last of them and stepped backwards as the vampire struggled to rise. "I thought you were trying to kill him."

"So you came out to defend me?" Tristan gave her a megawatt smile. "Princess...I'm so touched."

"Well I can't fault you for trying to protect someone." The stranger straightened up and smiled at her. He wasn't as drop dead handsome as Tristan but he had a certain roguish charm about him. "I'm Will."

"Nice to meet you Will. I'm Oceana." She took the hand he offered and winced again. "I really am sorry."

"It's okay. I can feel it healing." He flexed his back muscles tentatively. "I don't think it'll be permanent." His nostrils flared and he leaned into her. "Are you bleeding?"

"Look at your feet." Tristan sighed and they all looked down. "You've cut them to shreds on the glass."

"Yeah well, next time I won't be in so much of a hurry to save your ass. Do you always demolish the scenery when you're sparring?" She grumbled. Now that she was aware of the mess her feet were in they were starting to hurt.

"Oh no, you can come and save me in your nightwear anytime princess." He smirked. At least she was wearing a half decent nightgown and not her onesie or something equally embarrassing. "Let's get you inside and cleaned up." He scooped her off her feet and carried her into the house, seating her on the kitchen table and grabbing a towel to protect the floor. "You just sit here a minute. I'll need to find a medical kit."

Will put the kettle on while they waited for Tristan to return and brewed up some coffee. It wasn't long before Tristan returned and he took a seat in one of the chairs, lifting Oceana's feet up so he could take a closer look.

"I'm going to have to pick the glass out of these." He told her. "It's probably going to hurt."

She sighed. "Well I guess it has to come out. Just do it." She bore it patiently and without tears as he picked all the glass slivers out of her feet with tweezers. By the time he was done there was blood everywhere...all up her legs, all down his shirt, on the chair, on the floor...it looked like a scene from a horror movie.

"What do you want to do?" He asked her. "Do you want me to bite them or bandage them to heal naturally?"

She thought about it. "Either way will put me out of action for a few days." She pointed out. "I don't think we're ready to do the whole biting thing yet. Just bandage them please."

"You should probably clean them first." He let her feet down again and stood up to scoop her up. "I'll take you into the bathroom and we can bandage them when you're clean." He carried her to her bathroom and sat her in the bath, bringing a towel over so she could reach it from where she was sitting. He got the water from the shower tap to the right temperature and perched it on the side so she could get it when she was undressed and then he straightened up. "Not now and probably not today, but at some point in the not too distant future you and I are going to have a long talk about what you just did." He promised her, and with that he was gone.

She washed as best she could with the shower head and pulled herself up onto the edge of the bath to use the towel. Her feet were still bleeding and she didn't know what to do. If she tried to walk or crawl into the bedroom she was going to get blood everywhere.

"Are you done?" Tristan called from the other side of the door. He must have heard the water going off.

"Yes." She called back and he came in.

"Okay. Hold onto your towel." She held it up with one hand and put the other around his neck as he easily lifted her into his arms and carried her through to her room. While she had been washing he'd brought the bandages and gauze upstairs and laid them out neatly on her bed. Without any fussing he sat her on the pillows and set about fixing her feet. It didn't take long and then he fetched her clothes and left her to get dressed.

She was contemplating the journey to the mirror to put make-up on when he reappeared. "I've spoken to Mrs Wells. She's going to bring your breakfast straight to the office." He told her, lifting her again. "I don't want you walking on these feet at least until the cuts have sealed up so if you need anything just yell and I'll come and get you."

"I don't think that's really necessary." She protested but he gave her a look that brooked no argument.

"You might be able to walk on them but that doesn't mean you should. If you won't let me bite you then you damn well follow the rules I lay down."

"Fine." Feeling slightly huffy, since she had been injured in his defence anyway, she let herself be taken through to the study and settled in a plush office chair. The journals were all within reach and there was a neat stack of folders on the desk. The computer was already switched on and there was a cup of coffee by the monitor.

"Let me know if you have any issues with the software." He told her as he headed for the door. "I was assured it is the closest possible match to the software you work with at the Police."

"I'm sure I'll figure it out." Already forgetting that he was there she opened up the window on her screens and settled in to work.

By lunchtime she had all of her documents registered and most of the nominals created from the files – basic descriptions of names, dates of turning, known family, addresses etc. From Tristan's surveillance and photographs she had populated habits, clothing and vehicle details but so far nothing obvious was popping out. By the time he came to fetch her she was contemplating the first set of journals.

"How are you getting on?" He asked, noting that she'd barely touched her breakfast tray.

"Pretty well." She rolled her shoulders to ease the stiffness in her neck from focusing on the screen. "All of the documents and main nominals are on. I was going to start on the journals next."

"That's good." He smiled encouragingly. "What are these?" There was a neat stack of printed papers on the edge of the desk.

"Actions." She shrugged. "In a major investigation when something comes up in a document an action is raised to follow it up. So if a witness mentioned in their statement meeting someone else at a certain time an action would be raised to track that person down and take a statement from them and so on. These are all things to follow on from what I found in the files. I'm hoping you'll be able to answer most of them."

"I'll come up with you after lunch and we'll go through them." He seemed strangely enthused by the idea.

"Before I forget, is there somewhere I can photocopy these journals?" She asked. "I'll need to mark them up as I read them and I don't want to draw all over these people's memories. It's disrespectful."

"I don't have a photocopier." He looked mildly sheepish. "I'll order one this afternoon for delivery tomorrow. You'll just have to have a short afternoon."

"I'm sure I'll find something to do."

***

In the early afternoon they trawled through the actions looking for things that Tristan could do right away. He was happy to give her his kill lists for her timeline and managed to identify several people or places in his surveillance notes but some of it would just have to wait until she started on the journals and even then they probably wouldn't find most of the answers. His enthusiasm was waning slightly as he realised the task he had set for her.

"It never occurred to me that it would be so detailed." He admitted as he watched her marking up a surveillance sheet for indexing. "It's like a massive spiderweb that just keeps spreading exponentially."

"Catching murderers is a detailed job." She had pointed out in reply. "It's always the tiny things that trip them up."

He watched her for a while as she marked up sheets but eventually got bored and went back downstairs. She didn't realise that Will was still in the house until he came to get her for dinner.

"I'm sure I can walk." She protested, unhappy that a stranger she'd tried hard to hurt that morning was going to be carting her about but he shrugged and picked her up anyway.

"You might be able to get away with being cheeky to the Master and disobeying his orders but I most certainly can't." He told her in a tone that brooked no argument. "I have no idea why he hasn't killed you yet but if he orders me to carry you, I carry."

Because he could still use her. It was an unkind thought but it still popped into her head and refused to leave. Uncomfortably she changed the topic. "How long have you guys known each other?" She asked, hoping it wasn't too personal a question.

"Four centuries, give or take a couple of decades." He replied easily in the way that most people would have said four years.

"How did you meet?" Tristan had told her very little about his life...just the odd anecdotes here and there. "The way he speaks you'd think he didn't have time for anything other than work."

"He sired me." She bobbed up and down as he shrugged. "He needed a training partner. I was a damn good soldier. It was a win-win situation all round. Getting beaten up occasionally is a price worth paying for eternal life and I heal quickly."

She wasn't convinced that immortality was all that and a bag of chips but she wasn't going to argue with him. "How is your back?"

She bobbed up and down again as he flexed the muscles. "Right as rain." He grinned at her and she noted absently that his teeth were nowhere near as perfect as Tristan's. "They're an excellent invention though. I'm almost terrified of what Tristan says you need me to test."

For a moment she was confused and then she remembered the wards. "I needed to see if I could make a ward specific to a single vampire." She explained. "I don't think they hurt. Tristan's walked into them before. He'd know if there's any pain involved."

"Knowing and telling are two entirely separate things Princess." Tristan's voice floated from the kitchen. "Stop gossiping and get in here. Your dinner will go cold."

Yes oh great and glorious master... She thought sourly. As though reading her mind Will winked at her and she grinned back. Perhaps her enforced sabbatical wouldn't be as bad as she had thought.

It didn't take long for that idea to fly out the window. "Why do I have to sleep in here?" She demanded furiously as Tristan carted her from her bathroom through to his bedroom that night. "I've cut my goddamn feet. It's not like I'm going to die in the night. Take me back!"

"No can do princess." He smirked lazily, depositing her on the bed. "What if you need to get up in the night?"

"I'm 26, not 70!" She protested. "I can go a whole night without a visit to the bathroom and I'm sure if I got that desperate I could damn well walk!"

"Now now..." He remonstrated mildly in that infuriating manner. "I'm only thinking of what's best for you."

"Like hell you are!" She narrowed her eyes. "This is payback for letting you get naked when you were high isn't it?"

"I wasn't naked." He grinned. "But I can be...?"

"No." She averted her eyes as he started getting ready for bed himself. "Just take me back to my own room."

"No." She heard clothes rustling as he stripped and she flopped ungraciously to lie flat, knowing that a dash on her injured feet would get her nowhere. "Is it really so hard for you to accept that I may genuinely be trying to look out for you?" He asked, climbing onto the bed.

"There's so little humanity in you that I can't see why you'd bother." She replied bluntly, frustrated at her situation. "I thought maybe yesterday I was seeing something warm and caring in you when I watched you healing Mia but it occurred to me afterwards that you petted her the way you would a dog. You thought no more of healing her than you would about taking an animal to the vet. If that's how you feel towards women that have served you for years I don't know what I am to you other than someone you can use."

He actually thought about it. "You're a challenge." He said eventually. "I've never had anyone say no to me before. I could take your bracelet off and have you any time I wanted but it feels good to challenge myself mentally to seduce you."

"This is a seduction?" It was so absurd that she actually started to laugh. "Wow...well now I know why cavemen had to abduct their women. They were certainly lacking in charm back at the dawn of time."

"Let me ask you a question." He sounded stubborn. "Why is it that you keep refusing me? Is it really such a hardship to let loose and have a little fun?"

"I..." She started to protest automatically and then she actually thought about it. He was a good-looking, rich, powerful and extraordinarily charming man. She had no idea why she wasn't leaping at the chance to get naked with him...aside from the fact that he had quite neatly wrecked her life, obviously. But now that she was here and what was done was done, why was she not making the most of a bad situation? She certainly seemed to find it impossible to stay mad at him. Every time he did something ruthless or destructive he gave her that twinkling, errant-child look and she instantly forgave him. She studied him in the lamplight...the way his hair glimmered and shone like someone had spun it straight from the night sky, those astonishing cornflower eyes that seemed as though they were looking into your soul, the curve of those sensual lips that she knew from experience were soft yet skilled... "Because I'm afraid." She whispered. Whatever he had been expecting it wasn't that and he almost imperceptibly flinched.

"Why are you afraid?" He asked, just as softly as though he didn't want to hear the answer.

"Because if I give you my body I will end up giving you my heart and I don't know that I will survive you breaking it." Her honesty was brutal.

"How do you know I would break it?" He wasn't offended, just very serious.

"Tris, you have lived maybe fifty times my life span and in that time you have hunted and killed people for a living. I don't know that you can value human life in a meaningful enough way to ever love one of us. I don't believe you're as cold and amoral as you think you are but I also don't think there is enough humanity in there for love. However hard you try, however much you want me...you are vampire and I am not."

For a long moment she thought he would protest, tell her that he could try and regain some of his humanity, but in the end he nodded once, respecting her opinion. "You're still sleeping in here." He told her gently and she smiled, realising they had moved into unfamiliar territory.

"I know." He helped her under the covers and then they lay together with his arms around her, holding her close until her breathing began to even out.

"Cean?" He whispered just as she was drifting off.

"Hmm?"

"Do you think there'll ever be a time when you're not afraid to risk it?" He sounded strangely vulnerable and even in her hazy state Oceana thought about her answer.

"Maybe. One day. None of us knows what the future holds. You've had plenty of centuries practice storming the walls of cities...maybe one day you'll manage to scale the walls around my heart."

He chuckled softly in the darkness, his skin sliding against her back. "Maybe."

CHAPTER SEVEN

It took Oceana most of the next two days to copy all the journals she was going to use. Will had carried up one of the high stools from the breakfast bar for her so she could sit by the copier scanning page after page, neatly numbering them with a pencil. After that she spent another six days reading through them and annotating them. Some of the writing was particularly dreadful and she did what she could with them but on the whole most were pretty clear. After she'd marked them up she read them all end to end again, this time actually reading them rather than focusing on the links. They were fascinating. She learned a great deal about the vampire world...the way they feed, the interactions they had with humans and with each other...it was almost like reading a work of fiction. If she'd read them without ever coming into contact with Tristan she would have thought they were a work of fiction.

Eventually Will came and forcibly dragged her away from her desk. "It's not healthy!" He declared laughingly. "Your feet are better now. I told Tristan I was taking you out for some fresh air. You've been cooped up in that office for more than a week."

"But I'm enjoying it!" She protested indignantly as he stuffed her feet into a pair of her shoes as though she was a recalcitrant child. "I'm just reading!"

"So surely you have questions?" He grinned engagingly at her. "Which you can ask me as we take a walk in the sunshine." Rising, he took her arm and strolled out the front door towing her inexorably along.

"What happens to the people he kills?" She asked once they were a few hundred metres from the house. "I assume someone comes in and cleans up the bodies etc?"

"There's a whole department of liquidation." He told her cheerfully, inhaling deeply. Someone had been out and mown the lawn and it smelled of freshly cut grass drying in the warm summer sunshine. "There's a team of humans that goes in and cleans up the mess. Once the organics have been extracted, the dead vamp's assets are then turned over to another team of humans who inventory them...houses, possessions, bank accounts, mates and so on. Then the findings are passed to a team of vamps. What happens then depends on the dead vampire. If he has a lineage and has named an heir the assets generally pass to them as it would under human law...the next of kin so to speak. If the vampire hasn't named an heir for whatever reason, the team will reallocate any assets they feel are useful within the council and then liquidate the rest to enrich the council's coffers."

"Did it never occur to Tristan that perhaps these vampires are being eliminated because the council wants their assets?" It was the obvious answer.

"I'm sure it did but the group were all so varied in age and social caste. A few of them weren't particularly wealthy. I personally can't see anything they'd have that the council would want. Besides, most of them had named heirs, particularly the older and wealthier ones, and they weren't stupid. They've managed their assets in such a way that the council can't touch them even if they tried to bypass the lore makers."

They walked in silence for a while as Oceana processed this. Eventually she sighed. "If he goes up against the council he's not going to survive is he?"

For the first time Will's tone became guarded. "He may not have to." He told her firmly. "There may be a perfectly reasonable explanation for all of this. There's no point borrowing trouble."

"That's for sure." Moodily Oceana kicked a pebble but then she tried to shake it mood off. "We can't afford to pay the interest." Will burst out laughing and squeezed her arm.

"You're right. We can't."

They walked the entire perimeter of the estate. Oceana hadn't realised when they arrived how big it was or that there was a wall built all the way around it. She was mostly chatting to Will but part of her was absently calculating how long it would take to create a chain long enough to encircle the grounds. Too long was the answer. It was a very long way. But then it occurred to her that there was nothing to stop them purchasing lengths of pre-made chain, joining them together and adding charms to it. The length of leather she had knotted back home when she was under attack had served to block the attic hatch. She resolved to speak to Tristan about it when they got in. It wouldn't hurt to have more than one line of defence if it came to it.

By the time they returned to the house Tristan was in the hallway to meet them. He'd been out most of the morning and called them into the kitchen for Oceana to eat lunch while he talked. There was a plate of salads waiting for her with a cold glass of apple juice and she sat at the table to eat as Tristan laid out some paperwork next to her.

"These are your account details." He laid out a pair of cards. "These are credit and debit cards linked to your account. PINs are in the paperwork." He laid out a set of keys. "These are the keys I promised you to the house and the outbuildings." Oceana tried not to smile when she saw he'd neatly labelled each key. He laid out another piece of paper. "These are the codes for the keypads. You'll need to memorise them and then destroy this piece of paper. Don't ever take it out of the house."

"Will do." She tucked that piece of paper into her jeans pocket after a cursory scan.

"And I need you to sign these." He slid several documents in front of her and handed over a pen. "They're for direct debits from your new account to your old account in the same amount as your old salary from the Police so Inland Revenue don't get suspicious. They don't have access to your new account. Don't want you paying tax on your new wage but if you pay it on your old one it won't raise any eyebrows."

"Doesn't that mean they'll have access to my new account?" Oceana was confused.

"No." He grinned. "That's why there's so many documents to sign. We've done the paper trail equivalent of encryption. Your new account is with the vampire bank but the steps between your old account and your new one are multiple and convoluted through several different companies that they'll never trace. If they can even be bothered to look."

"Fine." Oceana scribbled her signature at the bottom of each page where the crosses indicated. "Do I even want to ask why my new salary needs to fly under the radar?"

"Because it's obscenely large." Tristan winked at her and she sighed.

"I knew I didn't want to ask."

"This bothers you why?" Will didn't get it.

"She thinks I'm trying to control her life again." Tristan explained ruefully. "And she's right. But I fucked it up so I might as well try and recompense some of the trouble I've caused."

"As if I'm ever going to get to spend any of it." Oceana grumbled. "The minute I've finished this job you're going to find me another one and then another one until eventually I'm a wizened old lady that won't appreciate the joy of shopping."

"You want to go shopping? I'll take you shopping." Tristan gathered up the signed papers. "Will, the car please."

"Of course." With a broad grin Will got up and left the kitchen.

"Where are we going shopping?" Oceana had no idea what their nearest town was.

"London of course." He said it as though it was completely obvious. "You might want to pack a toothbrush but don't worry about anything else. We'll buy it while we're there." He blinked. "In fact don't even bother with a toothbrush. We'll get one there. Finish your salad." He got up from the table and pulled out his mobile phone, dialling as he left the kitchen. "Joseph it's me. Please prepare the flat for three guests tonight..." He wandered off in the direction of the study leaving Oceana to stare after him in astonishment. Of course. They were just going to drop everything for a shopping trip in London. Why not... Shaking her head she did as ordered and finished her salad.

They arrived in London late in the afternoon and headed straight for the shops. Tristan insisted on purchasing clothes, nightwear and expensive toiletries for Oceana, despite her wanting to use her own money. The more she protested at the expense, the more he bought until eventually she gave up and let him get on with it. Will left them to it, saying he needed to order a new suit, but he did return in time to admire the soft cashmere sweater Oceana made Tristan buy for himself. They arrived at Tristan's flat in Kensington just after seven laden down with shopping bags and Oceana sighed at the mountain of them.

"I should probably put these away." She said guiltily. They had probably spent close to her previous annual salary in a few short hours, or at least Tristan had anyway. It was an obscene amount of money. "Where is the bedroom?"

"Ah yes..." Tristan's yes were twinkling wickedly. "About that...there's only 2 bedrooms."

She didn't skip a beat. "Looks like you and Will will be sharing then." She smiled coquettishly and lowered her gaze. "Unless maybe I share with Will..."

Will opened his mouth to speak but Tristan silenced him with a glare. "Must we play this game always?" He demanded, not really irritated but exasperation was creeping into his tone. "I'm not going to jump you."

"Are you sure?" Oceana couldn't help herself. "Didn't you see some of the nightwear we just purchased? Totally unnecessarily I might add."

Tristan ran his hands through his hair and pulled himself together, realising she was winding him up. "Top of the stairs, down the hall and to the left." He told her curtly. "Dress for dinner. We're going out."

"When you say dress for dinner does that mean smart casual or eye-wateringly up-market?" She sighed. "It's not all about sartorial elegance for women you know? There are levels."

"Aim for somewhere in the middle. Cocktail length. I'll be up shortly to change."

"Yes oh gracious lord and master..." She winked at him and both men watched her walk up the stairs with a healthy measure of appreciation.

"Don't say it." Tristan warned Will once she was out of earshot. "You've been alive too long to risk me destroying you now."

"Yes master." But Will was grinning as he too went to change for dinner.

***

"This is kind of weird." Oceana felt distinctly uncomfortable sat at a table in a high class restaurant with two men when she was the only one that had a plate in front of her. "Couldn't you guys at least pretend to eat something?"

"We ordered soup for the main course." Tristan pointed out. The restaurant had a clear consommé on the menu that wouldn't interfere with the vampire digestive system. "Unfortunately we couldn't get in at the restaurant run by our own kind tonight. We'll eat there tomorrow but I assure you it will be just as uncomfortable."

"You're not really selling it to me." She pointed out sarcastically, finishing the last scallop on her plate and settling back. "Are we staying tomorrow night as well?"

"Will was right. You've been cooped up in the office all week." Tristan sipped his wine. "It will do you good to have a couple of days off. I'll have Joseph book us tickets for the theatre tomorrow night."

"Count me out." Will traced a precise finger around the rim of his wine glass. "I have business in the city tomorrow. I'll meet you back at the flat the morning after."

Tristan nodded. "Sure." He returned that cornflower gaze to Oceana. "We'll have to buy you a dress. A spectacular dress. An opera-worthy dress. And then we can spend the rest of the day doing whatever you want."

"Can we go to the natural history museum?" She asked. "I've always wanted to go there."

Tristan turned to Will. "If you laugh I will kill you."

Will held his hands up in surrender. "No trace of mirth has passed these lips, I assure you."

Oceana stared at them both. "I don't get it. What's wrong with the natural history museum?"

"Never mind." Tristan sat back in his seat. "Never mind."

***

The following morning Will left shortly after breakfast and Tristan took Oceana into Soho. He seemed to know exactly where they were going so she didn't complain, following him in silence until he turned into a non-descript shop with nothing except a vase of orchids in the shop window. If Oceana had been alone she would never have guessed it was a clothes shop.

"Master." As Tristan moved out the way she could see a statuesque blonde heading towards them with a wide smile of greeting on her lips.

"Caroline." Tristan nodded and gestured to Oceana. "Oceana this is Caroline, Caroline – Oceana."

"Nice to meet you." Oceana knew she was pretty but she felt like a bug next to this Caroline who was all grace and legs a mile long.

"You too." Caroline sounded genuinely pleased. "What can I do for you?"

"Oceana needs a dress." Tristan didn't waste any time with small talk. "Something impressive. We're going to the opera and then to Hedon for a late dinner."

"No red please." Oceana just had to get that in. She'd be damned if she spent the night feeling like Julia Roberts in Pretty Woman.

"As you wish. Please follow me." She turned on heels that would have broken Oceana's ankles and swayed off with Oceana trailing behind.

"I'll just sit out here." Tristan folded himself into a nearby armchair and waited for the show to commence. Oceana paraded three or four dresses, each more elaborate than the last before Tristan shook his head. "She needs something more alive, more vibrant." He told Caroline. "These aren't right."

Caroline pursed her lips while Oceana tried to be quiet. She'd thought all the dresses were lovely. "I may have something..." Caroline mused, herding Oceana back into the dressing room.

When they emerged again, Tristan nodded. "That's it. That's the one." It was a shimmering floor-length strapless gown of teal taffeta that shone in rainbow colours like petrol spilled across water. The upper bodice was folded into complex pleats that spiralled around Oceana's body, curving around her back and over her left hip and the pleats were set with jewels to give the impression of a waterfall. The full skirt moved fluidly around her feet like ripples of chiffon as she turned slowly for him.

"Are you sure?" He could tell she was hopeful by the tone of her voice and he nodded, unable to say any more. He couldn't tell her it was so beautiful it made his fangs ache.

"Excellent." Caroline grinned. "I'll box it up with some appropriate shoes and have it delivered to the flat this afternoon."

"Charge it to my account." Tristan gave Oceana a warning glare not to challenge him and she meekly went back to the dressing room leaving Caroline to smile at him.

"Of course."

***

Tristan and Oceana spent the afternoon at the Natural History Museum as promised and returned to the flat shortly after 5 to find the dress laid out on the bed along with Tristan's finest suit.

"Thank you. For this I mean." Oceana touched the fabric of the dress gently and reverently. "It's probably the most beautiful thing I've ever owned."

"You're welcome." He was tempted to make some joke about repayment but decided not to. She'd been too genuine in her gratitude. "You might as well get used to it. The more time you spend in my life the more you'll need to wear outfits like these." He didn't explain that statement any further and Oceana didn't ask. She was sure she'd find out soon enough.

They left for the opera at 7 and despite her best efforts Oceana cried through some of it. She'd never been to the opera before and was utterly entranced by it. She'd thought she would struggle to understand as none of it was in English but it hadn't been too hard to follow the story and despite never listening to opera on the radio she found the soaring voices powerful and intense in a way that transcended music.

"That was incredible!" She breathed as they left the theatre arm in arm. Her eyes were shining and Tristan burst out laughing.

"I'm glad you enjoyed it. Next time we'll go to the ballet."

She sighed happily. "Best. Job. Ever." She enunciated. "I feel like a princess."

"Good." He patted her arm and they continued to stroll along the street. It wasn't far to the club and it was such a busy night in the capital that it was pointless trying to find a taxi. From the outside it didn't look like a club at all. It was a non-descript and unsigned door in the centre of a building facade with blacked out windows. If you hadn't known it was there you'd have assumed it was just a house. Tristan knocked on the door and flashed his fangs at a tiny camera mounted in the door frame. There was a moment's pause and then a buzzing noise as the door swung open. "Do not speak to anyone unless spoken to." Tristan warned her quietly as he led her through the door. "This is a dangerous place."

"Okay." Her exuberance slightly dampened, Oceana followed Tristan through an oak-panelled hall into a large dining area. It was done in muted forest colours but Oceana barely noticed it as the entire room had gone silent when they entered, spreading out from them like ripples in a pond. She was painfully aware of all the eyes on them.

"Executioner." A passing member of wait staff greeted him respectfully, careful not to look into his eyes. "Table for two?"

"Please." Ignoring the stairs Tristan guided Oceana after the waiter to a table in a secluded corner. As they were seated conversations started up again and eventually people turned away. "Is there anyone I should acknowledge?" Tristan was asking the waiter who shook his head.

"No sir. There are no council members in tonight." He thought for a second. "There are some visiting Americans but none higher than a fifth."

"Thank you." Tristan smiled encouragingly at Oceana. "Menus for both of us. What are the specials?"

"For you sir there is an extremely unusual Native American B positive or an A positive from the Canary Islands and for the lady the starter special is a selection of fine cheeses with rosemary crisps and sage and onion ice cream. The main special is Monkfish *en papillote*."

Oceana waited for him to return with menus before she started asking questions. "How did he know I was human?" She asked and Tristan shrugged.

"Practice." He told her simply. "That and they don't recognise your face. Most of the waiters have been around on the scene for long enough to be able to spot the differences."

"What did he mean when he said none of the Americans were above a fifth?" She asked curiously and he set his menu aside.

"It's to do with lineages." He explained. "The head of a line is counted as the first of his line. The vampires he or she sires are the seconds of the line, the ones they create are thirds and so on. Generally speaking, the closer to the top you are the older and more powerful you are. If the head of the line dies everybody sired by the successor moves up a level so you could say that the higher up they are the closer they are to ruling the family too."

"So what level are you?" She winced. "Or is that rude to ask?"

"It is a little rude but you are not from our world so it can be excused." He winked at her. "It's a social nightmare attempting to place people without asking straight up. There are lists of lineages at the council for anyone that wants to know but, since you asked, I am a first. I am the master of my line."

"So your maker is dead?" She asked before she realised it was probably another rude question but he just nodded.

"He died centuries ago. I have been the master of my line since the 16th Century."

Oceana's mind boggled at the time span so she backed away from it. "So if you're the first that would make Will a second?"

"Yes and any vampires he creates would be thirds."

She was frowning trying to piece it together. "So...if you died would Will be the master of your line or the master of his own line?"

"The master of my line...my family. Say I made you a vampire too. You and Will would both be my seconds. If Will then ascended to become the first, you would remain a second and any vampires you had sired would still be at the same level but everyone on Will's side would move up one in line with his rise in status."

"So who decides who moves up? I presume most vampires sire more than one?"

"Ah." He smiled. "That's complicated. Generally the master of a line will nominate an heir. If no heir is nominated it would go to the second who is oldest and strongest. That's the official line. Unofficially it's the equivalent of a civil war. Even when an heir is nominated, someone may challenge them to become a first if the nominated heir is an unpopular choice."

Oceana smiled drily. "That's something common to vamps and humans. Death does funny things to people. The most rational of mourners will still challenge inheritances."

"I don't suppose human contests involve decapitation..." He chuckled and Oceana burst out laughing, the sound startling in the hushed restaurant.

"No they don't." She giggled all the way through the waiter taking their orders and then returned to her questioning. "So, different blood types and races actually taste different?"

"It's subtle but yes. It's similar to wine...the educated palate can taste the difference but it's something that very much comes with age." He blinked. "And understanding. Most Native Americans are O type. A B positive is incredibly unusual. It's like finding an extremely rare bottle of Chateau Margeaux."

"And the granita? Is that really a bowl of frozen blood sorbet?" She wasn't sure she'd be able to watch him eating that. Somehow it seemed even more weird than sucking a blood bag.

"That's exactly it. Sometimes we just fancy a change in texture." Oceana wanted to freak out but she remembered her brief flirtation with vegetarianism when she'd felt like her teeth were wasting away from not tearing up steaks and realised it was similar. "If it bothers you I won't eat it." He offered quietly but she shook her head.

"No it's okay." She forced a smile. "It's infinitely less disturbing than having a live person laid out on the table for your delectation."

"I'm sure that could be arranged..." His grin was wicked and she burst out laughing again. For all he was a sociopathic killer he was certainly a charming dinner companion.

The food was excellent and throughout the course of the evening several vampires approached the table, mostly just to pay their respects to Tristan. Oceana did as she had been warned and didn't speak to anyone that didn't greet her directly but it was a weird feeling to realise that Tristan was by far and away the most powerful man in the room. Up until then she'd been able to ignore any thought of his job or society because it was just the two of them, three if you counted Will. But here, amongst his own kind, he was obviously a class apart. She felt a little out of place. There were a couple of other humans eating from regular plates dotted around but none of them moved or spoke the way that she did with Tristan. They were all fixated on their plates, unable to meet their master's eyes and she realised they were all pets of one kind or another. That shook her more than the other vampires' obeisance.

"You seem quiet." Tristan remarked as they climbed into a waiting cab when dinner was over. "Has something distressed you? Was it the granita?"

Actually the granita hadn't been distressing at all. It had just looked like a high quality raspberry ice cream. "It was the people." She blurted out. "The other humans. They were all so obviously pets. It made me wonder what I must look like to others."

He laughed, a rich warm sound. "Trust me princess, nobody mistook you for a pet. I wouldn't be at all surprised if someone tried to steal you out of sheer curiosity."

"Steal me?" She had a sudden vision of being hauled away over someone's shoulder.

"You aren't my property." He told her mildly. "Someone may try and make you a better offer and if that didn't work they'd probably try and kidnap you."

She closed her eyes and fought for calm. "Remind me again why you thought it would be an excellent idea to parade me in a vampire establishment?"

"Because people are talking about you." He wound one of her blonde curls around his finger. "Better for them to see that you and I have a united front. It's less likely that someone would attempt to bribe you away from me and I'd rather face a frontal assault than someone going behind my back."

"And you didn't think to ask me my opinion on this?" She had the uneasy feeling that he wasn't telling her the truth but didn't know what to do about it.

"You don't know this world like I do." He pointed out. "The politics are dangerous and complicated. I know I haven't given you much cause to, but I need you to trust me. I will do my level best to keep you out of harm's way but you need to do as I tell you."

"I'll try." It was the most she could offer, especially since she knew he wasn't being entirely straight with her.

They sat the rest of the way to the flat in silence and went to bed without much conversation. It was late and they were both tired. Oceana hung the gorgeous dress up with one last reverent touch of the fabric and dreamed of an ocean of jewelled teal taffeta.

The following morning Oceana awoke alone in the bed to the smell of fried food and followed her growling stomach down to the kitchen where Will was frying bacon and eggs.

"What are you doing?" She was sleepy and confused.

"Hey! Nice pyjamas." He smirked at her. "I thought I'd make you breakfast."

"Oh. Uh, thanks I guess. That was nice of you." And it was. He couldn't eat it so he really had made it just for her.

"I'm a nice kind of guy. Take a seat. Tea?"

"Yes please." She sat at the small table. "I guess this means you've totally forgiven me for trying to kill you the day we met?"

He chuckled. "Yeah I've forgiven you. If only because I want to be pretty damn sure you're on my side if we ever get into a fight."

That took some of the joy out of the morning. "I'll tell you the same as I told Tristan. I don't mind warding or defending but I won't make weapons."

"First rule of war my lovely." He gave her a dazzling grin as he set a mug in front of her. "Sometimes the best form of defence is offence."

"Whatever." She mumbled, accepting the tea. "Where is Tris this morning?"

"He was summoned to the council." He didn't sound unduly concerned but as far as Oceana was concerned an unexpected summons was never good.

"Did they say what for?" She asked when he wasn't forthcoming with any other information but he shrugged.

"No. I suspect they're just going to give him his next kill list. He's about due."

"Oh." That was just a little too coincidental. "How long will he be? I thought we were going back this morning?"

"We are." He placed a monstrously huge plate of food in front of her. "If he's not back by ten he said for us to go and he would follow after."

"Oh." With little else to say she tucked into the food and Will sat opposite her with a mug of coffee.

"He likes you." He suddenly said abruptly and Oceana froze with the fork in her mouth. "Sorry that was rude." He apologised.

"No it's okay." She swallowed what was in her mouth and gave him a steady look. "He doesn't like me that way. I'm interesting to him. That's all."

"Are you kidding?" He didn't know whether to be amused or horrified. "If anyone else was half as cheeky to him as you were he'd have taken their heads off for disobedience. And to let you sleep with him?" He shook his head in disbelief. "I've seen that man go through pets like they were yesterday's washing. They never stayed the night."

"Yeah but that's all we're doing. Sleeping." She pointed out. "There's nothing intimate going on between us. I'm just a novelty to him...someone with a heart beat that doesn't freeze up any time he's close by. He'll get bored of the novelty soon enough."

"Oceana..." He blew out a sigh. "Just be careful okay? I've known him for many times your life span. He doesn't think like a human any more and eventually he'll get bored of you saying no. In his own, twisted way he's utterly captivated by you and if you play it wrong you could end up getting badly hurt."

"How did you retain so much of your humanity?" She asked curiously, pointedly ignoring his concerns and he shrugged.

"I don't kill people for a living." Good point. "I've also been dead a lot less time than he has. Who knows? Maybe in a few centuries I'll be as inhuman as he is." He looked troubled by the thought and stared moodily into his coffee.

"I'm sorry." Oceana offered after a few minutes of silence. "I shouldn't have asked."

"It's okay." His shoulders lifted slightly. "It's been a long time since anyone had a proper conversation with me."

"What do you do when you're not training with Tristan?" She asked curiously and the smile lit on his face again.

"I work as a freelance editor. Mostly novel manuscripts."

That was unexpected and Oceana laughed. "How on earth did a soldier get into editing?"

"I know." Almost self-consciously he brushed a strand of hair from his forehead. "It's a bit of a leap. I think it was maybe 50 years after I was turned...it began to strike me that eternity was actually a really long time to just do nothing with myself, to not better myself somehow. I figured I could do with being a little more educated so I enrolled in a university near where we were living at the time. Back then there was a lot less paperwork and bureaucracy. It was pretty easy to fudge it. Started a lifelong love of learning. I keep going back...universities all over the world have given me degrees, mostly in languages and literature. Sometimes I do night classes instead...it's a lot less intense."

"Wow." Oceana stared at him, her delicious breakfast momentarily forgotten. "How many languages do you speak? How many degrees do you have?"

He laughed. "I've lost count of the degrees. I have them all filed away somewhere at home. As for languages..." He shrugged. "I speak most of the modern ones...Spanish, French, German, some of the oriental dialects."

"And the older languages?" She was fascinated.

"Latin, obviously. Some of the older European ones too. Old Norse, that sort of thing."

"Wow." She knew she sounded inane repeating that word but he really had surprised her.

"It's not that amazing." He sounded almost self-conscious. "I've had a lot of time to study. Don't let your breakfast go cold." He gestured at her plate and she automatically lifted her fork again. "While I remember, I got you something yesterday." He got up and left the room, returning a few moments later with a gift wrapped parcel in expensive tissue paper.

"A gift? Why?" A little bemused, she accepted the parcel. "Can I open it now?"

"Of course." He returned to his seat. "It's nothing special. I just thought it was something you might appreciate now that you're part of our world. It's hard to speak to anyone outside. It's from the same company that make mine."

She unwrapped the tissue paper to reveal a leather-bound journal. It was gorgeous – the leather was turquoise with a small design tooled into the cover that was something between a celtic knot and a wave pattern. The paper was thick and handmade but of the highest quality. It must have cost a fortune. "Will! I don't know what to say! This is gorgeous!" She ran her fingers across the leather, marvelling at the supple softness of it. "Thank you so much!"

"You're welcome." He gave her a smile that was almost as dazzling as one of Tristan's and for the first time she realised that he really was quite handsome. Whenever Tristan was about everyone else paled into ordinariness, but here and alone Will was beautiful. The morning sun was catching his hair making it shine with chestnut and auburn colours and she'd never noticed the pale green flecks in his hazel eyes before. Where Tristan was pale arctic midnight perfection, Will was all warm golden colours.

Realising she was staring she dropped her eyes and got up to give him a hug. "Thank you. Really. It's beautiful."

Looking slightly awkward he returned the hug. "Just use it wisely." He made light of the gift but she could tell he was pleased by her reaction. "Finish your breakfast!"

"Yes sir!"

She was just about finished when her mobile rang. She answered it but Tristan didn't even let her say hello before he launched urgently and quietly into instructions. "Cean, I don't have long. I'm not coming back with you. Go study the Books of Shadows, ward the house as soon as you can. Tell William the word 'Pegasus'. He'll understand. Follow his orders exactly as you would follow mine and I'll return as soon as I'm able. Be safe." He hung up and Oceana gaped at her phone in astonishment.

"Did he say Pegasus?" Will had gone white and Oceana nodded.

"I think so. He was speaking so fast."

"Get in the shower. Get dressed. We're leaving now." He flew into action and Oceana didn't argue. Tristan had sounded almost...not frightened, but definitely concerned.

"What's Pegasus?" She asked less than an hour later as they barrelled through the countryside towards Tristan's country home in the forest. "Will, please tell me what's happening."

"I don't know what's happening." He wouldn't look at her, paying attention to the road instead. "The Pegasus Protocol means something big is going on and we need to circle the wagons."

"Circle the wagons as in defend ourselves?" Oceana's heart was racing. "Are we going to get attacked?"

"I don't know." He replied helplessly. "He didn't exactly give us much to go on."

Realising that he knew no more than she did Oceana resumed gazing out the window as the countryside flew by. Whatever it was, if the vampires were scared it wasn't something she wanted to be involved in.

By the time they arrived back Oceana was so tense she felt like a walking chunk of granite. Accepting a cup of tea from Mrs Wells she headed straight for the library as Tristan had ordered and began taking down books from the shelves he had shown her when she first arrived.

"We have something of a problem." She told Will in dismay several hours later when he came to check on her. "I've found a couple that might help going by the pictures but they're all in old languages. I have no idea what they're saying."

"Let me look." He gently lifted the huge book out of her hands and placed it on the reading cradle on the desk, scanning pages with an educated eye. "Not this one." He told her eventually. "They're mostly illustrations rather than spells. Which others?"

She handed him several more books but on the third he frowned and leaned in closer. It was the oldest book she had given him so far and he was nodding as he tried to decipher the spidery scrawl on the pages.

"Is that one useful?" Oceana asked hopefully and he nodded slowly.

"I think so. This is a family grimoire though. While I translate this can you see if there are any others in here from this line of witches? We're maybe looking for something even earlier."

"Okay." Oceana turned back to the shelves just as her stomach roared embarrassingly loudly. It was mid-afternoon and she hadn't eaten since breakfast. Without missing a beat, Will absently lifted the phone to his ear and dialled Mrs Wells, requesting lunch in the library. Oceana smiled gratefully at him but he was too absorbed in his reading to even notice so she continued her search.

The light was fading and dinner was long past when Will finally presented her with several sheets of paper. "I think this is what you need but it's an approximate translation." He shrugged. "My ancient Greek isn't great."

"Ancient Greek?" Oceana gaped at him. "How old are these books?"

"Thousands of years some of them." He looked around. "It's the magic in them that has preserved them. They've faded slightly over the years with no magic in the house but now that you are here and using them they'll remain preserved."

"I had no idea." She felt weirdly guilty for not knowing. "Maybe I can make something that will translate them?"

"It's a good thought." He smiled and briefly touched her shoulder. "It's getting late. Why don't you go to bed and you can take this into the workshop first thing and see if it's workable."

"Okay." She hadn't realised how tired she was until she stood and he steadied her as she swayed slightly, yawning. "Goodnight Will. Sleep well."

"You too Oceana." He leaned down and kissed her cheek. He smelled like the autumn...late sunshine and warm spices...and she impulsively hugged him. Startled, he froze at first and then relaxed into it. She wondered how long it had been since anyone had held him. Tristan certainly wasn't a touchy-feely kind of master. She released him with something akin to regret and went to bed alone.

CHAPTER EIGHT

She slept late the following morning and awoke to several voices downstairs. Warily she had a quick shower and dressed, tucking a couple of death stars into her jeans pocket along with the keys to the outbuildings. There wasn't any shouting or signs of fighting but it didn't hurt to be careful. She crept along to the top of the stairs but as soon as she had left her bedroom the ground floor went silent.

"It's okay to come down." Will appeared in the hallway. "Please try not to kill anyone. These are all friends and they're just leaving." She tried to keep a straight face but her hand twitched and Will's eyes dropped to the bulge in her pocket. He hid a smirk. "I'm glad you're prepared though. Keep them on you."

Yeah, because that was so reassuring. "I'll just go through to-" She started but he cut her off.

"No, you'll have breakfast first." He told her firmly.

"Who died and made you boss?" She grinned, more amused than snarky, and he shrugged with a twinkle in his eye.

"When Tristan's not here I'm in charge. Now, do you want me to hold you down and force-feed you or will you come quietly?" She pursed her lips, wondering if she'd be able to get a death star out in the time it took him to haul her over his shoulder, and he gaped. "You're not seriously thinking about disobeying me are you?" He demanded and she sighed.

"I'm not a pet Will. You don't get to boss me around. Ask me nicely and I'll stop trying to prove a point."

"Not a hope." He was up the stairs before she could blink and easily lifted her into his arms like a child. "You are one painfully stubborn woman." He told her conversationally as he carted her down the stairs.

"It's part of my charm." She agreed and he chuckled.

"Am I going to have to sit on you while Mrs Wells makes pancakes or will you behave now?"

She opened her mouth to make a smart comment and then closed it again realising it was probably time to give in gracefully. "I'll behave."

"Excellent." He dropped her gently to her feet at the kitchen door and pushed it open. "I'd probably squash you if I had to sit on you. We'd never get the pancakes in."

"As if." She snorted. "Where did everyone go? I heard voices down here just now."

"I told you they were leaving." Will pulled out a stool at the breakfast bar for her. "I didn't know if Tristan's plans included you meeting everyone yet."

"Who were they?"

"Our family. The vampires Tristan and I have sired. Or at least some of them anyway. There have been a few over the years."

This was news to Oceana. "How many has Tristan made?" She asked curiously. "I thought you were the only one?"

"No there are 3 of us." He sat next to her, watching Mrs Wells make pancakes. "Catherine is over in America somewhere. I couldn't get hold of her but Alathea is here. She doesn't live too far away."

Oceana refused to dwell on the fact that they were both women and Tristan only ever did things because he wanted something. "So the others are vampires you've made?"

"Yes." He suddenly looked sheepish. "I went through a lonely phase in my middle years. A lot of them didn't survive...I wasn't very good at choosing them at first."

"How many are left?"

He shrugged. "6 or 7. I haven't heard from Esther for a while but last I heard she was somewhere in France. Robbie is still on his way from Scotland so he wasn't here this morning and Christine is flying back from Canada today. A couple of the others are running errands for Tristan at the moment but Charlie and Xav were here this morning."

"And how big is the family?" She accepted a plate of pancakes without diverting her attention from Will. "I presume the vamps you've sired have made others? I guess Catherine and Alathea have made some too?" She stumbled over Alathea's name. It was unusual.

"I don't know exactly but I think it's somewhere in the region of 100. We're a pretty small and close-knit family. It's unusual."

"How so?" The pancakes were really delicious and she surreptitiously drizzled maple syrup all over them.

Will's eyes were on her plate. "Vampires can be quite possessive and territorial. It doesn't make for close family ties. It also takes a long time to come to terms with being subservient to your highers. When you're an immortal, almost invincible being you don't feel like you should bend the knee to anyone. Most families create new vampires, use them for a few years and then discard them. It's unusual to create so few and keep in close contact with them."

"Possessive and territorial huh?" Oceana was amused. "Like I hadn't noticed that..." She remembered Tristan threatening to rip the throat out of any man she flirted with. "Well, I guess if you're all close I'll probably meet everyone eventually. I can't see Tristan letting me go back to my old life after this." She felt a brief pang of homesickness for her sunny conservatory and her own bedroom back in the West Country.

"Probably not but he may let you go home." He offered reassuringly as though he was reading her mind. "When you're more in control of your gift you'd be better placed to protect yourself and you never know...one of us might come with you to watch over you." Something in his tone made her really look at him and to her astonishment she realised he was almost blushing, diverting his eyes to her pancakes once more. Wondering what the hell that was all about she took a big swallow of apple juice.

"We'll see." She replied eventually. "It's going to take me a few weeks to finish indexing the journals before I can even start studying the witchy stuff."

"And somewhere in that we're going to teach you self defence as well." He reminded her.

"Yeah." She sighed. "So it'll be a few months at least."

"It'll fly by." He promised, bumping her arm gently. "You're already gifted with the jewellery. It won't take you long to learn enough to defend yourself. Tristan told me how you'd managed to ward your house just by guesswork."

"They still nearly got me though." She replied doubtfully. "I have a lot to learn and unless I can come up with a translation spell I can't leave here until I have begged you to translate every useful Book of Shadows."

"If I get time over the next couple of days I'll see if I can find a translation spell." He promised. "I'm sure there'll be one somewhere in all those books."

"Okay." They sat in companionable silence as she finished her pancakes.

"Another cup of tea dear?" Mrs Wells asked, clearing her empty plate, and Oceana nodded.

"Yes please Mrs Wells. I'll take it through to the workshop with me."

"Right you are." She poured a fresh cup and added milk, setting it in front of Oceana and whisking the empty mug away. Oceana smiled at her thinking uneasily that she could get used to this lifestyle...having someone else clear up after her all the time. She hated that she was already changing.

"Will you need any help?" Will asked and Oceana shook her head.

"No I'll be fine thanks Will." She slipped off the bar stool and took her mug.

"Well work hard and I'll come get you when lunch is ready." He flashed her another dazzling smile and she couldn't help but grin back. Touching his arm companionably, she left him to whatever he needed to do and headed for the workshop.

***

Taking stock of the supplies Tristan had provided Oceana was pleased. At some point he had obviously tasked someone to bring her things from her workshop back home, including her large bead trays. There were also multiple spools of wire in different metals and gauges that were obviously new but were in sizes she regularly used. Her favourite pliers and cutters were there too. Satisfied, she pulled out a new sketchpad and pencil from the drawer she had found in the work desk and sat down to sketch with the translated pages and the Book of Shadows in front of her.

Straight off she discarded the traditional setting. According to the spell book she had to make the ward and then lay it in the foundations surrounded by a circle of salt incorporating the five elements with earth, air, fire and water at the compass points and 'spirit' overlaying the whole. As far as Oceana was concerned her jewellery had always been magical items in and of themselves so it made sense to incorporate the protection into the actual object. She had no idea if it would work or not but Tristan had told her to trust her instinct and her instinct was telling her it would be fine.

With that in mind she selected a bead that had a wooden bore through a clay outer to represent earth. For water she selected a piece of turquoise sea glass that she hadn't been saving for anything else. For fire she selected a fire-polished glass bead that shone brilliantly with orange and gold iridescence. For air she found another glass bead. It was a solid top-drilled teardrop of glass with bubbles air-blown into it. She kept intending to make a pendant with it and then never getting around to it so she figured it was as good a bead to use as any.

For the salt circle she found some slim, hollow plastic tubing that she sometimes used for structural work when she was building chainmail items and, after a quick trip to the kitchen to fill it from the salt box, she looped it into a large circle, joining the ends together and binding it so that the salt was in an unbroken ring. That would be the frame of the ward.

Once that was decided she doodled on the paper waiting for inspiration to strike. She needed to get the beads into the right places but wasn't sure how to actually fit them into the structure of the ward and she had no idea at all how to put spirit into it. Frustrated, she read Will's writing again and again but it didn't help. Whoever had written it assumed the witch casting the ward had a basic understanding of spell casting.

Finally she closed her eyes and tried to imagine herself at home in her sunny workshop, looking out across the tiered garden with the sunlight dappling the fish ponds. There was music playing softly from the kitchen and overhead the sun catchers were refracting light in jewelled tones across the walls.

Smiling she realised she had it. She'd design it like a sun catcher crossed with a dream catcher. Dreams would be a good representation of spirit since they were born of the subconscious. Grabbing the pencil she sketched out a curving, looping band in heavy gauge wire which would be fixed to the salt-filled tubing and would frame her elemental beads. That would form the magic circle providing the power to the ward. Within that was another slightly thinner concentric band in a different coloured wire which would represent the perimeter wall of the estate. Referring to the Book of Shadows she wondered how accurate the representations of the buildings had to be but the pictures seemed approximate so she figured she had some leeway over the actual design. Within the perimeter band she sketched in a band of fine looping whorls in a loose circular Viking weave which would represent the grounds around the house. Within that she sketched the dream catcher section in the finest wire with small clusters of beads on representing the approximate locations and sizes of the various buildings. There was a small hole at the centre which, on a dream catcher, would be where the good dreams passed through, representing spirit. Smiling she studied the design. It was perfect.

Scribbling a few notes, she collected all her beads and wires, took a moment to collect her thoughts and then set to work.

***

Two hours later she had both the outer rings done but the Viking weave was a painstaking and lengthy process. The tension of the wire had to be exactly right to ensure all the knots went in a straight line and didn't warp the circle. Tubular weave was much more forgiving because of the compression but this had to be perfect. The ward was going to be protecting the house for a very long time and she didn't want future generations to think her a sloppy worker. It was difficult to concentrate on the process at the same time as fixing in her head the intent of what she wanted the ward to do. There were so many facets of the protection she was weaving into each section.

Taking a break she set the ward down on the worktop and stretched, her back cracking as she straightened up. There was a timid knock on the door behind her and she swung round to see a young woman standing there shyly. Searching her thoughts quickly she came up with a name.

"Mia!" She smiled. "How are you feeling? Is your leg better?"

"Much better thank you." Mia responded politely, blushing. "I'm sorry, I saw there was someone in here so I decided to come and say hi. I don't really remember meeting you the first time. I was on morphine. It all seemed a bit dreamlike."

"That's okay. It's good to see you up and about. Did you want to come in?" She gestured to an empty chair beside one of the windows and Mia hesitated. "It's okay." Oceana encouraged. "Tristan said I could hang around with you guys so I didn't get lonely."

"I wasn't sure." She stepped into the room and moved to the chair to sit down. "We don't usually get to meet guests."

Oceana couldn't help smirking. "I don't think he's ever had a guest quite like me before. Do you drink tea?" When Mia nodded Oceana picked up the phone at the far corner of the bench and spoke to Mrs Wells, requesting a pot of tea with two cups. It didn't take long to arrive and Oceana poured for them both, settling back into a chair more comfortable than her work stool.

"So when did you come round?" She asked curiously. "Tris had to bite you twice so they weren't sure how long you'd stay under for."

"The fever broke yesterday so they let me wake up this morning." Her eyes widened. "Does the master let you call him Tris?"

"He's never complained." Oceana shrugged and Mia gasped as though it was scandalous.

"You must be high in his regard." She whispered with awe.

"I think he just needs me to do my job more than he needs me to behave." Oceana chuckled, refusing to think she was in any way special to him. "Do you ever meet the other vampires?"

"Only Master Will." Mia's face softened. "When the master is away for long periods of time he sometimes comes to check if we need anything. Sometimes he takes us out shopping too, when we've been inside for a long time."

"You don't go out on your own?" Oceana wasn't sure why she was surprised by that.

"It's not safe." It was Mia's turn to shrug. "Finding pets isn't as easy as you'd think so attacking us is a good way of inconveniencing the master."

"How did you come to work for him?" Oceana asked curiously. She'd never really thought about it but looking at it now she realised she'd never have agreed to become a pet, for any price.

"Through the Women's Refuge." She said it like it was totally normal. "There was a woman there who gave me a number." Oceana felt her face grow hot with anger and Mia realised she was unhappy. "It wasn't like that." She tried to explain. "They didn't take advantage of a poor abused woman. I was taken there from the hospital. I had been badly beaten and it had been going on for years. I'd had enough. I just wanted to die. I did all the counselling and courses that they wanted me to do and even though I sort of understood how I came to be the way I was I didn't trust myself not to walk right into another relationship that was exactly the same. You have no idea how terrifying it was." Her eyes were bright with tears. "Finally this woman came to me with the number and said it was an option to think about. Yes, in some ways my relationship with the master could be termed as abusive, but there are strict boundaries and rules. He has never beaten me, never shown me anything but kindness. He pays me well and I live in luxury. I can have anything I want with no questions asked. He fixes us when we're injured and the truth is I love the women I live with. We bicker sometimes but we are all like sisters. Above all he has never lied to me. When I came for my interview he told me straight off why he recruited through the refuges – because he needed women of a submissive nature and because if our families had overlooked the abuse they'd probably also overlook an unusual lifestyle." She brushed her hair back self-consciously. "It's not for everyone but I have never once regretted the decision to come here. So few people have job security these days. We watch the news. We know what's going on out there. I'm set for life...even when I'm old and grey and can't give blood any more I'll be retired to one of his other homes to live out my days in peace and quiet."

Despite herself Oceana was fascinated. "So was it weird? The first time he bit you?"

"Not so much weird as disconcerting. Has he ever snared you with his gaze?"

"Once." Oceana shifted uncomfortably at the memory.

"Then you know what it's like. It's almost like having general anaesthetic. One minute you're chattering away to the nurse, the next you're waking up in the recovery room with no idea how you got there and no memory of what happened in between. The bite is very similar. You're looking into his eyes and the next thing you're waking up 3 days later feeling like you had a really good sleep." She smiled. "Sometimes if the fever is bad you have incredible dreams too."

"But it doesn't hurt?"

"Not at all. You don't feel anything once he's captured you."

Oceana's lips tingled with the memory of Tristan telling her he'd kissed her while she was snared and she refused to touch them. "Do you have family?" She asked abruptly, moving away from the subject of bites. "Do you get to see them?"

"Just my parents and I visit them sometimes. They think I'm working as a live-in housekeeper."

"And your ex?" She had to ask. She'd seen enough cases of domestic abuse in her job to know that they never released their claws that easily. "Did he ever try and track you down?"

"The master killed him." She said it calmly and matter-of-factly and Oceana's jaw dropped.

"He what?"

"He killed him." Mia shrugged. "When I first came here the Master asked me about it and when I told him some of the things that had been done to me he flew into a rage and left the house for two days. When he returned he told me that my ex was dead." She smiled faintly. "They never found the body."

"And you were okay with that?" Oceana almost felt like she was missing something.

"I am but for a lot of reasons." Mia sipped her tea. "It's not just what he did to me. I used to lie awake at night hating myself for not putting him through the courts. I couldn't face a prosecution but it was eating me up inside that he might treat another woman the way he treated me. They don't change. Now I can sleep at night knowing he'll never hurt a woman again, never put anyone else through what I went through."

Oceana's anger had slowly dissipated and she was left feeling almost guilty for condoning what Tristan had done but the truth was that she was glad the unnamed abuser would never hurt another woman. She'd been in the justice system long enough to know how hard it was to prosecute these guys and even if he had gone to jail it wouldn't have been long before he was out and ready to hurt someone else. Tristan's justice might have been savage but at least it was absolute. The fact that he had done it in revenge for Mia's suffering also made him seem a little more human in her eyes. If he didn't care for her he wouldn't have wasted the time or the energy.

"I can't be angry with him for killing someone." She confessed to Mia. "But it's wrong. I work for the Police...or at least I used to."

"Don't you ever think that perhaps the human justice system has too many shades of grey?" Mia asked her gently. "That it's too easy for people to get away with lenient sentences or unpunished altogether?"

"Sometimes, but the law has to be that way for a reason." She didn't know why she was arguing. She agreed with what Mia was saying. It was hard not to get militant about crime and punishment when you saw people get away, literally, with murder.

"The thing with the master is that he lives in absolutes. There is right and wrong, duty and pleasure, love and hate...nothing in between." Mia sipped her tea again, smiling like Mona Lisa. "He lives in black and white, not shades of grey, and I think it's a wonderful way to live. You have to give all that you are to everything that you do otherwise life isn't worth living."

Oceana thought about Tristan's kill lists, the vampires he was taking down because he had been told to and it was his duty even though he didn't think they deserved to die. When it was a question between right and duty, how did he choose? She knew the answer even as she thought the question. He would choose whichever had a greater possibility of self-preservation.

Mia allowed her to think in silence, eyes roaming the trays of beads and spools of wire with curiosity. Her eyes fell on the ward and she studied it for several moments, admiring the way the light caught the fire-polished bead. She looked at the sketch propped up to work from and the pages Will had translated from the ancient Book of Shadows.

"It's a ward for the estate." Oceana explained, realising what Mia was looking at. "I'm not entirely sure what's going on but Tris wanted the house protected."

"It's a good idea." Mia leaned over and pulled the sheets to her, studying the translations. "I like how you made the circle part of the ward. Pretty and functional."

"You know about this stuff?" Oceana was surprised and Mia blushed.

"I went through a phase as a teenager. Learned the basics. I don't have any ability though...my spells didn't work. It's more the philosophy that I like."

"The philosophy?" Oceana repeated blankly.

"Yeah. You know that most witches believe that what you send out comes back to you threefold so it makes sense to only do good." Oceana was still looking at her blankly and Mia blinked. "You've never learned this stuff?"

"I didn't know I was a witch until a couple of weeks ago." Oceana pointed out. "I only know what I've read in Tristan's library."

"Wow." Mia pursed her lips and whistled softly. "Then maybe I can help. I'm sure I've got some of my old books. I'll request them from storage."

"Thanks." Oceana smiled. "I'd really appreciate that. Most of these books read like manuals or recipe books. There's no explanation behind them."

"I'll call up to the house when they come in and you can come over for tea." Mia sipped her tea again. "It usually only takes a day or two."

"Thanks."

"No problem." Finishing her cup, Mia set it back on the tray and got to her feet. "I'll leave you to it. When the master wants something he usually wants it yesterday."

"That's for sure." Oceana chuckled and then surprised them both by getting up and hugging Mia. "Thanks for stopping in. It's kinda lonely here."

"You're always welcome at the house." Looking shy but pleased, Mia dipped her head and left the workshop leaving Oceana to get on with the ward.

***

It was past six when she put the finishing touches to the ward and she set it down on the worktop, stretching her back which cracked loudly in the silence.

"That didn't sound so good." Will said from the doorway and Oceana yelped, almost toppling off her stool as she jumped.

"You scared the hell out of me!" She accused, embarrassed and he grinned, walking in to stand behind her.

"Sorry. I was watching you work. Didn't want to disturb you." Strong hands rested on her shoulders as his thumbs began kneading the tense muscles in her neck, sore from working all that wire.

"Mmmm." She slumped in relief. "How long have you been standing there?"

"Not long. Maybe twenty minutes or so."

Okay, so that was kind of creepy. He'd been watching her for 20 minutes and she'd had no idea he was there. "You should have said something." She grumbled half-heartedly, making a small noise of satisfaction when he hit a particularly tense spot.

"Why? It was nice watching you work. It's beautiful by the way." His hands didn't stop but he leaned over her shoulder to study the ward. "Even the plastic tubing fits, weird as it is."

"It's the magic circle part of it." Oceana explained, resisting the urge to lean back into him. She was so tired and he was there and warm. "Figured it would be longer lasting than a circle poured onto the ground. And if I made the water symbolic we wouldn't have to keep topping it up ad infinitum."

"Excellent plan." He approved, hands now working on her upper neck and into her hairline.

"Oh my god that feels so good." She closed her eyes and dipped her head as a headache she didn't even know she had eased considerably.

"If you keep saying things like that we might never make it to dinner." Will sounded amused. She blushed but didn't make any move to stop him.

"Is that why you came over? Is it dinner time?"

"It'll be ready at seven. You have a little while yet. I just came to warn you in case you wanted a shower or anything."

"No I'll just wash my hands now and have a soak in the bath later." If she made it that far. She was tired and his soothing hands were making her sleepy.

"Do you always get this tense when you're working?" He asked curiously and she gathered enough energy to shrug.

"With the bigger pieces. I get really focused and when there are a lot of things to manipulate into place my muscles are always engaged. It's a lot more physical than it looks."

"So I see." He sounded more concerned than amused this time and Oceana sighed, opening her eyes again to look at the ward.

"It is pretty isn't it?" With a gentle finger she traced the clusters of beads representing the buildings. "I hope it works. I'll be gutted if I have to start again."

"I'm sure it will. Tristan was impressed with the wards at your house."

"They were crayola drawings to an impressionist masterpiece in comparison to this ward." She allowed a small touch of pride into her voice. "I'm not going to tell you what it does but if it works it's going to be awesome."

"Not going to tell me huh?" His voice was playful. "And yet I get the feeling you'll need me to test the ward."

"I won't hurt you." She grinned. "Well, nothing you can't heal at any rate."

"Great." His voice was still light and playful. "In other words it is going to hurt but there'll be no loss of body parts?"

"Something like that." She chuckled.

"It's just as well I trust you." His hands were working their way back down her neck and he reached down to raise her left arm, manipulating her shoulder.

"Have you had some training in this?" She asked curiously and he snorted with amusement.

"If I told you the answer to that it would take away all the mystery of whether I know what I'm doing or just like the skin to skin friction with a beautiful woman."

Something coiled low in her belly and she suppressed it. "Are you flirting with me Will?" She tried to keep it light but her voice hitched with something...anticipation?

"I do believe I am, yes." His tone had dropped into something huskier, sexier, but still playful.

"To what end?"

"Skin to skin friction is an end all of its own." He teased. Oceana bit her lip as an involuntary image of full body skin to skin friction flashed through her mind.

"Are you sure that it's a safe idea?" She asked, hating that her voice sounded breathy. "You know Tristan considers me his."

"That is unfortunate." He just sounded amused and Oceana had no idea what to make of it. "Perhaps I am tired of existing and intend to flame out in a blaze of glory." He teased. "There's a certain poetic justice to being destroyed by my maker, don't you think?"

"Don't even joke about it." She shuddered. "Your peculiar brand of sanity is what makes being stuck here bearable."

"Glad to hear it princess." His hands slowly left her aching muscles. "You'd better go get ready for dinner before I go too far."

For the briefest moment she considered staying where she was but she didn't want to provoke Tristan into a rage and if she played with Will that's what would happen. "As you wish." Unable to look at him for fear of something flaring between them, she left the ward on the table and left the room wondering what the hell had just happened.

***

The next morning he brought her breakfast in bed. "How are you feeling?" He asked cheerfully.

"Sore." She groaned, hauling herself gracelessly upright. "I feel like someone put me through a mangle."

"Did you have a bath after dinner?" He handed her the tray and sat across from her in the chair beneath the window.

"I did but it didn't help much." She squeezed lemon syrup onto her pancakes and wondered if she had drool or anything on her face.

"Well I was going to take you into the gym this afternoon but I think we'll just do yoga." He frowned. "There's no point further straining already damaged muscles."

"You don't have to keep me company just because Tristan's not here." She tried not to sound ungrateful but it didn't come out as gently as she'd expected.

"I need to teach you to defend yourself." He explained. "The others are doing what must be done. My role is to hold the fort until its Master comes back and that means ensuring everyone in it is safe and capable of defending it."

"Where are all the others?" She asked curiously. She hadn't seen any of them since that first morning.

"Here and there. They're keeping out of sight for now. We don't want anyone else to know that the master is gathering his forces."

"Well they can't be on the grounds when I cast the ward." Oceana winced. "If they are I can't guarantee they'll survive it."

Will looked impressed. "It's that strong?"

She shrugged, her stiff muscles screaming in protest. "It's designed to be. Whether or not it does as it's supposed to is open to question. I've never made anything like that before."

"We'll see. I've had the room behind the wine cellar opened up for you. Do you need anything to cast the ward? Is there a ritual?"

"I have no idea." She grinned at him. "I'm just going to take it down there and do whatever feels right."

"Well I'll have my mobile if you do need anything and I'm sure Mia would come over and help if you needed her to."

"I'll be fine." She projected a confidence she didn't feel and he graciously let it slide.

"I thought once the wards are set up I might pop out for a bit." He changed the subject. "I've got to run some errands. Did you want to watch a film tonight? I can pick up a DVD while I'm out."

"Doesn't Tris have films? He's certainly set up for them."

"He likes weird arthouse and indie films, usually in foreign languages." Will grimaced. "Give me a good old-fashioned action movie any day."

"Fair enough." She laughed. "I'd like that. Just don't choose anything too gruesome. And nothing scary. I don't do horror films."

"I think I can remember that." He waited until she was done with her breakfast tray and then left her to get showered and dressed.

He was waiting in the hallway when she finally came down the stairs. "Do I need to clear everyone out or just me?" He asked curiously and she thought about it.

"Just you I think." She smiled to soften the sting. "I made it specifically with vamps in mind. I never thought they'd attack with humans. I'll maybe have to make another ward eventually."

"How far out do I have to go?"

"Past the front gates, please." She murmured, slipping her shoes on. He gasped and she blinked up at him. "What?"

"It covers the whole estate?" He seemed dumbfounded.

"That was the idea, wasn't it?"

"Just exactly how strong are you?" He asked, a new respect in his eyes.

"I have no idea. Still learning, remember? Go on, get somewhere safe. I'll come find you when it's done."

"I'll be by the front gates." He slid his feet into his shoes and walked out the front door, streaking off towards the gates of the estate in the sunshine.

It only took Oceana a few minutes to fetch the ward from her workshop and she headed down into the basement, past the carefully climate controlled wine cellar and into a small room that had probably been used for storage at some stage but was now just empty. Will had thoughtfully left candles burning in there for her as there was no light and it made the room seem kind of cosy. Well, as cosy as a small concrete box with a reinforced steel door could get anyway.

Not really sure of what to do she laid the ward on the ground in the centre of the room and, following some inbuilt instinct, she moved the candles so they were standing in a circle around her. The metal gleamed so brightly, twinkling in the candlelight that she got to her knees on impulse and laid her hands gently on it. Some stray thought told her to close her eyes so she did, letting them drift shut as she breathed in the silent, musty air and focused on the metal beneath her fingertips. It seemed almost warm where she touched it and she ran her fingers over the intricate patterning, realising that it felt almost alive. It felt like the scaly, gnarly skin of some ancient dragon with its clusters of beads and intricately knotted mesh.

She was so at one with the ward that there was no mistaking the sensation when it rippled beneath her fingers. Startled into yelping, she ripped her hands away and leaped backwards, stumbling into the wall as she stared at the ward. It was no longer sat on the surface of the concrete, it had sunk into it, expanding slightly and becoming somehow...more. It was beautiful, shining with a soft golden light that shimmered in a faint lilac iridescence. She studied it for a few moments more but her heart told her it was done and so she blew out the candles and went to find Will.

"Is it ready?" He asked as she approached the gate and she nodded.

"I think so. Wait until you see it." She shuddered. "Weirdest damn thing I've ever seen."

"Really?" He grinned like the nerd kid at a science fair. "Then let's get this over with." Before she could warn him, he tried to step through the gate. Instantly a deafening clanging started up, like the wind chimes of a thunder god. "Wow." He staggered backwards and the clanging stopped. "Early warning system. Excellent thinking." He shook his head looking a little dazed. "What's making the noise?"

"No idea." She replied cheerfully, delighted that it was working so far. "I just willed it to be and there it was."

"You are one scary lady." He narrowed his eyes at her but it was obvious he was teasing.

"And don't you forget it!" Grinning she beckoned him forward. "You may step through the gates." Without flinching he stepped across the gate and her heart warmed that he trusted her word enough to take it on faith. There was absolute silence, no clanging of the damned. Excellent. "Now come slowly this time." She warned him. "This one might hurt."

Without stepping forward he raised his arm and tried to push it in front of him. "That burns." He hissed as his hand began to smoke barely a centimetre past the inside of the perimeter wall. He tried to snatch his hand back but it was stuck where he had pushed it, held into the air as though superglued there with faint curls of smoke rising from it.

"Burning enough to kill?" She asked quickly, wanting it over and done with. She hated hurting him.

"I think so." He gritted out through clenched teeth.

"You may come into the grounds." She garbled out and instantly his hand dropped to his side.

"Thank fuck for that." He shook it out, waiting for the smoking to stop. "That hurt. I'm impressed."

"I'm sorry." She sounded so miserable that he laughed out loud.

"Don't be. You're keeping us all safe. Someone had to test it."

"Well I'm sorry it had to be you." She took his undamaged hand and they strolled back towards the house.

"How many more layers are there?" He asked and she shrugged.

"I'm not sure. There's definitely one for the house as a whole and one for the room where the ward is to protect it but it's worked so well I'm thinking you might actually have to be invited into every building in the compound."

He shook his head in wonder. "The master is going to go nuts when he sees this." He grinned at her. "He'll have the most impenetrable fortress in creation."

"Regular people can still get in." She reminded him. "I'll have to fix that when I get a moment."

"I'm sure you'll figure it out." He squeezed her hand reassuringly as they arrived at the front door.

"You're not testing this one. It might kill you." She told him, releasing his hand and stepping through the door ahead of him. "Will, you may enter this house."

Gingerly he stepped across the threshold and let out a breath of relief. "I didn't get charred to a crisp, it's all good." Smiling he went past her towards the kitchen and went sprawling as he tried to walk through the door. "What the...?"

It was Oceana's turn to gape as he got to his feet and stared accusingly at the open doorway. "It warded every damn room?" She wondered aloud, astonished, and he turned to stare at her.

"You mean you have to invite me into every room of this house individually?" He sounded just as astonished as she was.

"Looks like it." She shrugged helplessly. "That was never my intention. It was obviously just stronger than I thought it would be."

"Ye gods..." He just stared at her and then his shoulders slumped. "You'd best get inviting then. Lead the way..."

They did the whole ground floor and the outbuildings first. The ward had indeed protected every individual room. It was totally unexpected and Oceana was more than a little freaked out but Will kept reminding her that it was a good thing. Every room between her and a vampire was another line of defence. It was somewhat reassuring. By the time they were done with those rooms it was almost 11am and Oceana was thirsty.

"You might as well grab a drink. I'll head into town but I won't be long. We can have lunch when I get back." Will suggested and Oceana sighed.

"You don't have to watch me eating all the time Will." The argument was getting old but she felt bad taking up so much time in his day.

"I like the routine." He shrugged. "Breaks my day up a little. If it makes you feel better I'll empty a blood bag into a soup bowl."

"No, you're alright." She turned her back on his laughter and fetched a freshly squeezed lemonade from the fridge. Mrs Wells had gone into overdrive on the summer foods with a human in the house to feed and as Oceana sipped the tart liquid she felt well and truly spoilt.

"I'll be back in a bit." He squeezed her shoulder and she pressed her cheek to the back of his hand briefly in affection.

"Drive safely."

"I always do." He released her and stepped away.

She listened to him leaving the house and wondered what to do next. There wasn't enough time to boot up the database and start another day of the journal she was currently working on. It was slow going. The few she had done so far didn't appear to have anything in common so every place, phone number and person visited or mentioned in each document had to be created from scratch. She decided to go out to the workshop instead. The ward had bothered her that morning, the way it had rippled and moved beneath her fingers. She didn't know if it was the nature of the ward or just her magic working on the metal. She knew she had several spools of wire to mess about with so she took her glass of lemonade out through the walkways into the workshop and set it on her bench.

Scanning the spools of wire she wondered if her magic had an affinity for a particular type of metal. The original starfish she had made as weapons were steel but the unbreakable chain had been aluminium and the ward had been mostly made of gold. Presumably they stored the magic but she didn't know if some metals stored more than others or for longer. She didn't know if some of them were easier to connect to. Guessing there was only one way to find out she collected a spool of each kind of wire she had in the workshop and laid them out on the bench. Grabbing a piece of paper she carefully wrote down 'Aluminium' and set to work.

CHAPTER NINE

When Will came looking for her just before one he pushed open the door of the workroom to the most bizarre sight. "What the hell is that?" He blurted out and Oceana jumped. The moment she lost her focus the strands of copper that had been twining themselves slowly in a cage around her wrist recoiled and one of them snapped back, whipping across her face and slashing her cheek open from nose to ear.

"Damn it!" She cursed, yanking her hand out of the metal and pressing it to her cheek which was bleeding.

"Sorry." Mortified, Will rushed in. "I didn't realise you were so focused." He took her face in his hands and tilted the cut towards the light. "Here, let me."

"What are you doing?" She squeaked as he moved in and he blinked.

"Sorry, I forgot you're new to this. I'm going to lick it. There's enough venom in my saliva to heal it up without scarring."

"Eww." She made a face but that made the cut sting so she gestured for him to get on with it. She'd rather deal with that than go to a hospital for stitches. The first touch of his tongue to her skin made her flinch slightly but she forced herself to remain still as he swiped a long, slow lick the length of her cheekbone.

"It's slightly deeper than I thought." He murmured, pulling back to study it slightly. "This might sting." Without waiting for an argument he leaned down again and this time pushed his tongue into the cut in delicate, gentle movements, easing the sting with soothing strokes after each invasion. Oceana tried to relax into him but it hurt and she had never been great with pain. Trying to distract herself she tried to recapture the feeling of working with the metal magic, trying to release what was going on around her enough to zone out. She was so intent on ignoring what was going on that she totally missed the moment when Will's tongue was replaced with his lips and the healing strokes were replaced with fluttering kisses. It wasn't until his lips found hers that she realised something had changed and by then it was too late. His mouth was gentle on hers but demanding, his fingers curling into her hair as he held her to him. Oceana froze briefly and then abandoned her senses to the kiss, helpless to do anything else.

When he finally released her after an infinity she took a deep breath and opened her eyes, wobbling slightly on knees that wanted her to fall into him. "What was that for?" It was a silly question but it was the first thing that popped into her head.

"You tasted so good. I couldn't seem to stop." His pupils were dilated deep with desire. "It's been so long." He brushed her lips with his thumb and they tingled.

"We can't do this Will." She whispered sadly. "Tristan will go nuts."

"Is that the only reason?"

Not quite sure what he wanted her to say, she frowned. "It's a very good reason. He could kill both of us faster than we could blink."

"That's not what I was asking." He pressed his forehead to hers and closed his eyes. "You're an amazing woman Oceana." He sighed, his hands sliding around to the back of her neck. "I want you. Probably more than I've ever wanted anything in my very long existence."

"It must be lonely." She almost couldn't bear to think of it. All those hundreds of years alone in the service of a master who had forgotten his humanity. She reached up and squeezed his forearms comfortingly. "He'll get bored of me soon enough, Will. When this job is done and I've made him all the wards he could ever possibly use he'll let me go."

"He wants you as a person, not just as a tool." He argued but she sighed.

"No he doesn't. He wants the novelty of being with a woman that can't be snared. I can make bracelets like mine for all his pets. For any woman he chooses. He just needs to realise that."

"I know him." He insisted. "It's you. Not your magic."

"He can't force me to stay Will. I'm more than capable of protecting myself now that I'm really getting to grips with my magic."

"And I'll spend the rest of my existence afraid for you." He let out a shaky laugh and finally released her. "What were you doing when I came in and startled you? How were the wires moving like that?"

"It started this morning." Oceana bent down and retrieved the mass of tangled wires on the floor, slowly turning it over in her hands as she wondered how to explain it. "I didn't know what I was doing, how I cast the ward to protect the house. So I laid my hands on it and closed my eyes and tried to focus on it and after a few moments it rippled under my hands and sank right into the floor. I wondered if I could recreate it so I was messing round with some wire in here when you came in."

"What were you making?" He asked curiously and she looked embarrassed.

"Armour. Of a sort. But it's really hard to maintain focus long enough for it to all weave together." She set the wire tangle on the bench behind her. "The minute I lose it, the whole thing falls apart. I'm thinking it's probably a good idea to just make things the old fashioned way and then finish them with the magic."

"Or just learn to focus absolutely." He shrugged. "We were going to do yoga after lunch anyway. I can teach you some meditation techniques at the same time. It would be handy to be able to use anything you come across if you ever got stuck in a dangerous situation."

"That would be great." She smiled at him just as her stomach rumbled. "Sorry." She clapped a hand to it as though that would fix it and he laughed.

"Let's go get you fed."

***

Three days of intense yoga and meditation later the entire household was awoken in the early hours of the morning by the clanging chimes of the warning ward. Oceana jumped out of bed and pulled a dressing gown on, yanking open her door just as Will blew across the landing in a rush and took the stairs in one long, graceful leap.

"Stay here." He threw back over his shoulder in her direction as he left through the front door to investigate. Shivering, Oceana ran back to her room and collected her bag of chainmail, tipping the jumbled starfish into her palm in readiness. Her system was so full of adrenaline the rings clinked together in her shaking hands and she wished Tristan was there. She trusted the ward to hold but it was only the two of them in the house to defend the staff and the pets. She was just wondering whether to head to the workshop for more metal when the front door crashed open and Will reappeared looking like something from a horror movie. It had been raining outside and he was covered in blood.

"Oh my God!" Oceana dropped the starfish and ran down the stairs, barely noticing the crumpled heap he was carrying gently in his arms.

"Someone left her at the gates." He sounded a bit dazed and Oceana drew up just short of crashing into him.

"What?"

He raised the bundle in his arms. "She was left at the gates. In the middle of the road."

Oceana looked at the bundle, only then realising it was a person wrapped in a tattered, bloodstained blanket. "Is she alive?"

"Barely."

Oceana reached for the blanket covering the woman's face and pulled it back. Instantly the blood drained out of her face and she sank slowly to the floor, knees in the slowly spreading pool of rainwater tinged with blood around Will's feet. "No!" She wailed. "Nooooo!"

"You know her?" Will studied her face and she nodded.

"It's Jo. My best friend."

"Fuck." He hefted Jo in his arms. "We need to get her fixed up." He strode towards the kitchen bellowing for Mrs Wells who appeared looking flustered but fully dressed. Together they laid Jo out on the kitchen table while Oceana tried to pull herself together enough to get to her feet and follow them. They threw away the blanket and cut her clothes away, trying to see what damage had been inflicted. She had been brutally beaten, complex fractures all over her small frame. Cuts and slashes marred her pale skin and her lips were turning blue in the bright lights of the kitchen.

"She's lost too much blood." Mrs Wells said quietly to Will and he turned helplessly to Oceana who was hovering in the doorway.

"If I bite her enough times to fix this I can't guarantee that she'll survive." He raised his bloody hands in a gesture of sheer helplessness. "She's too badly injured to survive that much venom."

"You have to do something!" Oceana came into the room then and picked soggy tendrils of hair out of Jo's face. "Please fix her." She begged. "You have to try."

"You're not understanding what I'm saying." Will caught her by the chin and looked steadily into her eyes. "She will not survive but she might come back. As one of us."

"A vampire?" She whispered and he nodded. Oceana studied her friend, knowing she had only seconds in which to make the choice. "Then do it." She swallowed thickly, her head ringing with fear and anger. "If she doesn't want to exist that way I'll end it myself."

"Are you sure?" She nodded again and he released her. "Then you'll need to step back." She moved out of his way and Mrs Wells stepped back too.

"I'll go get Ellen." She told them. "If she makes it she'll need a transfusion."

"Good idea." Will took a deep breath as he studied where to go first. He'd have to bite her all over quickly to saturate her entire system with venom before her heart gave out. It was going to be touch and go as to whether he could work that fast. He could already hear her heart fluttering as it went into shock. With one last look at Oceana he steeled himself and attacked, his fangs puncturing and tearing flesh until his face was smeared with the girl's blood and his jaws were aching with producing so much venom.

After the first few frenzied moments Oceana couldn't watch any more and turned away feeling nauseous. It had to work. It just had to.

***

Jo awoke to the sound of gentle snoring and turned her head slightly to see Oceana asleep in an armchair by the bed she was lying in. The room was unfamiliar and she frowned slightly trying to figure out where she was. The last thing she remembered was stepping out of her front door to head for work. Confused, she looked up as the door opened and a total stranger came in carrying a large knitted blanket which he laid gently over Oceana and then he turned to Jo with a relieved smile on his lips.

"I'm Will." He whispered. "How are you feeling?"

It took a couple of attempts to speak. Her throat was dry and cracked and she was exhausted. "I've been better."

He nodded. "Do you think you can get up? We can talk downstairs, let Oceana sleep. She was up all night."

Jo struggled to push herself upright and as she did she was relieved to feel some strength flowing back into her body. She pushed the covers back and stared at the pyjamas she was wearing. "Why am I wearing Oceana's pyjamas?" She asked and a smile touched the corners of Will's mouth.

"The clothes you arrived in were beyond salvage. It was that or nakedness."

"Oh." Confused to the edge of hysteria, Jo allowed Will to help her out of bed and they quietly made their way downstairs to the living room to talk.

***

When Oceana awoke her eyes flew instantly to the bed and she panicked when she realised Jo wasn't there. Terrified that Jo might have died in the morning and no-one had told her she jumped up, tripping over the blanket someone had laid over her and scrabbled across to the door.

"It's okay." Will's voice called up from below. "We're down here."

"Oh thank God." Oceana ran across the landing and down the stairs, flying into Jo's arms hiccupping sobs and gulping breaths as she tried to speak through her tears. "I thought you were dead. I'm so sorry."

"Near as I can make out, I *am* dead." Jo grinned to show she was joking and then swatted Oceana's arm. "You're such an idiot. You should have told me about all this. I've been freaking out that you were being held by the government because some badass terrorist was trying to kill you."

"Because being held by a bunch of vampires is any less scary or unrealistic?" Will pointed out drily and Jo laughed.

"That's true. I wouldn't have believed you." She released Oceana who swiped unsuccessfully at the tears streaming down her face.

"Are you mad at me?" She asked in a small voice and Jo shook her head.

"It's not your fault. Will has explained the circumstances."

"And the whole..." she gestured vaguely at Jo. "...vampire thing. Are you okay with that?"

"I just want to live." Jo shrugged. "Will told me that if he hadn't turned me I would have died. It's too early to know how I feel about any of the rest of it. I've only been awake a couple of hours."

As though realising it was daylight, Oceana checked her watch. "It's lunchtime." Will said, noticing. "Mrs Wells is putting something together for you to eat. We were about to come and get you."

"I'm not really hungry." She said tiredly but Will just shrugged.

"Nevertheless, you will eat." His tone brooked no argument and she and Jo trailed after him through to the kitchen. The mess from the night before had all been cleaned away. There was no trace of blood anywhere on the floor or walls and the table looked as though it had been freshly sanded.

"Did you get some sleep?" Oceana asked Mrs Wells, running a hand along the unmarked tabletop and the housekeeper smiled.

"Yes Oceana, I got plenty. Thank you for asking."

"Thank you for your help this morning."

"You're welcome. You don't have to thank me." She carried a huge plate of food and a glass of lemonade over for Oceana and set them on the table where cutlery was already laid out. "Please eat."

Sighing inwardly at the mountain of food, Oceana did as she was told and sat down to eat. Jo watched her enviously. "That looks really good." She murmured, sitting opposite and Oceana winced.

"Sorry."

"Here you go." Mrs Wells placed large mugs in front of Will and Jo. "I warmed it up for you. I heard it was easier that way at first."

"Thank you Mrs Wells." Will smiled at her. "That was most thoughtful of you."

Jo sniffed suspiciously at the mug and then yelped, clapping her hands to her mouth as a cracking sound filled the room. Her eyes watered at the pain but Will reached across and rubbed her back soothingly.

"It hurts." She whimpered as her eyes watered and he nodded sympathetically.

"I know, I'm sorry. I forgot. It only happens the first time. It gets a lot easier."

"Your fangs?" Oceana asked with a blend of fascination and fear.

"Yeah, how freakin' weird is that?" She lisped slightly around her new teeth.

"I must say, you're taking this all rather calmly." Will remarked and Jo shrugged.

"What's done is done. I can't change it and with these bloody great big pointy things breaking out of my jaw I can't exactly be in denial can I? Right now I'm probably in shock. Ask me again tomorrow."

"Well we're not going anywhere." He reassured her. "It will seem strange at first but we'll get you through it."

They were just clearing away Oceana's plate when the clanging started up again. They all froze and then Will's mobile started ringing. "It's Tristan." He checked the screen. "He's probably wondering why he can't get into his house."

"He's back?" Oceana grinned, feeling relieved but at the same time slightly saddened that her alone time with Will was over. "I'll go get him." She dropped her plate in the sink and left as she heard Will telling Tristan she'd be right out. She ran all the way up to the gate and he grinned when he saw her.

"Well who's a clever little pumpkin?" He asked drily and she blinked.

"Did you just call me a pumpkin?" She burst out laughing. "That sounded so wrong coming from you. It's good to have you back."

"It's good to see you too." He unleashed his most dazzling smile on her and despite herself her libido did a little happy dance. "Are you going to invite me in?"

"Ooh I don't know about that." She smirked. "It's kinda fun having the house to ourselves..."

"Come on 'Cean. Let me in. You know you're just *dying* for a hug."

"Whatever." She stepped to the side but put a hand up in warning. "You can only step one step past the gates when I invite you and then I have to invite you over the next ward."

"Whatever." He mocked her and she sighed.

"Tristan, you may enter these gates."

He stepped forward and pulled her to him in a hug. "Was that a euphemism?" He breathed into her ear and she giggled.

"No it wasn't. You're not 'entering' anything of mine."

He sighed. "That may change when you hear the things I have to do for you." Releasing her he straightened up. "What happens with the next ward?" Without waiting for an answer he took another step forward and instantly froze mid-step, his flesh beginning to smoke and burn.

"Tristan!" Swearing at him Oceana rushed to stand in front of him. "Tristan you may enter this estate."

"Nasty." He straightened his collar and held his hand up to examine the fast-fading burns. "I'm impressed."

"You could have been killed you idiot!" She exploded and he smiled sardonically.

"Why, it actually sounds as though you care for me."

"You know I do. And you're still an idiot." She threw back at him. "Don't ever do that to me again. And don't step over the doorway to the house without being invited. You think this ward is nasty, wait until you get to the house. That one is twenty times worse."

"I can't wait." Smiling he went to fetch his car.

By the time she'd invited him into the house and into all the ground floor rooms he had introduced himself to Jo and looked askance at Will.

"She was attacked and left at the gates to die last night." Will explained succinctly and Tristan frowned.

"That's interesting."

"Interesting?" That was not the word Oceana would have chosen. "Someone attacks my best friend and leaves her to die on our doorstep and you think it's 'interesting'?"

"Well obviously it's awful and the paperwork is going to be a nightmare. Retrospective licence applications are a bitch. But I'm more concerned with who did it and why."

She shuddered. "It feels like a warning."

"That's exactly what it is. And it's aimed at you." He cupped her cheek in his palm. "We need to talk. All of us."

They sat around the kitchen table and Oceana sighed as Mrs Wells placed a cup of tea in front of her. "What do you mean the warning was aimed at me?" She asked Tristan as he took one of her hands in both of his.

"To explain that I need to tell you what happened." He interlaced her fingers with his and studied their linked hands. "I was summoned before the council to be given my kill list but when I arrived they questioned me extensively about you. It was an open council session."

"An open session?" Will was horrified and Tristan nodded.

"What does that mean?" Oceana looked between them. "Why is that so bad?"

"Because it means that everyone in that room knows everything about you. The place was packed with people wanting to know about my latest asset."

"Oh this is bad." Will muttered, getting up to pace.

"Luckily I could tell them truthfully that I didn't know the extent of your powers but it made no odds. I have received four challenges over my right of your ownership."

"But you don't own me. I don't understand." She hoped it didn't mean what she thought it did.

"In vampire terms you are my property. You are in my employ, you live under my roof and you sometimes share my bed. We were seen together in public. You know about our kind." He smiled to take the sting out of his words. "By our law that makes you mine."

"I knew you shouldn't have taken me to that restaurant." She yanked her hand out of his and got up to pace on the opposite side of the table to Will. "I told you."

"It wouldn't have made any difference." Tristan responded mildly. "Your existence was known about anyway. Some families have spies everywhere."

"So what does this mean? What does a challenge involve?"

"It's like an old-fashioned duel. Two opponents, the challenged nominates the weapon and then they duel to the death. Can you please sit down? I can't track you both at once. I'm good but not that good."

"A duel to the death?"

"So that's why you called in the reinforcements." Will ignored Oceana and focused on Tristan. "And why it was so important to defend the house in case someone tried to steal her. When will the challenges be held?"

"The council deliberated this morning and allowed them to stand. The challenges will be five days from now."

"All on the same day?" Will was shocked enough to stop pacing.

"I'll be fine." Tristan brushed it off but Oceana was about to lose her rag.

"A duel to the death?!" She shouted. "You mean you could actually die?"

"That's generally what death is all about, yes." He mocked her gently. "Don't be afraid princess. I am the finest warrior of my kind. There are none that can defeat me, not even four in a row. What does concern me is the dealings of the council in this."

"They must know about the journals." Will had connected the dots. "They can't move against you directly but they will encourage challenges over your property and try to rig it so that you fail."

"Which means that I have to keep taking on all comers until you can figure out what the secret is that they're trying so hard to keep covered up." Tristan told Oceana.

"I don't want you to die for me." She was shaking. "It's already happened once this week. I can't go through that again. Let me go Tristan. I'll go to whoever wants to take me. I don't want anyone to die."

"I'm not going to die." Faster than she could blink he was out of his chair and gathering her up in his arms. "'Cean don't worry. I'll be fine. I just need you to do your job. Let me worry about me."

"He's right." Will added slowly but quietly. "He is the best at what he does. He will not be harmed."

"But what if it's a trap?" Jo asked, the first thing she had said since the conversation started. "What if they're luring you there to fight all these people and then ambush you?"

"They can't." Tristan spoke over the top of Oceana's head. "Formal challenges have to take place in front of the assembled families. Everyone will be there and I have spent the last several days gathering allies. They can't ambush me without dividing our race."

"Do you have to go back?" Oceana's voice was muffled by his shirt. "Do you have to go gather more allies?"

"Yes but I needed to come and get you first. You have to come with me. As the prize for the winner the law states you must be present. That means you need clothes and so on. We can spend this afternoon packing and I'll get the indexing program transferred onto the laptop for you but we need to leave tomorrow morning."

"What was the point of making the house a fortress just to step outside it?" Oceana demanded futilely but Tristan just shrugged.

"It means we have somewhere safe to come back to." He replied mildly. "If you have wards you can take with you then all the better but you'll be with me and Will and we'll protect you."

"The others are here too." Will reminded him. "They're not at the house but I can ring round and have everyone meet us in London."

"Get them to meet us outside the gates." Tristan's voice had gone hard and the steel in it made Oceana shiver. "I'm not leaving any of this to chance. We'll travel down in convoy."

***

The following morning Tristan and Oceana had an argument over whether or not Jo was going to come with them. Tristan had asked her to stay overnight with him and she had felt so guilty over the threat to his life that she had conceded.

"She's taking it remarkably well." Tristan was saying in his calm, measured tone. "But I can't afford to have a fledgling embarrass us in front of the council and we haven't filed for a licence yet. We'll leave her here."

"She's only taking it well because this is a whole new and exciting world to her." Oceana argued back fiercely. "She hasn't realised yet how much she's lost but when she does she'll fall apart and I won't leave her to deal with that alone. She's my best friend Tris. She's in this mess because of me. Whether it happens now, tomorrow, or ten days from now it's suddenly going to occur to her that she'll never eat another meal, never have kids, never see her parents again...I can't let her deal with all that loss on her own."

"I don't have the resources to protect her in London." He stated bluntly. "Mine is only a small house and we'll be staying in a hotel that's open to all vampires."

"You don't have the resources but I can protect her." Her tone was pleading. "All I need is a spool of wire and a few minutes and I can make any room on earth totally impenetrable."

That gave him pause and finally his eyes narrowed. "If I agree to this you will owe me." He said shortly and Oceana sat back.

"What do you want?"

"You know what I want." He brushed a curl away from her face and tucked it gently behind her ear.

"You're asking if I'll give you my body to protect my friend?" She clarified and he sighed.

"You don't have to put it quite so crudely, but yes."

"Done." She didn't hesitate. "I'll go tell her to pack a bag." She made to get out of the bed but he caught her arm.

"Not so fast! We just made a deal. You need to complete your half of the bargain."

"Oh Tristan..." She smiled sweetly at him. "I might have agreed to your demand but I never gave you a timescale. For such an old dude you're surprisingly easy to work around." She patted his arm and climbed out of the bed, wrapping herself in a robe and leaving the room leaving him staring after her in chagrin.

"Only when it comes to you." He muttered as the door closed behind her. "Only when it comes to you."

***

He had booked them a suite at a hotel that Oceana had never heard of but which was clearly luxury and had a very exclusive clientele. She felt a little grubby in her regular jeans and soft cotton shirt as she looked around at the glossy, well-dressed people in the lobby.

"Do not speak to anyone or look at anyone." Tristan warned her and Jo quietly under his breath. "This is a vampire hotel and I'd like to avoid any diplomatic incidents. If anyone speaks to you keep it short and defer to me. Do you understand?"

"Yes master." Oceana lowered her eyes, painfully aware that their arrival had caused silence to ripple through the room as everyone turned to stare at them.

"Executioner." The Manager of the hotel rushed forward. "If you will come this way please." The silence held as they crossed the lobby and stepped into the elevators and even though all of Tristan's family were surrounding her protectively, Oceana felt as though her skin was crawling with the eyes turned on it. She wondered what they thought of her, this insignificant little human that the vampire executioner was prepared to fight to the death over. She concluded it probably wasn't very favourable.

"Well that was awkward." She muttered under her breath once the lift doors were closed and Will hid a grin, brushing his fingers across the back of her hand in an invisible gesture of comfort. Tristan said nothing as they rose towards the suite of rooms he had booked for them and Oceana sighed. It was going to be a long week.

***

Apart from a brief visit to Caroline's shop to find a suitable dress for the day of the duel and a few meditation sessions with Will, Oceana spent most of the remaining four days working methodically through the journals while the vampires went to various dinners and balls, cementing alliances. Tristan had debated the wisdom of leaving her and Jo alone in the hotel but Oceana had set up wards around the rooms and no-one could get in or out without her permission no matter how hard they battered at the invisible barriers and eventually he trusted her enough to leave them to it. Will continued his yoga classes until Oceana had almost completely mastered the art of single-minded focus. She was still having wobbles here and there but with Will on hand to heal any cuts caused by wire springing back she was making huge progress and could create a ward in a matter of moments.

The night before the duels Tristan found her standing gazing moodily out of the window across the city. They were high up on the 12th floor and the window faced out towards the river. "Do you regret bringing me into your life?" She asked without turning round, studying his reflection in the darkening glass.

"Not for a minute. Why?" He came to stand beside her and she leaned her head against his shoulder.

"Because this could have been so much simpler. There are other indexers out there who aren't witches. They could have done the job and remained in obscurity."

For a few moments Tristan was silent and then he tucked her under his arm and gazed out across the city with her. "I've existed for a very long time and that's all it has been...existing. Another woman, someone I could snare and order to do my bidding, wouldn't have changed that. But you?" He made a noise halfway between a sigh and a chuckle. "I can't remember the last time I actually really wanted something. I can't remember the last time I was frustrated or really amused or even what it feels like to actually care about something. I've been the stuff of nightmares for so long that I'd almost forgotten what the word 'no' sounded like." Subconsciously his hand ran up and down her arm. "I've had more fun in the last few weeks than I've had in the last few centuries combined. So no. I don't regret bringing you into my life, not even for a second."

"I'm scared." She whispered in a small voice and he squeezed her tightly.

"Don't be. I'll win tomorrow. And if by some freak of nature I don't then you'll be well provided for."

"You've written up a plan B?" Her heart sank. If he had thought about Plan B it meant he believed there was a chance he might not survive the next day.

"I don't expect to have to use it." He said easily but she couldn't let it go.

"Tris...tell me the truth. How dangerous is tomorrow going to be? Are you going to get hurt?"

"More than likely." She took a deep breath, her heart racing. "'Cean, it's okay." He pressed a kiss to the top of her head.

"No. It's not." She turned into him and buried her face in his chest. "Don't you dare die on me Tristan. I don't think I could bear it."

"Then give me a reason to live." He whispered, strong fingers under her chin tipping her face up to look at his.

For the first time she set aside her own fears and hang-ups and realised that she was looking into the eyes of a man who was prepared to bleed to protect her, to die to keep her safe. Whatever his motivations, his desire for personal gain, at the end of the day he was laying his life on the line for hers and she couldn't argue with that. "Okay." She whispered. "Take me to bed Tristan."

***

When the alarm went off at 6am the next morning they were already awake and sat on the edge of the bed together holding hands. "Do we have to do this?" She asked him quietly and he nodded, a smile touching the edges of his lips.

"Yes we do. But I'll be fine. Don't worry." He released one of his hands and traced the line of her neck with a gentle finger. "You look really beautiful today."

"In my dressing gown?" She gave a shaky laugh. "It's 6am and I've barely slept. I don't look beautiful."

"After last night you'll always be beautiful to me."

She ignored the shiver of lust that trembled at her core, blissfully sated but ready to stir at a moment's notice. "Even when I'm old and grey and wrinkly and losing my marbles?" She joked weakly.

"Even then." He sighed. "We should get dressed. The others are waking."

"Breakfast first." She laid a kiss on his bare shoulder. "Go get in the shower. I'll order room service."

"I hate that I love it when you boss me around." He sounded perplexed but amused and did as she asked, dropping the sheets covering his waist and strolling indolently into the bathroom. Oceana admired the view with a sigh. The man was sin on legs.

"How many am I ordering breakfast for?" She called as she headed into the main living area and counted the mumbled replies she heard. Tristan was right, they were all stirring. She picked up the phone and dialled reception, ordering for everyone and then turned and walked smack into Will.

"Sorry." He stepped back. "I thought you knew I was there."

"No I didn't hear you. I'm sorry, I should have looked where I was going." They stood there awkwardly, he in his cotton pyjama pants and her in her silk dressing gown.

"You slept with him." It wasn't a question and she didn't try to deny it.

"He asked me for a reason to live. It was the only answer I had to give him that I thought would actually mean something."

He nodded, accepting that, and pulled her into a hug. "How are you holding up?" He asked quietly as doors began opening and semi-dressed vampires stumbled into the room.

She wanted to lie and say she was fine but she knew he would know. Instead she sighed. "I've never been so scared in my life."

"Is this a two person hug or can anyone join in?" Jo asked from behind her and Oceana laughed, startled into forgetting her fear just for a moment.

"No, anyone can join in."

"Awesome." Jo's arms encircled her and then Caroline's, followed by Alathea's and Charlie's and Xavier's. By the time Tristan emerged from the bathroom, there was a large group hug going on in the centre of the suite and he surveyed it with disbelief.

"Well that's just plain disturbing." He ruffled his damp hair uncomfortably and the black locks fell in a sexy tousle about his face as though they were designed to.

"Stop being a sarcastic ass and join in." Oceana's voice was muffled at the centre of the huddle but it was still loud enough to make him grin.

"No I'm all right thanks." He gave them a wide berth as the group hug finally broke up. "I hope this little Kodak moment was nothing to do with you all thinking I'm going to lose today."

"It wasn't about you." Jo blinked. "It was about Oceana. And how she's struggling today and just needed a little moral support to help her through watching her lord and master dealing out death and destruction."

"Oh I see." He blinked back at her. "In that case..." He reached out one-handed and snagged Oceana into a bear-hug. "You'll be fine." He told her sternly and set her back on her feet. "Now man up and chase up breakfast. I'm hungry."

When room service arrived it was still one of the weirdest things Oceana had ever seen. There was a traditional tray for her with smoked salmon and scrambled eggs on toast, a pot of tea and a flower in a vase. The rest of the trolley was taken up with mugs of blood carefully warmed to body temperature and four or five carafes of coffee.

"I love this place." Charlie took a mug and sipped. "They never have preservatives in their blood."

"What does that mean?" Oceana whispered to Will and he winced.

"It means there's so little time between donor and cup that the blood doesn't have time to coagulate." He shifted uncomfortably on his feet. "The stuff that we usually drink from the blood bags is treated with anti-clotting preservatives."

"Eww." She made a face. "I wish I hadn't asked."

"You'll get used to it." Smiling he gestured towards the large dining table off to one side in an alcove and she sat in front of her plate. She wasn't hungry but she knew Tristan was watching her with concern so she tucked in with fake enthusiasm and eventually the others joined her at the table, laughing and sharing stories in the way that families who have been apart a long time can.

***

"What are you going to do with all of those?" Tristan asked after breakfast as they retired to the room to get dressed. Oceana had showered and was standing in her towel hefting a pile of wire spools in one hand and a pair of stockings in the other.

"I'm going to hide them around my ankles." She replied absently. "Do you think they'll pull the stockings?"

Tristan hid a grin. "If they do I'll personally buy you a new pair."

"Thanks." She laid the spools on the bed and contemplated the corset that had come with the dress. "You might have to help me into this." She held it up. "It looks complicated."

This time he didn't bother to hide his grin. "Not a problem at all..."

CHAPTER TEN

The council chambers were in Bow Road. Outside the building looked like a deserted warehouse, crumbling and unsafe and covered in graffiti. Inside, down a concealed staircase and through several layers of security, it was all glossy opulence. Gleaming marble colonnades lined each underground hall and the carpets were so plush they muffled every sound into silence. Black was the prevailing colour but it was saved from being morbid by slashes of brightly coloured tapestries here and there on the walls.

Tristan stalked along the hallways with lethal grace, totally calm and in control of his environment. The others marched behind him with Oceana at their centre and Will bringing up the rear, his eyes watchful for any sign of attack.

Oceana heard the council chamber before she saw the doors. There was an excited buzz of hundreds of voices carrying down the hallway and when the doors opened ahead of them it spilled out in a rush, flooding around them in a wall of sound. But just as suddenly it was cut off, like someone had pulled the switch. Tristan entered the room to dead and absolute silence. Willing her legs not to shake, Oceana followed him and tried not to stare too much at the room around her. It was shaped like an amphitheatre, a massive underground amphitheatre, and tiers upon tiers of faces stared down at their little group as it made its way across the expanse of stone as the carpet faded once more into marble.

"Executioner." A large blond man stepped into his path and clasped wrists with Tristan. "It's good to see you."

"And you my friend." Tristan sounded genuinely pleased and Oceana relaxed slightly. "I did not realise you would be here."

"I nearly didn't make it but I couldn't miss seeing the bright flower that has caused all the fuss." He glanced over Tristan's shoulder at Oceana and she instantly dipped her eyes as Tristan had told her to.

"You could have visited anytime." Tristan sounded vaguely reproving but he stepped aside and introduced them. "Wulfric this is Oceana. Oceana this is Wulfric. His House has been friend to mine since time immemorial."

"Nice to meet you." She curtsied slightly and he grinned, showing broad strong teeth.

"Nobody told me she'd be so pretty!" He joked to Tristan before taking Oceana's hand and laying a gallant kiss on the back of it. "The pleasure is all mine Oceana, truly."

He was about to say more but a loud booming interrupted the conversation and everyone turned to clear the floor, leaving Tristan's group along with four other groups standing alone in the centre of the massive space. There was a slight shuffling at the far end of the hall and then 6 vampires marched regally into the centre of the arena and looked around. A tall woman with striking bone structure stepped forward.

"Challenge has been laid and accepted." She announced briefly. "All here bear witness." Without any further ado they spun on their feet and went to sit in ringside seats.

"Oceana, Will, you stay and help. Everyone else go sit." Tristan ordered calmly and everyone except the 3 of them backed away. Tristan unslung the bag he had been carrying and opened it up, pulling out several well worn and scratched pieces of leather. "You're going to have to help me into these." He commanded, handing half to Oceana and half to Will. They instantly dropped to their knees and began buckling the light armour in place, for that's what it was. Oceana's fingers shook as she fed the leather thongs through the buckles. Leather was no match for swords, certainly not when wielded by vampire strength. He might as well be going out there naked.

They fastened on his shin guards, breastplate, shoulder guards and greaves before Will finally handed him his swords, helping him fit the belt across his back and snug at the waist. He looked beautiful and deadly and, staring at him, Oceana felt like her heart was about to break.

"You should go and sit with the others." He cupped her cheek in his palm briefly and she turned into it, kissing the callused skin.

"Come back to me Tristan." She fought the tears that trembled in her voice. "Otherwise I'll march into hell and haul your soul screaming back into existence, so help me god."

"Now that I'd like to see." His eyes were twinkling and she realised that this was what made him feel truly alive, dancing on the edge of death. There was no fear in him at all.

"And try not to mess up that pretty face of yours." Throwing protocol to the winds she leaned forward and kissed him full on the lips and he threw himself into it, pulling her to him and plundering her mouth with his tongue leaving her breathless and dizzy. The murmurings in the crowd rose to a crescendo until finally the icy woman's voice snapped across the room.

"Enough! Let us begin."

Tristan released Oceana and smiled at her. "I'll be fine. Go sit with the others."

With nothing else to say she did as she was bid and crossed the marble to sit with Tristan's family. They were seated about a quarter of the way up the tiers in a group and she stepped into the centre of them as they shuffled around to make room.

"Are you okay?" Xavier muttered quietly under his breath and Oceana took a deep breath.

"Not really but I'll deal with it. Just promise me if it gets bad that you'll shield me from it."

"On my honour." He bumped her shoulder gently and they turned to watch events unfolding in the arena.

Tristan was limbering up, stretching out his neck and arm muscles, flexing his wrists and pacing round. He was so beautiful he made Oceana's throat ache. He looked sleek and deadly like a panther, the muscles sliding under his skin in fluid motion. His face was calm as the council elder called for the first of the duels to start and a muscular young man stepped up opposite Tristan.

Oceana suddenly found she couldn't watch and turned away as the first clash of metal rang in the air. "This is no contest." Xavier whispered to her. "His opponent is grossly outmatched. The Master will win."

Barely moments later there was a sickening crunching sound followed by a wet thunk and Oceana risked a look at the combatants. Tristan was stripping the blood nonchalantly off his blade between his thumb and forefinger, flicking it at the headless body lying before him. Her stomach lurched and she looked away again.

"Are you going to be sick?" Charles sounded more curious than concerned and Oceana shook her head.

"No. I'm fine."

"Then you must watch." He told her gently. "You do him dishonour by not witnessing his bravery." She looked into his troubled eyes and tried to get control of herself.

"I'm sorry." She forced her chin up and looked down to where Tristan was just facing up to his second opponent. Wordlessly Xavier took her hand and she squeezed his tightly in thanks.

"This will be closer but the Master will still win." He continued his commentary quietly in her ear. "He'll be fine."

Oceana watched tensely as Tristan and the other vampire circled each other warily and then, at some invisible provocation, they ferociously attacked. Steel crashed and sparks flew, peppering the air with muffled grunts. Tristan drew first blood but almost immediately took a cut to the thigh. They drew apart quickly to assess their wounds before crashing together again. The fight raged back and forth across the open space and by the time Tristan had finally managed to defeat his opponent they were both bleeding heavily and the floor was slick with blood.

"Will they clean up?" Oceana studied the glistening marble apprehensively.

"Normally I'd say yes but the council has an agenda here." Xavier tilted his head as he appraised Tristan's third opponent. "It depends who they think it will inconvenience more."

It seemed they thought it would inconvenience Tristan as the blood was left where it had pooled and only the body was dragged away.

"How even is this match?" Oceana glanced at Xavier and he shrugged.

"The Master is the better swordsman but he is tiring. If he can finish it quickly he'll be fine. If it is dragged out he will still win but the fourth duel will be difficult."

It seemed Tristan had come to the same conclusion. The moment the signal was given to start he bulled towards his opponent, taking a punishing blow to the side of his breast plate without any attempt to deflect it, and hacked the vampire's head off in an epic show of strength, but the crack of breaking ribs had been clearly audible.

"Fuck." Oceana tried to rise to her feet to see how badly he was hurt but Xavier anchored her down.

"He will heal." He told her tersely. "There is no blood, for now."

Tristan returned to Will and handed over his sword for cleaning, taking a moment to swipe a damp towel over his face and neck to clean away some of the blood. It looked as though the cuts on his arms and legs were healing over already but the way he moved had lost some of its grace. He was clearly favouring his broken ribs.

"This match." Oceana turned to Xavier. "Will he win it?"

"He should but it will be brutal." Xavier shrugged. "He is going to get hurt."

Worse than he already was? Oceana swallowed as rage lit a fire in her belly. This was crazy. Before she knew what she was doing she had risen to her feet and her voice rang clearly across the chamber.

"I nominate myself as champion for the House of the Executioner to fight the next duel." She declared. Absolute silence fell as every pair of eyes in the room swung in her direction.

"Oceana...what...?" Will didn't get a chance to ask. The councilwoman stood up and turned to Tristan who was watching Oceana with something akin to horror on his face.

"Does this woman speak for you?" She asked clearly and Oceana pleaded with her eyes for him to trust her. She didn't know what he saw in her face but after a few moments he nodded just once.

"She does."

"Then clear the floor. Step down to the arena, witch."

"I will act as second." Xavier got to his feet and followed her down and she was grateful. She didn't know what was going on between her and Will or even her and Tristan and it wasn't fair to either of them to expect them to back her in this insane adventure. With barely a glance she swept past them as she walked out onto the floor, her rage floating her into a calm realm of serenity.

"Are you sure about this?" Xavier asked her uneasily and she nodded, cold and still as ice within her little bubble of fury.

"I'm certain." Without hesitation she mentally stepped within as Will had taught her and grasped her magic, flooding her body with it and fuelling it with her fury. Pushing the straps of her velvet dress from her shoulders she allowed it to pool around her feet and stepped out of the fabric, walking towards the centre of the arena as the coils of wire around her ankles curled up and flowed across her skin. There were gasps from the crowd as she drew to a halt and the wire continued to slither and flow across her skin. Holding out her hand she focused on it and some of the wire formed a delicate, spiralled spear.

"Come then, you who would challenge." She met the vampire's eyes fearlessly and for the first time he faltered.

"What magic is this?" He demanded and she shrugged.

"It is the magic you coveted without understanding. Attack me and have done." She waited for him to attack and his eyes flicked to the council members. They gazed back impassively and he winced as he realised they weren't going to intervene. Eventually he darted forward, slashing at her with his blade. It stopped a good half foot away from her body and she didn't even flinch. "Try harder." Her tone had slipped into something dark and vengeful and his face blanched. Furiously he attacked but his blade just slid away without ruffling a single hair of her head and all the time she just stood there watching him.

When she realised she had made her point she shifted her centre of balance without warning and threw her spear at him. He tried to duck it but it twisted and collapsed in mid-air into one long gleaming loop of wire that wrapped itself around his neck and sliced it clean off like a cheese wire through softened butter.

Absolute silence filled the room as the body hung motionless for a moment before toppling to the floor at her feet and Oceana looked around, turning on the spot as she gazed at the sea of faces around her. "Let this be a lesson to you all." She announced coldly when she had let the entire room feel the weight of her gaze. "And I suggest you learn it well. I serve only one master. I will only ever serve one master. You challenge him or you hurt someone I care about and I will hunt you down and slaughter you like an animal. I hope I have made myself clear." With a last pointed look around she stormed back across the marble towards Xavier, her heels clicking on the stone.

As she walked she let her magic slip away and the wire flowed back down her body to recoil itself around her ankles. He mutely held up her dress as she reached him and she stepped into it gratefully, allowing him to smooth the shoulder straps back into place. "That was well done." He squeezed her shoulder briefly with pride, respect and no small amount of fear and then stepped aside to allow Tristan to approach. His face said they would be discussing this at length later but he didn't say anything to her, turning instead to face the crowd.

"Are there any more challengers?" He demanded but the sullen silence reigned supreme. "Excellent." He sheathed his sword and gestured for the rest of his House to join them on the floor. Bowing respectfully to the council members who were looking chagrined and not hiding their dismay at all well, the familiar faces formed up around Oceana and together they left the room.

***

Tristan waited until they were back at the hotel and alone before he exploded. "What the hell were you thinking?" He roared at her. "You could have been killed!"

"How are your ribs?" She asked quietly, ignoring his question. "Do they need binding?"

"Do you have any idea how badly that could have gone wrong?" He was still shouting and so she began removing her dress. "I know you aren't in control of your magic. Will told me you were struggling to focus."

She slipped a coat hanger into the dress and went to hang it in the wardrobe. "Are you hungry?" She asked as she returned. "Would you like me to order room service?"

"No I don't want you to order me room service!" He was shaking with pent-up fury and delayed shock. "You could have been killed today Oceana!! What part of that are you not understanding?"

"Calm down and think about it and you'll realise you're totally missing the point." She said finally, sitting on the edge of the bed to remove her sandals and pull the coils of wire from her ankles. "I knew exactly what I was doing." Okay, so that was a small white lie but he didn't have to know that. "If it worked I knew it would stop people from coming after me and harming my family. I knew it would scare them enough to back off and stop challenging you. If it failed and I lost control of my magic and got killed then I'd have neatly removed the issue. No-one can try and claim me if I'm dead. There was also the added bonus that you wouldn't have had to fight another duel with a set of broken ribs. People feared you already. They will fear you even more now that they know how loyal I am to you and what I am capable of. It gives us the time I need to figure out what the connection is between the people the council wanted dead."

"How close are you to finding an answer?" He asked, slightly appeased, and she shrugged.

"I don't know. I'm still only halfway through the journals. I haven't found a pattern yet. Give me another few days and I'll be closer."

"A few days is all I can give you." He finally started loosening the buckles on his wrist guards. "There is someone on my new kill list that I really don't want to take out but I need to know what we're dealing with before I can plan."

"Well the house is warded." She pulled on her favourite pair of yoga pants and a vest top. "I can devote all my time to the indexing now and I've got Jo to help me. We'll work as many hours as it takes." She came to him as he started unbuckling his breastplate and took over, pushing his hands out of the way and deftly undoing the straps.

Suddenly he crushed her to him in a hug. "Don't you ever do that to me again." He said fiercely, laying a cheek against the top of her head. "I haven't felt fear in more than 5 centuries but I felt it this morning when you walked out into that arena."

"I'm not as fragile as you think I am." She responded gently, sliding her arms around him. "You saw the strength of my wards."

"All it takes is one slip of focus and you'd be dead. You've got to stop throwing yourself into these things. I warned you we would talk about that stunt you pulled the day you met Will and I think that now is the time to have that conversation." He reluctantly let her go and she returned to his armour, lifting the chest piece over his head and away.

"You can't ask me to change my nature." She replied mildly, dropping to her knees to work on his legs. "Asking me to stop doing the right thing, to stop fighting for the people I care about, is like asking the sky to stop being blue or asking the tide to stop rolling in and out. It's a natural instinct."

"One that will get you killed." He persisted but she looked up with a lopsided smile.

"Then I'll take that particular idiot gene out of the gene pool, won't I?"

"Do not make light of this, Oceana." He ran his hands through his hair. "You are not of our world. It's deadly and shadowed and nothing is as it seems and I can't bear to lose you to it."

She tossed the last piece of leather aside and looked up at him from where she knelt. "Some day you will have to let me go Tris. It is the way of life. You can keep me until I'm old and grey but you can't stop time and in the great scheme of things my life span will be like the blink of an eye to you."

"I could turn you." He insisted but she was already shaking her head.

"It's not what I want Tris. I want children. I want a life free of politics. You said it yourself – I'm too bright and vibrant to belong in your world. It's my mortality that makes me special, to me and to you. Life has to be short to be truly valued."

She held her arms up and he helped her to rise, pulling her into another embrace. "I can't understand how you've turned my nice, neat existence on its head in a few short weeks." He groused and she laughed.

"You came looking for me, remember? I was happy to live in blissful ignorance." She sighed, trying to peel away from him. "And now you've got blood all over my nice clean clothes."

"They'll wash." He didn't let her go. "I just don't understand why you're so determined to lose me. I can give you the world. You have only to ask. Why are you so convinced I will break your heart?"

"They had to make me watch you in the arena this morning." She winced at the memory. "I couldn't bring myself to look at you getting hurt. Every time you go on a job, have a meeting with the council...I'll be wondering if you're going to come back to me in a box. I can't live like that Tris. I can't invest everything I have in you knowing that it's only a temporary thing. You freaked out because I put myself in harm's way just twice and yet you do it every day and expect me to just accept it."

"That's different." He declared stubbornly and she laughed.

"Whatever." She tried to step back again. "You really should get in the shower. You're a mess."

"I guess." He still didn't let her go. "We're taking the rest of today off though. You can start the indexing tomorrow. Which means you can come have some fun with me in the shower."

She sighed mockingly, smothering a laugh. "Whatever my lord and master desires..."

***

That evening, perhaps to prove a point, Oceana didn't know, they went out on the town. They started at a restaurant where everyone except Oceana ordered soup. If the waiters thought it strange they certainly didn't comment. From there they went to a bar where Tristan ordered four bottles of champagne and when, finally, those were done they moved onto a club.

"Do you remember the last time we went clubbing together?" Tristan asked Oceana as they danced and she blushed at the memory.

"After the murder? Yeah I remember."

"Do you remember what happened when we got back to the hotel?" He was grinning and she burst out laughing.

"Yeah. You got me all fired up and then snared me into sleeping instead."

"I'm not making that mistake again." His hands slid up her thighs. "Tonight there will be no mercy."

"Is that really any way to speak to a lady in public?" A massive voice boomed from behind them and Oceana spun round, dropping into a defensive crouch.

"Wulfric." Tristan grinned. "Well met."

"I heard on the grapevine that you were out celebrating." He offered Tristan his hand. "I felt I should come and congratulate you in person." They shook and then Wulfric turned to Oceana. "Congratulations to you too, beautiful lady." He kissed her hand and she blushed again. Damn but these vamps could be charming. "I thought the council would go into conniptions when you so calmly messed up their plans for our friend here."

"One should never underestimate a woman." Tristan chuckled. "Never mind the council, I actually did have conniptions."

Wulfric gave a hearty, booming laugh and gripped Tristan on the shoulder in a brotherly manner. "It has been too long Tristan. We must catch up properly."

"When do you return to Orkney?" Tristan asked and Wulfric's eyes clouded over.

"I have some business in the city over the next few days but I don't have to fly back until next week."

"Then come out to the estate for a few days." Tristan suggested. "When your business is concluded, obviously."

"I would like that." Wulfric smiled at both of them. "I would like that very much."

"Excellent." Tristan gestured to where the others were sat in a booth at the edge of the dance floor. "If you would care to join us my family are seated over there. You are more than welcome."

"I would like to speak to Robert. Is he here?" Oceana remembered that Robbie was the one who had flown down from Scotland the previous week and wondered if they would be talking business.

"Yes, he's here." Tristan pointed him out where he was standing at the bar and Wulfric nodded.

"Then I shall leave you to it, my friend." As he turned to walk towards the Scottish vampire, Tristan's eyes flashed briefly with some unidentifiable emotion.

"You must find the answer soon." He whispered to Oceana. "I really don't want to kill him."

"Wulfric is on your list?" Oceana gaped and he pulled her against him, forcing her to move to the music.

"He is but I don't know how to get around it without knowing what I'm dealing with. I had hoped not to have to deal with it at all but his coming here has complicated things. The council will expect me to execute him while he is within easy reach."

Oceana glanced back at the huge blond vampire who was laughing out loud as he greeted Tristan's family and she shuddered. "I'll find you an answer. I promise."

***

The following morning they returned to the estate. With the immediate threat eliminated most of Tristan's family had gone to their own houses but as they pulled up at the gates Tristan sighed, half with amusement and half with irritation.

"I wish you would stop enchanting my children so." He muttered to Oceana. "Xav and Charlie have not stayed with me for centuries and suddenly they decide it's time for an extended visit?"

"How do you know it's not Jo they're interested in?" She responded sweetly, pushing the door open. "Go on up to the house. I'll invite them over the wards." She climbed out and waited for the second car. "I have to invite you across the wards." She explained as Charles rolled the window down and he nodded.

"Sure." They both got out and walked up to the gates.

"Charles and Xavier, you may enter these gates." She stepped back slightly and they came over the threshold.

"Before you invite us in can I test the second layer of wards?" Charles asked. "The master said they were impressive."

"If you must but don't step into it." She grimaced. "What is it with you men? It burns. It's designed to stop vampires and yet every damn one of you has just cheerfully strolled right into it."

"Not me." Xavier held his hands up. "I have no desire to burn."

"Pansy." Grinning with his fangs out, Charles extended his arm in front of him. Within a couple of seconds it had started so smoke. "That's incredible." He tried to pull his arm back experimentally but it held firm, frozen in mid air by an invisible power. "I am impressed." He let it hang for a couple of seconds more until his flesh actually blackened and then he turned to Oceana. "Please invite us over now."

"Charles and Xavier you may enter these grounds." She responded immediately and his hand dropped to his side. He lifted it to his face and examined the healing burns.

"That really is extraordinary. Would you come and do my house at some point?"

"Of course." Slightly chuffed to have been asked Oceana grinned at him. "I'm going to be working flat out for Tris over the next couple of weeks but after that I'm happy to make you a ward. I'll have to see your house first though. The ward is personal to the building."

"I will speak to him about arranging a visit."

"I suspect he will want you to do all our homes eventually." Xavier pointed out as they climbed into the car. "We are a small house but great in age and experience. It would damage him irreparably to lose any of us."

"Well whatever. I'm happy to do anyone's."

"Wonderful." He grinned at her. "I have no idea why the master lets you shorten his name so but if it's good enough for him it's certainly good enough for us. Please don't be so formal. You can call me Xav."

"And you can call me Charlie." Charles offered from the front seat and Oceana's face lit up in a smile.

"Thanks guys. You can call me whatever you like as long as it's not rude."

"No fear of that." Xav burst out laughing. "The master would flay our skins from our backs if we were ever disrespectful to the first lady of the house."

"I'm not the first lady of the house." Oceana shifted uncomfortably. "I'm an employee. Nothing more."

"Wow, you are in some kind of denial." Charlie stopped the car outside the house. "Take it from us Ana, I have never in all my years seen the master behave like this over anything. He is almost human again."

"In his line of work that's not a good thing." She said worriedly. "Being human makes him vulnerable. I would be wise to distance myself a little more than I have of late." Without giving them a chance to respond she got out and walked up to the front door which Tristan had left standing open. "Charles and Xavier, you may enter this house."

CHAPTER ELEVEN

The next few days flew past. Oceana had roped Jo in to helping her and she was running checks while Oceana did the indexing. After the first night when Tristan had tried to enter her room and been rebuffed by the ward, Oceana had carefully maintained her distance from him. He seemed perplexed but accepted her excuse that she needed the sleep to focus on the indexing at face value. She couldn't bring herself to admit that his fascination with her was making him weak. Even less could she admit that in giving him her body she had begun to give him her heart. Things had changed forever between them because she could not give one without the other…she could not make a conscious decision to give her whole self to him physically but withhold her affection. It just wasn't in her nature.

He was still insisting on joint mealtimes despite the fact that she was the only one actually eating and she quickly grew to look forward to them. Despite a slight tension between her and Tristan and her and Will, Charlie and Xav lightened the whole mood considerably. They were far more like Will than she had expected – charming, roguish and funny. More than once she found herself laughing at their antics until she felt like her sides would split. It was a happy time. She and Jo worked well together and she loved the complexities of the indexing. When she wasn't working she was laughing with new friends. It was almost enough to take away the pangs of homesickness for her home in the West Country.

Five days after their return to the estate the pieces all fell into place and Oceana dropped the last of the journals, leapt from her chair and did a victory dance.

"What are you so pleased about?" Jo asked drily and Oceana whooped.

"I've found it! I've found the link." Her brow wrinkled. "Or at least I think I have. I just have to fit one last piece of the puzzle." She rifled quickly through the pile of actions on the desk and held one out to Jo. "Can you take this to the guys and see if any of them knows this vampire. I need to know where he lives. Don't tell them I think I've cracked it. If I'm wrong he'll be disappointed."

"I'll be right back." Buoyed by Oceana's enthusiasm, Jo grabbed the piece of paper and left the room.

Oceana sat back at the computer and opened up a new graphical indexing chart and spreadsheet and started exporting data.

By late afternoon she was ready and summoned Tristan to the study.

"You found it?" He asked cautiously and she nodded.

"Take a seat." She shifted to the side and he pulled another chair over so he could see the screen. "I couldn't figure it out until I went to look for an address for a nominal I was registering this morning and realised there were a lot of cross-references to the city. When I followed them back to the sources and then referenced them against the sequence of events I realised I'd found the pattern." She brought up a table with the names of the dead vampires in. "They all visited the city of Cambridge on these dates." She clicked and the second column of the table filled up with dates. "These are the dates they appeared on your kill lists." She clicked again and the third column filled up with dates. "Do you see a pattern?"

Tristan looked back and forth across the dates and realised that each vampire had appeared on a kill list very shortly after visiting the city so whatever they were dying for was something they had seen in Cambridge. "So what's in Cambridge?" He asked but she waved the question away.

"I'll answer that in a second. There's more." She closed the table and brought up a graphical indexing screen. "When I charted the links to the city I realised that there were several other vampires mentioned in the journals who were also linked to Cambridge." She opened her chart and showed him the spiderweb of icons and cross references. "When I traced the lineages I realised that many of your journal writers had gone to the city to find a family member that had vanished. That's why the links weren't obvious. Many of them mentioned visiting people rather than places."

"Vampires are vanishing in Cambridge?" Tristan was astonished. He hadn't heard any rumours but something like that was difficult to cover up. That was a flashing warning sign that the council was involved. Only they had the power to cover up something that huge.

"At least 6 that I could make connection to." Oceana confirmed. "I suspect that if we dug deeper we'd probably find all of them are linked to a mis-per but the fact that it was so well covered up is probably why the connection wasn't immediately obvious to you. In any event, there's clearly something fishy going down in the city."

"And that's where I came in." Jo brought the laptop over and angled the screen so they could all see it. "I started canvassing companies and industries in the city that may have links to vampires and hit pay dirt almost immediately." She brought up a window with a little Ta-da! sound. "Lady and gentleman, I give you Venogen Corporation. On the surface it's a pharmaceutical company manufacturing medicines and beauty products but the owners and shareholders are a maze of shell companies and umbrella organisations. It makes organised crime look amateur."

Tristan scrolled up and down the company website with curiosity. "So what do they do? Why all the secrecy?"

"That's what we don't know." Oceana admitted uncomfortably. "We've exhausted all legal channels here. All evidence points to this being the only Vamp owned industry in the city where our vamps all went missing or got killed for visiting but we have no idea what's actually going on behind the walls."

"The scientific papers I found suggest that they are actually manufacturing at some scale." Jo added. "Not enough to account for the size of the complex but enough to provide a reasonably flawless facade to the untrained eye."

"So how do we find out?" Tristan ruffled his hair back from his face, the only sign of his frustration.

"Well we either break in or get someone to hack their network." Jo replied cheerfully and Oceana's face darkened.

"That's against the law." She pointed out and both Jo and Tristan stared at her as if to say 'So?'.

"Can you hack it?" Tristan asked Jo and she shook her head.

"I'm not that good. But I know someone who can."

"No. Absolutely not." Oceana glared at Jo. "Oliver is a criminal."

"He does more good than harm and you know it." Jo argued back just as hotly. "He just got carried away with curiosity that one time and he paid the price for it."

"Who is Oliver?" Interrupted Tristan and Oceana glowered mutely at her computer leaving Jo to explain.

"Oli is an online vigilante. He's crazy good with computers and does a lot of security testing for networks but in his free time he hunts down people that misuse the web and makes them very sorry for it."

"And how did he end up on the wrong side of the law?" Tristan asked levelly.

"He was tracking a paedophile ring." Jo sighed. "He'd picked up a lead in a chat room and was following the links back to the perpetrators. Unfortunately for him, or them, or perhaps both, two of said paedophiles worked for the government and had been a little lax in their security. He hacked their computers and was so incensed at what he found that he downloaded one of his little killer viruses, not realising that it would wipe out the entire government computer network of Bristol. He hacked the network again to fix it and restore the programming but came across some accounting documents that didn't add up and started investigating the city council. By the time he was arrested he'd created an airtight case against the council but he'd breached the Data Protection Act so many times they had to convict him."

"Is that an accurate accounting of events?" Tristan asked Oceana and she nodded unhappily. "And can this man be trusted to keep secrets?" He asked Jo and she nodded too. "Then call him. I want to get to the bottom of this ASAP. Wulfric will be here tomorrow night and we haven't a moment to waste."

***

The next morning Oceana's phone rang as she was sat in the workshop having tea with Mia. They'd spent the morning together passing her spools of wire through water, fire and salt, stringing each with a ceramic bead. She frowned at the unregistered number and then answered it, wondering who would have her encrypted number from Tristan.

"Good morning Starshine."

She sighed, realising she should have known. "Hello Oliver."

"After I've sat up all night working for you the least you could do is sound a little pleased to hear from me." He sounded too cheerful for someone that had been awake all night.

"You startled me. I wasn't expecting anyone on this number."

"Yes, your new employer is doing a good job of keeping you safe. I checked out the firewalls around his computers. It's almost impenetrable." He actually sounded impressed.

"Almost?" Queried Oceana and he laughed.

"Yeah almost. Any mobile devices linked to it can be implanted with a Trojan virus when they leave the estate I should think. Not that I've tested it. No-one has left the estate this morning."

Oceana closed her eyes and leaned her forehead on her work bench in weary resignation. "Why are you trying to hack my employer's network Oliver? It's not us you're investigating. It's Venogen."

"Let's say that I was so concerned by what I found that I wanted to check your employer was legit before I passed on any of the data."

Oceana's eyes flew open and she bolted upright. "You found something? What is it?"

"First there is the small matter of payment."

"How much do you want? Email me your bank details and I'll get it transferred immediately."

"I don't want money."

There was a long pause in which Oceana sighed, closed her eyes and rested her forehead back on the workbench. "What do you want then?"

"You know what I want Oceana. It's what I've always wanted."

"Season tickets to Wimbledon?" She offered hopefully but he wasn't amused.

"You know where I am."

"Oliver! Don't hang up!" She waited to see if he stayed on the line and then she swallowed. "Look, we only met the once and it was under difficult circumstances. If this is some revenge thing..."

"It's not about revenge." He sounded almost sincere. "You and I are kindred spirits, my lovely. I watched you sitting there in the witness box with your charts and graphics and you looked like a geek-chic angel. No-one else would have understood the complexities of the programming like you did. You built that case against me. It was impressive. And then to go after the council?" He blew out an amused breath. "It was almost worth going to jail for. You're the only woman I've ever met that even comes close to my level."

"So what? You want to dominate me to prove something to yourself, is that it?" She resisted the urge to bang her head against the bench.

"At the end of the day it doesn't matter what my reasons are." He said mildly. "That's the price. You pay it or you don't. Will you come?"

She closed her eyes and weighed it up. "I may have to bring guards." She said eventually in a small voice. "My new employer doesn't like letting me out alone. The situation is dangerous and it'll take me a while to get it organised. Tell me this and tell me straight. Is the information you have worth the price you want?"

For the first time he sounded shaken. "Yes. Yes it is." There was a soft click as the line disconnected and Oceana's heart sank. There was no way she could tell Tristan the price of his answer. His rage would be beyond words.

"That didn't sound like it went well." Mia, in her sweet gentle way, tried to offer help without asking a direct question.

"It didn't." She still had her head on the desk. "Tris is going to go apeshit."

"Over the cost or the data?"

"The cost definitely. I don't know about the data yet."

"And there's nothing else you can offer him as an alternative that won't send the master off the deep end?"

Oceana thought about it. "I don't know. It would appear the ward is not just protecting the estate, it's also firewalling our computer systems. I could offer to provide him with impenetrable computer security but given who he is and what he does I don't know what value he'd place on it. And I'd have to try and convince him that I have magic abilities and that it works. I don't know that I have time. I need to be back before Wulfric gets here."

"If you chose the simpler option the master would forgive you." Mia offered softly and Oceana closed her eyes again.

"I know. But he might kill Oliver. And for all the guy is a law unto himself he really is a force for good. He's taken out more criminals internationally than most countries have in the last year."

"The master is more understanding than you think."

Oceana finally raised her head, looking grim. "He's going to have to be."

***

"Tris, I have to go out." She leaned against the doorway of the training room where he was sparring with Will. "I need to go alone."

"Where and why?" He stalked towards her across the exercise mats, all feline grace and deadly beauty.

"Oliver has your information. He has insisted I collect it in person and alone."

"It's too dangerous." He came to a stop in front of her. "Why does he want you to go?"

"It's not too dangerous." Oceana insisted. "I'll be warded up to the eyeballs, practically bulletproof. I'm not a complete idiot." She raised the spool of wire in her hand as though to demonstrate.

"I still don't want you out there on your own."

"Then I'll take Charlie or Xav but they'll have to wait in the car." Sensing he was about to ask why her again she continued on in a rush. "And no-one can take any mobile phones or laptops or anything off the estate until I've had a chance to ward them."

"Why?"

"Because it seems the ward is protecting our computer system too. Oliver tested them overnight and couldn't get in." She allowed herself a brief smile. "It must be driving him nuts. But he mentioned planting a Trojan in one of our portable devices so nothing can leave. That includes the sat nav systems in the cars but I'll ward the one I'm taking."

"I never thought of the car as having a computer on board." Tristan sounded a little taken aback.

"Most devices can take some sort of programming these days." She forced a smile. "I'll go make the ward and pick up one of the guys. We'll be back long before Wulfric arrives." With that little reminder that they couldn't afford to delay she walked away, praying he wouldn't call her back and demand an explanation. Luckily he let her go and her shoulders slumped with relief the moment she was out of sight and into the house.

For a long moment she considered just heading out alone but the chances of getting caught before she made it to the end of the driveway were too high and there was no reason to make Tristan's rage even greater on her return. Just as she was crossing the hall to go up to her room Xav appeared in the front doorway.

"Are you busy this morning?" She asked him and he shook his head cheerfully.

"Not at all. I was just out enjoying the sunshine."

"I need to run an errand. Tris said I had to take one of you with me. We'll be out for a few hours if you're up for it."

He bowed gallantly, a broad grin on his face. "My lady, I am wholly at your service."

***

It was almost four o'clock by the time they returned and Xav was no longer smiling. They entered the house in icy silence just as Jo was descending the stairs. "Hey!" She greeted and then her smile wilted. "What's wrong?" She scented the air around them and suddenly her face paled. "You didn't?"

"She did." Xavier walked away stiffly and Oceana let him go.

"You knew the price when you called him." She turned to Jo and looked her right in the eye. "Don't you dare judge me for something you set up."

"I'm sorry." Jo came the rest of the way down the stairs. "I didn't think he'd actually do it."

"Well he did. Take this to Tristan. I'm going to get in the shower." She handed over a portable hard drive and walked past her friend to the stairs. "Don't let him take it out on Xav. He didn't know until it was too late."

"I'll try." Jo turned to go find Tristan but then she stopped. "I really am sorry." She said quietly and Oceana's shoulders slumped.

"I know." Before she could start crying she ran up the stairs two at a time and went to get in the shower.

She heard Tristan's rage even over the spray of the shower and was grateful she had never invited him into her room after the ward was laid. She needed to be alone to get clean. She scrubbed her skin until it was almost raw, feeling shamed by what had been asked of her. She had bought information with her body and it felt like prostitution. It felt like she'd never be clean again. Part of her couldn't believe she'd actually done it, that she thought any information would be worth that price, but people were dying and she was the only one with the ability to stop it. In the great scheme of things it wasn't that great a price to pay and at least Oliver was a relatively decent guy. He fought for those that couldn't defend themselves and he wasn't bad looking.

The water finally ran cold and she switched off the spray, snuggling into the largest towel on her radiator as she stepped through to the bedroom.

"Let me in!" Tristan roared through the door.

"I'll be out in a minute." She muttered, wondering what the hell to wear.

"Open this goddamn door right now Oceana or so help me I will get one of the pets to take up that fucking ward with a crowbar!"

That caught her attention and she strode to the door, flinging it open so hard it bounced off the wall. "What the hell do you want Tristan?" She demanded. "You employed me to find you answers. I got you answers. There is nothing more to say."

"Are you okay?" His eyes roamed her anxiously and abruptly Oceana realised that it wasn't rage in his voice, it was anguish. What the hell was that all about?

Slightly off-kilter she swallowed. "I'm fine."

"Let me in." He pushed up against the ward but she shook her head.

"No. I need my sanctuary Tris. Please understand that. Give me a few moments to put some clothes on and I'll come to your room."

Stepping back he ruffled his hair and for the first time it looked out of place, stuck up at odd angles. "I'll wait right here." Realising he wasn't going to budge, Oceana nodded tightly.

"Fine." She closed the door and pulled on some soft yoga pants and a T-shirt, dragging her fingers quickly through her curls to give them some semblance of order. When she opened the door again he was pacing up and down the landing waiting for her.

"Are you going to be okay?" Will's voice sounded uncertain and Oceana stepped out to see him standing at the top of the stairs.

"We'll be fine. Just give us a few moments." She looked back as Tristan took her hand and nodded reassuringly at him. "I'll be fine." She mouthed silently but he didn't move, staying where he was as though torn.

Tristan pulled her into his room and immediately enfolded her in a smothering embrace. "Why didn't you tell me?" He demanded. "You should have said and we could have worked something out."

"We didn't have time Tristan. Wulfric will be here any minute and you needed your answers."

"I'm going to kill him!" He was actually shaking. "You didn't have to do that, not for me. Not for Wulfric."

"I did and you know it." She tried to relax into him but he was squashing her. "Ease up Tris. I can't breathe."

"You will never do that again. You're mine. Do you understand me? Mine."

"I'm not a possession Tris." She pushed at his chest, trying to get some air. "You can't take away my free will."

"Did you want to do it?" He demanded and she gave up struggling, going completely limp.

"No I didn't. But I still chose to. For you, for the people you've killed and for those that are still missing. So don't let my sacrifice have been for nothing." Her face was flushing red as he stifled her. "Tristan please, I can't breathe."

He finally stopped squeezing but didn't let her go. "You will sleep in here tonight." It wasn't a question. "I don't want you to be alone."

"Then I can sleep with Jo." She argued stubbornly.

"For once you will do as I tell you." He roared, anger finally seeping through, and Oceana went still. He was terrifying when he was like this.

"Okay." She replied quietly. "I'll sleep in here. Now, please go and read what's on that drive. It's important."

"Come on then." He squeezed her briefly again and then let her go. "It's in the study."

Oliver had given Oceana a brief overview of what he had found in the Venogen computer system so she was able to bring up the salient documents relatively easily. "These are all invoices for supplies they've ordered in; cages, medical equipment etc. Individually it's not much to be concerned with until you reach this."

"And what is that?" Tristan asked as she opened up a transaction sheet.

"This, according to Oliver, is a series of transactions relating to the black market purchase of missiles."

"Missiles?" Tristan stared at the screen. "This is about arms deals?"

"Not quite. They're purchasing the ordnance but they're manufacturing what they're putting in them." Oceana closed that window and opened the next document. "These are the results of their test studies although I'm not sure if the subjects are animal, human or vamp. You'll notice that the results across the board are showing a coma response to exposure to the agent."

"Bio warfare?" He was stunned.

"It looks like it. But not just any bio warfare. Oliver found hundreds of log entries relating to subjects in captivity where the output was measured in millilitres." She found one and opened it up to show him. "I didn't connect the dots at first but then I remembered something you said ages ago and realised it's the missing vamps. They're milking their venom, hence the output measured in volume."

"And then making the nerve agent from the venom." He finished, staring at the screen with an unreadable expression.

"What I can't understand is why." Oceana sat back slightly from the screen. "Why on earth would the council, who presumably have millions of pounds in assets, start dealing in black market missiles? It's a risky venture."

"They're not going to sell them. They're going to use them." Tristan closed his eyes and rested his head in his hands. "War is good for us 'Cean." He explained. "All those dead and dying people...ripe for the picking. We make good soldiers and with all those bodies to feed from you are sated in a way that you never will be by drinking from bags. The problem is that there are very few first world warzones left. They're all in the third world and no vampire would voluntarily live somewhere less luxurious just because the food is easy to come by."

"So they're just going to start one?" Oceana was floored. "Out of what? Boredom?" The scale of what they had uncovered was mind-boggling.

"My guess is that they'll ship these around the world to enclaves in the States and across Europe and then start randomly firing them at each others' cities. As soon as the inhabitants are out cold they'll go in en masse and start ripping throats out. They could slaughter whole cities in a matter of days...hours even."

"But if they've breathed in the venom won't they just turn into vampires?" Oceana asked and he shrugged.

"It's hit and miss. You have to have a lot of venom in you to make the transition. My guess is that they're modifying it in the labs somehow before putting it in the warheads."

"What are we going to do?" No matter how daunting the prospect, Oceana couldn't just sit idly by and wait for world war 3 to break out.

"First things first I think we need to find out what Wulfric knows. If it's just speculation on his part then we need to break into Venogen and confirm our suspicions before we do anything rash."

"And if we're right?" She had gone pale and he took her hand.

"If we're right then we take them down." He said flatly. "Every last one of them."

CHAPTER TWELVE

Tristan brought up the subject gently over dinner. They were sat around the dining table drinking soup while Oceana ate.

"Have you visited England in the last couple of months at all?" He asked Wulfric gently and Wulfric nodded around his spoon.

"Yes. I came down while you were in Somerset to follow up a couple of leads on a family matter. I stopped by but you weren't home."

"A family matter?" Picking up the subterfuge, Will joined the conversation.

"Yes, four members of my family have gone missing over the last year. I have been trying to find out what happened to them and picked up where my investigators left off."

"And where did those leads take you?" Tristan asked, knowing the answer but needing to hear it all the same.

"I tracked them to Cambridge and then I lost them."

Tristan took a deep breath. "Wulfric, do you have any idea why the council wants me to execute you?" He asked gently. The blond vampire froze as he rushed through the exits in his mind but he knew he didn't have a hope and slumped in his chair.

"I don't know." He carefully laid down his spoon. "Unless they have something to do with the missing members of my family then I have no issue with them and they have no issue with me." He shifted uncomfortably in his seat. "Tristan, you are my oldest ally. Are you going to kill me when I don't know what I've done wrong?" Interesting wording thought Oceana. Oldest ally...not friend.

"Likewise, you are my oldest ally." Tristan levelled a clear and steady gaze at him. "I have no intention of executing you but you must know that you have walked into a dark and dangerous can of worms here. We may well have to fake your death to buy some time."

"Buy some time for what?" Wulfric looked around at the unsurprised faces. "You know why I am on your death list don't you?"

"Tell me." Tristan leaned back in his chair and swirled his glass. The deep red liquid in it glistened thickly in the light. "Have you ever heard of a company called Venogen?"

"Venogen?" Wulfric said it slowly as though that might jog his memory. "It doesn't sound familiar. Why?"

"It's a company owned by the council operating in Cambridge. We believe it's directly linked to the missing vampires. Your family is not the only one that has lost members."

"You know where my family members are?" Surprised enough to have forgotten his fright Wulfric leaned forward. "Are they alive?"

"We're not sure." Tristan admitted. "But we have some recent documents that may help us to shed some light on that if you can give us the details of your missing family members and when they went missing."

"I'll give you what I can."

"I'll run them through the system after dinner." Oceana offered and Tristan smiled at her.

"Why would you have to fake my death?" Wulfric asked and Tristan sighed.

"Because Venogen is a cover for something much bigger and we need a lot more information before we can decide what to do. My conscience is telling me I need to fight the council on this but mine is a small house and risking it without being fully prepared would be suicide."

"My house is also small." Wulfric said carefully. "Small but, like yours, powerful." The two men gazed at each other across the expanse of tabletop. "Tristan what is so bad that you feel you must oppose the council over it?" The blond vampire asked eventually and Tristan did not blink.

"Before I can tell you that I need to know if you are with me on this." He set his glass back on the table. "I know that I'm not giving you much information to go on but what I can tell you is that the council are directly responsible for the kidnap, captivity and abuse of your missing vampires, amongst many others. They have used me as a private assassin to kill at least 12 prominent members of various families for no reason other than that it suits their own ends. You too would be on that list if I had not started to question what was happening. I can tell you that what they're planning is big and it will probably destroy everything about the world as we know it."

His words hung in the air in brief silence before Wulfric shook himself out of the trance Tristan's voice had induced. "This event that they are planning...will it benefit vampire kind? Why are they doing it?"

"It will briefly satisfy the blood lust of vampires less civilised than us." Tristan conceded. "There may also be an argument that the council could make a rich profit off the back of it. But the ends do not, in any way, justify the means. On that you have my word."

Wulfric studied the table before him, minutely adjusting the spoon where it lay against the edge of the bowl. "I know you are a man of honour." He spoke softly. "I know that you feel justified in your stance on this. That is good enough for me."

"I have your backing on this?" Tristan clarified and Wulfric nodded.

"My house and your house have ever been allied. We will stand with you on this. So tell me now what suicide mission I have pledged my house to."

"For that it would help if we could show you the documents we have found. Are you almost done Oceana?"

She ate the last morsel of food on her plate and set down her cutlery. "Yeah I'm done. I'll go get the laptop. Ask Mrs Wells to save dessert for me for later."

"Will do." Tristan grinned and sent Will to find Mrs Wells to clear the table while Oceana fetched the laptop. They set it up at the end of the table and Oceana sat next to Wulfric so she could explain what she was showing him.

She started right at the beginning with the vampires Tristan had executed, with the diaries he had collected and how she had indexed them to find the links. She showed him the same table she had shown Tris: the names of their vampires who had gone missing, the names of the vampires Tristan had killed, the dates they arrived in Cambridge and the dates they appeared on his kill list. Once that link had been established she gave him a brief rundown of Jo's search of companies in the area and explained how they had come across Venogen Corporation. She showed him the list of companies they had started tracking back from the shell company and the tangled maze of shell and umbrella companies, some of which they found had links to vampire owned conglomerates and which confirmed that Venogen was owned, circumstantially at least, by the council. Then she closed down her indexing program and brought up the stolen files that Oliver had provided them, showing the invoices for the ordnance and the scientific purchases that could be used to make the payload. When that was explained she brought up the subject logs and explained how they thought it was the kidnapped vampires being milked for their venom.

At that stage Wulfric's shock turned to anger. "They're keeping my family captive and milking them?" He demanded.

"They haven't given the subjects names." Oceana told him apologetically. "There are lists of vital statistics though and we can track the logs back to the dates they started to find an approximate date of capture."

"How many have they got?" His rage was turning ice cold and Oceana actually leaned away from him as the force of it seethed under his words.

"I think it's about 20." She hazarded a guess. "I'm not too sure about the scientific data but from what I've managed to look up on the internet it's showing some sort of distillation process. They're not milking them every day either. Whatever they're doing it's taking them a long time."

"Which is to our advantage." Tristan said quietly and Wulfric nodded.

"There's one more thing." Oceana admitted with trepidation. "When I had a closer look at some of this data before you arrived Wulfric, it's become apparent that they also have human captives. I found more subject logs relating to the testing. These are not animals."

"That complicates things." Will got up to pace. "I presume we are destroying this lab of theirs?"

"Whatever happens we have to get our people out of there." Wulfric said adamantly. "I don't care one way or the other about the humans but I won't allow my people to be destroyed."

"We have to destroy the lab and destroy the data." Tristan looked utterly composed as though it was an ordinary, every day occurrence. "We need to do some thorough reconnaissance on the property before we can plan everything."

"They'll have back-up drives of the data somewhere." Oceana pointed out. "There is absolutely nothing to stop them just setting this up somewhere else. They've certainly got the finances behind them to do it."

"Let me get this straight." Wulfric looked slowly between her and Tristan. "Are we talking about taking down the council? As in the actual council members?"

"It's the only way." Tristan still sounded absolutely calm. "We can do it. We just need to plan."

"It's not the only way." Oceana couldn't look at him. "Oliver could-"

"Oliver is going to die." Tristan said flatly. "He will have nothing to do with this."

"He could take out their computer and security systems." Oceana argued. "He could track every byte of data and destroy it, stop this from happening anywhere else with nowhere near as much danger to those involved."

"At what cost?" This from Will. "We all know what you paid for this data and every one of us wants him dead. He will not survive the month."

"There is no-one on earth who could get into their security systems as absolutely as Oliver." For all she was angry and upset at the price he had demanded for the data she didn't want him to die for it. "He could really help us. Look around you Tris. Look at the faces of these men and ask yourself how many you're prepared to lose over some territorial pissing match."

"You stood up in front of the leaders of vampire kind and told them you only served one master." He told her mildly. "You are mine."

"I am not yours and you know it." Angry now, Oceana stood up. "Excuse me gentlemen, I'm going to eat my dessert now. You don't need to watch." She snapped the laptop shut and walked out the room, leaving an uncomfortable silence behind.

Mrs Wells had left a dish of chocolate and raspberry tart in the fridge for her and she pulled it out, accessorising it with a healthy dollop of homemade vanilla ice cream. After a second's thought she made herself a cup of tea too.

"Is there enough water in the kettle for me?" Xav asked quietly from the kitchen door and she turned round, surprised he had followed her.

"Yeah sure. Tea or coffee?"

"I'll have one of those weird herbal things she hides in the back of the cupboard." He smiled and pulled himself up onto a stool at the breakfast bar as she poured him a mug, sliding it across to him.

"So..." she smiled awkwardly. "On a scale of 1 to 10 how angry with me are you?"

"Maybe a 2." He sighed. "I'm not really angry at you. I'm angry at the situation. I'm angry at that sleaze for asking that of you. I'm angry at Jo for bringing him into this knowing what the cost would be. You're probably the only thing I'm not angry about."

"That's good." She was relieved. "The thought of everyone hating me was worse than the thought of actually doing it."

He actually shook his head in disbelief. "You really have no idea do you?"

"About what?" She had to resist moaning with delight as the chocolate and raspberry slid across her taste buds.

"About how utterly captivating you are to my kind?" He chuckled, dunking his tea bag up and down. "It's impossible not to fall for you. You're so vibrant and full of attitude. We're predators...we live for the hunt. The minute you say no to anything, the moment you challenge us, you start pushing all our buttons. We all have that crazy alpha male need to dominate anything that looks vaguely powerful. Add to that you're funny and smart and charming..." He shrugged. "It's like someone gave you the master key to hotwire our engines."

"That's a terrible analogy." She burst out laughing, trying not to blush. "You don't use a key to hotwire an engine."

"Okay, it's like someone gave you the master key to our chastity belts." He laughed with her. "Someone gave you the world's sharpest wire cutters to hotwire our engines."

"Chastity belts, huh?"

"Oh yeah." Xav was still laughing. "I swear to God, you get that look in your eye like you're about to hold someone's nuts hostage and it dials a hotline straight to my pants."

She actually choked she was laughing so hard. "It's totally a rock and a hard place situation!" She snorted through the giggles. "I say no to you guys and you get a hard on, I say yes to you and I become a slut."

"It's more of a Greek tragedy situation." He joked, half seriously. "If you said yes to any of us Tristan would kill us without question. So you continue to say no and that just makes us want you even more."

"I'm sorry." She tried to stop laughing enough to apologise seriously but she had the proper giggles and couldn't get it together.

"It's okay. I'm totally glad I met you." He gave her a dazzling smile and bumped her shoulder gently. "Life round here has been a lot more interesting since you arrived."

"I'm so glad I could entertain." She tried to gather herself and returned to her dessert before her ice cream could melt and they finally subsided into companionable silence.

***

The guys stayed up late into the night and Oceana was so tired she went to bed without even saying goodnight. She didn't want to get into another fight with Tristan, even though she'd promised she'd stay with him. After the row they'd had she wasn't in any mood to concede to his demands. She woke up briefly in the early hours of the morning when she heard hushed, angry voices on the landing and then a few moments later Jo slipped into bed with her.

"You okay?" Her friend whispered and Oceana mumbled she was fine before drifting back off to sleep with Jo's arms around her.

When she got up the next day it was early and the others were all still asleep. Mrs Wells had just arrived in the kitchen and made her some fresh fruit salad and pancakes for breakfast and she sat looking out across the courtyard wondering what to do with her day. Now that her indexing was done and there was no way that Tristan would allow her to take part in the assault on the labs she was kind of at a loose end. Her job was done. It was time for her to go home. She just wasn't sure how to communicate that to a man that saw her as a possession. *His* possession.

Will was the first up and he took one look at her face and suggested they go for a walk. It had rained overnight and there was a soft mist rising from the grass as the summer heat began to light up the day. It was spectacularly beautiful and arm-in-arm they walked in silence around the walls of the estate for much of the way. Finally, when they were almost back to the house, Oceana spoke up.

"It's time for me to go home Will."

He laid a hand over hers where they were joined and sighed. "He won't let you go."

"I know but he can't keep me captive here. I have no further purpose to serve."

At that he smiled. "You will always have a purpose to serve. I heard just yesterday that Xavier and Charles were putting in requests to have their houses warded."

"It takes me a day to do each house." Oceana pointed out stubbornly. "I could do his whole family in the next two weeks and then go home. Hell, I can make those wards from home. I don't need to be here."

"I don't want you to go." He said softly as they drew level with the door.

"You want to go round again?" Oceana gestured at the wall in the distance and he nodded. "Come on then."

""I don't want you to go." He repeated softly as they reached the wall and Oceana sighed.

"Will, Xav explained to me how I...push your buttons. Surely my being far away from you is a good thing? To constantly be inadvertently teasing you when you know that Tris would kill you for touching me must be the worst kind of torture."

"I would rather live in an agony of want than be far from you." A self-deprecating smile made the statement poignant. "You remind me what it's like to be alive. You're fascinating."

"And doesn't that hurt?" She persisted. "Doesn't it hurt to be reminded of something you will never have again?"

"I made peace with what I am a very long time ago." He laughed. "But you are beautiful and fresh to me, like a flower. Something that must be protected and cherished and not a moment missed for the brief span of your existence."

"I'm a person Will, not a flower." She reminded him. "You can't keep me prisoner just because I fascinate you."

"I wouldn't keep you here." He smiled wistfully. "I'd travel with you. We'd go all over the world. I'd come visit you at your home in between exotic trips and sit in your workshop and watch you make pretty stuff."

"And what about your job?" She persisted. "You can't give up everything that you are, everything that you do because you want to watch me like some science project."

"I can edit from anywhere in the world." He replied easily. "All I need is a computer and an internet connection. I could have a corner of your workshop to write in."

"And what about Tris?" She persisted. "Will, if we ran away together he would hunt you down."

"There are ways and means." He sounded like he had thought about this at length. "I could petition to declare you as my mate."

"As I understand it, if you did that and Tristan killed you anyway I would automatically revert to him." She frowned.

"It's not as simple as that. When it's within a family it makes it more complicated. There are traditions and rules that must be observed."

"He'd still go apeshit."

"True." Will let her arm slide down his until he could take her hand and he interlaced his fingers with hers. "But I would risk it if I knew what you were thinking...how you felt."

"Will..." She trailed off, trying to find a way to put her thoughts into words. "I've only known you a few weeks. I know it's been intense and difficult and we've really hit it off but if you were just a regular guy and I was just a regular girl I still couldn't agree to any commitment to you right now, let alone a lifetime commitment. It's just not long enough to know it would work. If you were someone I'd met at the office we'd still be in the early stages of dating."

"But you care for me?" He persisted and she blushed.

"Of course I do. You're a great guy and handsome too."

"You could feel like that about a brother." He pulled her to a stop and made her turn to face him. "Do you want me Oceana? And not like a brother. Do you want me as a lover?"

She looked at him. *Really* looked at him. Yeah, he wasn't as flawlessly beautiful as Tristan was but he seemed infinitely more...real somehow, as though his tiny imperfections were what made him more human. She'd be lying if she said the memory of his hands on her neck didn't stir something primal in her. He was an attractive man. Funny, intelligent and charming too. Tristan was like a holiday romance, that brief fling you had with the insanely attractive guy that you never saw or heard from again after that one holiday. But Will...he was more down to earth, less demanding, more able to read her needs and desires. He wasn't as possessive as Tristan. A life with him would give her more room to breathe. Would she ever consider him for a lover? If all else was taken out of the picture, if the whole dream of children wasn't an issue, if they were just a man and woman apart from this whole mess, would she consider giving him her all?

"Yes." She whispered. "I would consider taking you for a lover Will. But it would only ever be temporary. I'll tell you the same as I told Tristan – I want children. You can't give them to me. You could never give a family a normal life."

"Nothing is impossible." He responded lightly, buoyed by the first part of her answer. "Given a little hope I can work with anything."

"You should abandon all hope Will." She told him bitterly. "Your world and mine were never meant to collide."

"But you are of our world." He argued stubbornly. "You have magic. It's only in our world that you'd be able to learn how to use it. And I know that you thought you were happy before when you didn't know you had a gift but you can't guarantee that your children or their children would have the same gift as you. Magic is as wide and varied as the shades of the ocean. When the time comes for them to learn, you are better off being part of our world. We have contacts that can help."

"I will not have my future children bound in slavery to vampires!" She wanted to walk away but he was still holding her by the shoulders. "It's bad enough that I'm 'indefinitely employed' by Tristan. I won't have my children tied against their wishes to creatures that would never give them freedom."

"We are not all like Tristan." He insisted. "I would let you have a normal life. I wouldn't expect you to work for me full time."

"But you are bound in slavery all of your own. You have ties to a house and a master that you cannot ignore. If he commands you to do something you must do it and if that command involves me or mine you are duty and tradition-bound to honour it, whatever my feelings on the matter."

"He is a good master." He was shaking his head. "If he knew I felt strongly about something he would not ask it of me."

"That's bullshit and you know it." She replied flatly. "Tristan will do whatever he feels he has to if he thinks it will profit or protect his House. You know as well as I do how little humanity there is left in him. You only have to imagine what he would do if you went to him and asked for me to see how wrong your statement is."

"If he truly thought I loved you..." He trailed off uncertainly.

"It would make no difference." Oceana finished gently for him. "Tristan will not allow me to go until he is bored of me or can find no further use for my skills. Maybe now that I know what sets him off he'll get bored of me quicker but until then you would do well to find another to love."

"So that's your answer?" Angry now he let her go. "You'll keep saying yes to him until he's used up your life in the hope that he'll let you go?"

"What else can I do?" She asked helplessly. Instead of answering he crushed her to him in a kiss. It was frustrated and angry and not at all gentle but fiery and passionate and it made her knees weak. For a moment she froze but the assault on her senses was so overwhelming she abandoned herself to the kiss, allowing his tongue to seek hers out in something closer to a duel than a dance. It wasn't until he released her and they laid their foreheads together, breathing raggedly, that she realised they could be seen from the house. She jerked away and spun round to study the windows but the sun was shining directly on them and she couldn't see through the glare. "What if someone saw?" She whispered fearfully but Will just shrugged, pulling her back to him and enfolding her into a hug.

"Let them see. The master will not kill me now, not when he needs his House whole and undivided." He laughed and it was both breathlessly light and bitter. "No doubt I will pay dearly for that kiss later but it was worth it." He kissed her again, laughingly. "*So* worth it."

"Cut it out Will." She tried to be angry with him but it was hard. "I have no desire to die today."

"Me either. Not when I have such riches to live for." He tucked a curl behind her ear. "Come, we should return to the house. The others will be awake by now. There is much planning to be done."

***

The others were all up and drinking coffee in the dining room when they arrived back at the house. If anyone had seen their tryst by the wall no-one said anything. Tristan levelled them a steady, searching look when they arrived but, instead of disciplining them, got straight to the matter at hand.

"Oceana, I know you swore to me you would never make weapons but I'd like you to rethink that." He gave her his most winning smile. "If there's anything you could make us that would help we'd appreciate it."

"I'll see what I can do." She responded stiffly. "What's the plan? Are you breaking into Venogen?"

"Eventually but that is only step 3 in the plan."

"What are steps 1 and 2?" Will asked, taking a seat beside Charlie.

"Firstly we need to stage Wulfric's fake execution." Tristan nodded at the blond. "The council knows he's on my kill list. They are already suspicious of my intentions. If he leaves here in one piece they will know I am opposed to them and will move against me immediately. Phase 2 is to bring his family here, ostensibly to gain revenge on my house for the unjust execution of their sire but once all is in place we will go for the third part which is to destroy Venogen."

"The council will retaliate almost immediately." Wulfric warned him, his deep bass rumble full of concern.

"And we will be ready for them. The estate is a fortress. We can gather here in safety until we are ready to strike. Our forces will be marshalled long before the council's."

It all just seemed too simple to Oceana. "This is not as easy or as simple as you're making it out to be." She protested. "You know as well as I do that the council are watching us closely and probably monitoring our calls and those of Wulfric's family. How do you intend to get a message to them that he's not really dead? And how can we stage a visible fake execution to allay their concerns? The only way to kill a vampire is to chop off his head. That's not something that can be easily faked. As for destroying Venogen, that might take weeks of surveillance. We don't even know if the captives are being held at the Cambridge facility. We have no idea what the layout is of the building or what the security issues are. Even if you manage to get past that hurdle with relative ease you can't just come back here and hole up and wait for the council to realise what you did. I might have made it a fortress but you have humans living here. You guys are okay for food but if they lay siege to us before we're ready to attack them it won't be long before me and the other ladies are dead. You have to be ready ahead of time to make a pre-emptive strike. Which means you need to carry out surveillance on the council members and find out exactly where they'll be and what they're doing so you can pick them off one by one. You need to know how closely they monitor Venogen. For all you know we could cross the security fence there in Cambridge and an alarm could go off down in London and lay waste to all your planning."

Wulfric was gazing at her with admiration. "When you're ready to become a vampire you just let me know." He told her, grinning. "You'd be a great asset to my family."

"One, I'm not going to become a vampire. Two, if I was ever forced to make that decision I don't want to be around when you and Tris duke it out over which family gets me." Oceana turned back to Tristan. "Tell me you're taking this seriously and you're not just going in all gung-ho vampire ninja because you're the Executioner and you're invincible?"

His lips actually twitched. "Of course I'm going to plan it meticulously. I haven't survived this long by being all...what did you call it?...gung-ho vampire ninja. But I'm curious to know how you would plan it out."

Feeling slightly foolish for doubting his wisdom, Oceana cleared her throat. "If I was planning it I would obtain the blue-prints for the facility in Cambridge, see if there is anywhere suitable for holding captives. If there isn't then I'd start searching for other facilities possibly owned by the council. If there is somewhere there, I would get a computer expert to hack the system. Find the security logs, camera locations, alarm settings and so on. If he's a really good hacker he could probably disable the security system completely during the assault to make the invasion easier. In the meantime I'd get some photos made up or stolen of a decapitated blond and send them to Wulfric's family up in Orkney with a message to come collect his body. That way no-one has to die and if they're monitoring emails or texts or however you do it, that's all the proof they need. I'd also find some way of planting trackers on the council members. It cuts down the surveillance time required and would also mean that if something went wrong at Venogen and they were alerted that we were on the offensive, we wouldn't be attacked out of the blue. We'd have some warning that they were coming for us."

"I have several issues with that plan." Tristan was taking her seriously but they needed to poke holes in any idea that was put forward to make sure it was foolproof. "Not least of which is that I will not work with a man I intend to kill. That hacker's days are numbered."

"Well that's your ego interfering with your practicality." She shot back. "For someone so old you're being pretty fucking immature about this." There was a collective gasp as everyone froze, waiting for him to kill her for her rudeness.

"When it comes to you I am unreasonable, I fully agree." He conceded, ignoring the horrified faces around them. "The fact remains that if I see him again I will kill him."

"No-one said you had to go skinny-dipping with him!" She pointed out. "You don't even have to deal with him directly. One of the others can do it." She expelled an angry breath. "Tris, I hate this as much as you do. I don't ever want to see him again either but the fact remains that he is the best in the business at what he does. If anyone can get us in and out of that building alive with all the information we need and without alerting the council, it's Oliver."

"And what happens when he demands payment from you again?" Xavier interrupted. "You just put out again?"

"No." She shuddered. "But we'll have more time to negotiate this time around. I have information that may be useful enough to him to buy the help we need. I can make him enough wards between now and then to make ample payment." She turned back to Tristan. "Promise me you will at least think about it?"

"I'll ask my contacts if anyone knows of a good hacker." He compromised. "If no-one comes back with another name then, and only then, will I consider it. Second issue, where would you obtain photographs of a decapitated blond?"

"From work." Jo piped up excitedly. "We had a decapitation case a couple of years ago. The vic was about Wulfric's height and build."

"You actually had a case where someone was decapitated?" Will was astonished and Jo grinned at him.

"It was a freak accident. We thought it was murder but it turned out to be a bizarre sequence of events involving a clothes horse, a tile, a lorry and a duck."

"What?" Now they were all staring at her.

"That's a story for another time." Oceana rescued her from retelling the incident. "That's a great idea but I don't know enough about the technical side of it. The images were digital and I don't know if they'd have a way of seeing the date stamp on the picture. They'll know it's a fake if they can see it was taken 2 years ago. We need a computer expert."

"Or a way of making up fresh photographs to look like a decapitated person..." Tristan mulled the idea over.

Oceana's eyes widened. "Do you still speak to Mr AppleMac?" She asked Jo who blushed.

"Not for a few weeks but yeah, he rings every now and then."

"Who is Mr AppleMac?" Tristan asked and Oceana grinned.

"It's this guy who works in special effects. He left his rucksack with some expensive photography equipment and his AppleMac in it behind in a layby about a year ago and he called the station a couple of times asking if anyone had handed it in. One thing led to another and he's pretty sweet on our Jo. He calls *all* the time."

"He does not!" Jo blurted out, cheeks aflame, and everyone laughed.

"He does. She speaks to him at least once a month." Oceana poked fun at her but then turned serious. "I'm sure he does make-up for movies and TV. I'm sure he could make up some pictures for us and photoshop anything that needs digital editing without it being obvious." She winked at Jo. "He's certainly got the software. Or should that be hardware...?"

"Fine, I'll call him." Jo groused. "Just get over it okay? We've never even met in person and it was really expensive equipment. A decent person would have handed it in, that's all he was expecting."

"But you still have his number?" Oceana teased. "I rest my case. What's issue 3?"

"Issue 3 is how the hell you think we're going to get anywhere near close enough to any of the council members to plant trackers on them." Tristan said and she shrugged.

"As I see it the only option is for me to try and use magic. That way I don't have to get close to them per se, I just need to get close to somewhere they're going to be."

"If you can get me their addresses I can access the Police Computer system and find out which vehicles are registered to their postcodes." Jo offered, relieved the subject had changed. "Do they drive anywhere?"

"No, they all have drivers." This from Wulfric who was following the conversation with astonishment.

"So the vehicles won't be registered to them. That's a shame." Jo's face fell.

"What about their seats?" Oceana wondered out loud. "At the council chambers, do they always sit in the same seats?"

"They do but we can't guarantee that they'll have a council meeting between now and when we need to find them." Tristan said. "Realistically we need to get this all in place in the next couple of weeks if we're to have any hope of stopping them from manufacturing those warheads. They've been working on it for months already."

"Can we not call a council meeting?" Wulfric suggested. "I'm sure between us we could come up with some pretence as to why the council would need to convene in your presence."

"Why don't I offer to do some work for them as a peace offering?" Oceana suggested but Tristan shook his head vehemently.

"I will not allow you to bind yourself to the council. You'll be in over your head before you know it."

"Which is kind of a moot point when you intend to kill them all." She persisted. "That is your intention, is it not?"

"It may not be possible." Tristan replied flatly. "They are old and powerful. It would be a suicide mission to go up against them all at once. They have to be picked off, one at a time, and chances are we won't get to all of them before they realise what's going on and come for us."

"You could make them gifts as peace offerings." Charlie spoke for the first time. "It was obvious to everyone at the duels that you have fallen into some disfavour. Perhaps you could offer to make public gifts of enchanted jewellery made by your own witch to them as a show of humility."

"They're probably just about arrogant enough to fall for that." Wulfric nodded. "And they'd want all the aristocracy there to witness your fall from grace. The plan has merit Tristan."

"And that way we could plant several trackers." Oceana was trying to follow the thought through. "I'm still not entirely sure how it would work so I could put them in the jewellery too and then if they happen to be wearing them when we're looking for them, all the better."

"Fine." Tristan consulted his watch. "It's two hours until lunch time. Oceana, I suggest you go to the workshop and start planning what materials you need. Wulfric, I want you to send an email to your family back home. Tell them you're having an amicable time but make out that the atmosphere is strained. We need to make this believable. Jo, go call this Mr AppleMac of yours. Do whatever you have to for him to help. I may have a complete inability to bargain with Oceana's person but I have no such qualms about yours. Do you understand me?" It was said coldly but Jo was in so much guilt over having brought Oliver into it in the first place that she just nodded miserably. "Charles and Xavier, I want you to access the public records and obtain the blue prints for the Venogen complex. Start plotting out possible surveillance routes for us to take. While you're at it, take stock of my surveillance equipment and draw up a list of anything else you think we may need." He gestured them all away and then turned to Will with a look on his face that would have chilled ice. "As for you" he said softly "you have some explaining to do, William. I suggest you take the time between now and the room clearing to come up with a damn good excuse as to why I should not rip your head from your shoulders with my bare hands." It felt as though the temperature in the room had dropped by several degrees.

"Leave it." Charlie murmured softly to Oceana before she could go to Will's defence. "This is for them to sort out." He physically bundled her from the room and the door slammed closed behind them. "The master will not kill him. Not yet."

"Yeah, because that makes me feel a whole hell of a lot better..."

CHAPTER THIRTEEN

Oceana started in the workshop but her mind was churning over what was happening between Will and Tristan and she couldn't focus on anything. Feeling jittery and panicky she decided she needed some sort of distraction and ended up going to the vault to have a closer look at some of Tristan's treasures. Locking the door again behind her she made her way to the back of the room and spent some time just gazing at the chain mail haubergeon, marvelling at its antiquity and how well preserved it was. It really was a thing of extraordinary beauty, if only for its rarity.

Finally tearing herself away from that display case she wandered across to a set of glass topped archive trays and slid the top one out. It appeared to be full of Saxon and Viking jewellery. Oceana was tempted to try and feel the resonance of the metal – after all she'd never seen that much gold in one place before – but with the state her mind was in she didn't trust herself not to do something stupid and melt it into a big mass of destruction. The second tray was more jewellery – crowns, circlets and a woman's belt in intricately wrought silver. The waist it must have encircled was tiny judging by the size of it and Oceana couldn't help but wonder who it had belonged to. The third tray was like a museum collection displaying the history of the pocket watch from its first rudimentary incarnations to the kind commonly worn in the 50's and 60's. It struck her as immensely ironic that an immortal would have such a fascination with the minutiae of time. The fourth tray, surprisingly, was full of masquerade masks that looked like they dated back to Tudor times. Clearly that had been a time of heavy partying for Tristan. Many of them she recognised from her research before the ball as being of French design and if the gemstones were real Tristan had clearly spent time at the French royal court. She wondered if he'd ever met any of the Louis' or even Marie Antoinette. The concept gave her the shivers but looking at them gave Oceana an idea and she made a mental note of it for dealing with the council.

Assuming the rest of that set of trays were jewellery related she left them for closer inspection at a later date and moved onto the next cabinet. These were all documents...lost works of Shakespeare and Kit Marlowe amongst them. After the second tray her hands were shaking so badly she couldn't bear to look at any more. Her heart was going into palpitations. There was a love letter from Queen Victoria in there and god only knew how he had managed to get hold of that little snippet of history. At least that was what she thought until she saw who it was addressed to. That was just wrong all over.

From there she gave up on looking methodically going through the cabinets, instead just opening trays at random and finding all sorts of weird, fascinating, spectacular, beautiful and priceless things. Perfectly preserved extinct creatures, ancient artefacts alongside photographs of early excavations, gadgets and inventions from the dawn of the technological revolution, works of art...it was incredible. One tray she opened contained nothing but neatly twisted locks of hair, neatly labelled in Tristan's precise script with names of famous historical figures. It was like he was a man centuries ahead of himself in time. Whatever his reasons for collecting them over the years, he could never have known that they held genetic secrets that the present day would be able to unravel if only they were allowed access. For the longest moment she contemplated the idea of cloning one of those extraordinary people...what would Galileo make of the modern world? What would Da Vinci invent with the tools of today? The idea totally freaked her out and she carefully slid the drawer shut, drawing back from the possibilities. That way lay madness.

She moved onto the display cabinets of weapons. There were beautiful examples from all over the world including a perfectly preserved Roman gladius and helm, a full set of original Japanese Samurai armour enamelled in a gorgeous shade of cerulean blue, a late mediaeval Claymore that was longer than she was tall and a set of armour like nothing she had ever seen before. Leaning in closer to study it she realised it was dress armour. It was too light and ornate to be of any use in combat but it sure was pretty to look at. Made of tooled and moulded leather it was inlaid with precious metals and gemstones. It would probably fall apart if a masculine man so much as sneezed near it, let alone bashed it with a sword. But if it was made with magic...now there was a concept. There was a concept indeed...with a smile on her face, Oceana went to find a piece of paper and began writing her shopping list.

"We can finish this how we started it." She explained to Tristan over lunch. "With a masquerade ball. Find some reason to celebrate. Maybe someone in your house is getting mated or siring a new fledgling, whatever you call them. I don't care. Announce a grand ball and in the weeks before it we can present the council with handmade masks with wondrous properties as a gesture of humility. We can cover up our preparations and gatherings under the guise of being towards the planning for the ball. It'll be an insane amount of work but if we're clever about it we can sail the destruction of Venogen through the chaos almost unnoticed. We might even be able to take out a couple of council members at the ball before they have any clue what's happening. It'll be on our terms, to our timescale and at a place of our choosing."

"Are you really sure you don't want me to turn you?" He asked, amused. "It's like you were born for this stuff."

"Yes I'm sure." She replied stiffly, not really sure what he was implying. "It's just my training. That's what indexers do – we see a string of events and items and find all the webs that connect them."

"Whatever." He grinned at her. "It's a great idea though. You just let me know what you need and I'll get it ordered."

"I wrote a list." She slid it across the table to him. "There's other stuff on there too, stuff I'll need to make for you guys."

"What do you need all this leather for?" Tristan scanned the list, a little bemused at the random nature of some of the requests.

"That's a surprise." She replied impishly, relaxing a little. "If I told you what it was for I'd have to kill you."

***

Will did not reappear all afternoon or at dinner. In the early evening Jo and Oceana watched a film together while the men played cards and discussed whatever they were planning for the surveillance. At ten o'clock Oceana yawned and looked at the clock on the mantelpiece in the living room.

"Well, lady and gentlemen, it's time for me to go to bed." She announced, getting slowly to her feet. "Long day tomorrow in the workshop."

"You will go to my room." Tristan did not look up from his cards. Oceana wanted to argue but she was tired and she knew that this talk was going to have to happen sooner or later. He had clearly seen Will kissing her in the grounds that morning and the longer she defied him the worse it would be when it eventually happened.

"Fine. I'll shower in my room and then come through."

"I won't be long."

As she dragged herself wearily up the stairs she pondered whether that was a promise or a threat. She was pretty sure he wouldn't hurt her. He'd been light and more than civil all day so it wasn't as though he was suddenly going to turn on her. He was unpredictable but he didn't appear to suffer from some sort of multiple personality disorder.

Putting up her hair and donning a shower cap so she didn't get it wet, she took a leisurely shower, soaking her aching body in the warm water and soothing her jangled senses with a sweet, spicy shower milk. Feeling slightly better when she got out, she pulled on her favourite brushed cotton pyjamas and trundled on through to Tristan's room. He'd beaten her there and was lounging on the bed half-dressed, idly flicking through a book.

"Sonnets from the Portuguese?" She raised an eyebrow. What on earth was the big bad bogeyman of the vampires doing lying in bed reading love poetry?

"You are familiar with them?" He seemed almost as surprised as she was.

"She's one of my favourites." Oceana confessed. "I might be a highly logical person but there's still a hopeless romantic in there somewhere."

"Will quoted her to me this morning." He lifted the book. "He was right. It reminded me so much of you – '*Could it mean To last, a love set pendulous between Sorrow and sorrow*?'"

"Well that's depressing." She moved across the room and climbed into bed next to him, taking the book from his hands. "That's not how I see myself, or you, at all." She flicked through the pages, smiling at the familiar words. "'*Love that endures from life that disappears*'." She read softly. "That's more appropriate." The words of sonnet 18 were particularly poignant after her discoveries in what she thought of as the treasure room. It was about the giving of a lock of hair. Closing the book she leaned back into the pillows, turning slightly so she could look at him.

"I don't know how to let you be anything other than mine." It wasn't what she had expected him to say. Anger yes, betrayal definitely. This sorrow was so incongruous with his personality that it caught her totally by surprise. "Will is in love with you."

"It's too early for that." She disagreed. "It's only been a few weeks. He's fascinated by me, sure, but love? No."

"How can I argue with his words when it's how I feel?"

Oceana blinked. Had he really just told her he was in love with her? Surely not. She must have misheard him. There was no way he'd just said that. "I'm sorry, what?" She managed weakly.

"I said I can't tell Will he's not in love with you because I'm in love with you myself and I know how it feels."

"But..." She couldn't seem to scramble her thoughts into any coherent sort of meaning. "That's not possible."

He gave a bitter smile. "I know you think I am incapable of any feelings. Hell, *I* thought I was incapable of any feelings. But the fact remains that you've stirred something in my dark and shadowed soul that I thought was long dead and, for whatever it's worth, my withered and dusty heart will probably continue to love you long after you are buried and gone."

"Tristan, I..." Words failed her.

"It's okay." He flicked the bedside lamp off, moved across and gathered her into him. "I don't expect you to say anything yet. The fact that you don't think love is possible after such a short time tells me that you do not love me. Or Will for that matter, although I have known you several weeks longer than he has."

She lay in his arms a little bemused by the situation. There was nothing she could say. She genuinely didn't believe that either of them loved her. Fascination, sure. Infatuation, possibly. After all she was something new and exotic to them and they had admitted that she set off every predatorial instinct they had. Perhaps it had been so long since they had truly felt anything that they were mistaking this minor crush for love but she couldn't suggest that without belittling them and that was something she desperately didn't want to do.

"Are you angry with me?" She asked eventually. "For kissing Will back I mean?"

"It's not so much anger as it is a raging need to dominate." His grip tightened almost subconsciously. "There were screaming instincts in my head saying 'MINE'. If I'd given into it I'd have ripped William's head right off his body and taken you there and then over his cooling corpse."

"For the record I'm glad you didn't do that." She tried to keep it light but couldn't contain the shudder that rippled lightly through her.

"I still feel like doing it." He admitted quietly. "Not so much the whole head-ripping thing but the need to mark you is still there."

Oceana carefully kept any fear out of her voice, knowing that would trigger his predator instincts. "I guess that's what happens when you have too many alpha males and only one female under the same roof."

"I never thought of it like that."

"It *is* like a pack. Think about it. You have this weirdly close-knit family. You're all hunters. There is one head of the family, the alpha if you like. Women tend to be mates or pets. You never have alpha females in the pack because it's so rare to have females in a position of strength or authority."

"Or just plain crazy-ass fearless." He joked, half-seriously. "It's true, you're right. That doesn't give us an answer to the problem. Unless you're suggesting we bring more alpha type females into the pack?"

There was an idea she'd never considered. "I don't know if you could. They'd have to be human. I don't understand what your hold is over Jo...I don't understand the whole master, subservient bond. Before her change she'd have definitely been alpha female material. Now you crook a finger and she just complies."

"Face it, you're a rare and special creature." He nuzzled the side of her neck, laying fluttering kisses behind her ear before nipping the lobe of it gently.

"What about that council woman?" She asked. "She's in a position of authority. Definitely alpha female material."

"She outranks me." He said as though it was the simplest thing in the world. "You challenge me and I find it endearing and sexy and it makes me feel like a man to impose my will on you. If she challenged me I would have to comply. It's somewhat emasculating."

"It's no wonder you're single." She was smiling in the darkness. "You're so picky."

"That's where you're wrong." He sounded amused. "I'm not single. You're *mine*."

***

Oceana spent the next few days in the workshop. The items Tris had ordered for her hadn't arrived yet but she had enough wire and beads to be getting on with making the masquerade masks. It was tempting to make them with magic but she wasn't sure she could control her anger or dislike long enough to make items that wouldn't kill the wearer that put it on so she was making them the traditional way. Mia came in and offered to help. She seemed so starved of company that Oceana agreed, letting her string beads and cut wire for her. When the leather arrived Oceana sent Mia up to the house to get measurements from everybody and then gave her the task of cutting out and stitching all the panels and buckles she needed. By that time she'd completed 4 of the 6 masks she needed for the council members and she could move on to the armour.

When the panels were done she sketched designs onto them with Mia's help, researched from one of her pagan symbology books which had arrived from storage, and then let Mia cut slight grooves out of the surface of the leather in which she would eventually work her wire. When that was as complete as she could manage without actually moulding them onto bodies for the final fit, they turned their attention to weapons.

Will and Xav surrendered theirs without question but Tris was reluctant and Charlie even more so. Oceana had to throw a full scale argument before they let her take all their daggers, swords, throwing knives and various other items into her workshop for modification.

After 10 days they were as ready as they could be. Both women's hands were blistered and aching from working so much wire but they surveyed their handiwork with immense pride. "You're pretty good at this." Oceana remarked to Mia who blushed.

"Thanks. It's just nice to feel useful I guess. I didn't realise how bored I was getting."

"Well you know you can come help me any time. It doesn't look like Tris is going to let me go."

Mia smiled at her. "I'm glad. Life has been a lot more interesting since you arrived."

Oceana burst out laughing. "That's what everyone says. I'm not sure if it's a gift or a curse. Come on, let's get the high and mighty executioner in here and kit him out."

When Tristan arrived he looked uncertainly at the soft sheets of leather Oceana was holding up. "What is that?" He asked and she smiled.

"It will be armour once I've finished it. Remove your shirt and raise your arms please."

In weary resignation he shucked off his T-shirt, raised his arms and allowed them to buckle the shapeless top around his torso. "Now stand very still." Oceana warned, allowing her intuition to choose a metal for her. Selecting a spool of copper by some unknown instinct, she slid it over her wrist, placed her hands lightly on Tristan's hips at the bottom of the leather and closed her eyes, focusing on what she needed. As she connected with her magic she could feel the first slithers of wire over her hand and Tristan flinched almost imperceptibly as it climbed up his broad chest, flowing through the grooves they had cut in the dark leather.

It seemed as though they stood there for an eternity but eventually he leaned down and kissed her eyelids. "It's done." He murmured. She opened her eyes and studied her work. The leather was now hardened and moulded to his form, defining his muscles and accentuating his stature.

"How does it feel?" She asked and he flexed his torso, twisting this way and that.

"Almost ridiculously comfortable." He conceded. "It's so soft. Are you sure it's going to stop anything?"

"Mia hand me a dagger." She responded seriously, holding her hand out. Mia hesitated so she crooked her fingers gesturing her to get on with it and, reluctantly, the young woman handed her one of the weapons from the pile on the work bench. "How much do you trust me?" Oceana grinned up at Tristan and he shrugged.

"With my life." He held his arms out, presenting her with his chest.

"Excellent." Before she could overthink what she was about to do, Oceana drove the dagger firmly towards his heart with both hands and as much leverage as she could muster. He didn't even step back or flinch as the dagger hit the leather and deflected off without leaving so much as a scratch.

"Oh my god!" Mia gasped but Tristan just stared down at his chest.

"I didn't feel a thing." His voice was almost painfully neutral to cover his shock and Oceana burst out laughing.

"That was kind of the point. They're thin enough to fit under your every day wear. I'll have to make special ones for the ladies if they're going to be worn under ball-gowns but you can send the rest of the guys on down and I'll get them kitted out."

"I'll send them straight down." He held his arms out for them to unbuckle the armour which was now holding the shape of his body. "How are you getting on with the masks?"

"They're all done and in the boxes." She gestured to where they were stacked with her chin as she wrestled with a buckle which was stiff.

"Excellent." He let them lift away the leather and then asked Mia to leave them alone for a moment. He waited until the door was closed and then cupped Oceana's cheek in his palm. "If I send Will on down here and he takes his shirt off is anything going to happen between you two?"

"I think I can restrain myself." She snorted. "I'm not into exhibitionism and Mia will be here if you're that concerned."

"It's not funny." He drew her to him and she leaned into the warm planes of his chest, rubbing her skin against the smooth perfection of it. "You drive me crazy. I can't be held responsible for what happens if I find he has betrayed me again."

"It takes two to tango Tristan." She pointed out. "We would have both betrayed you, not just Will."

"Well, when it comes to you, all the normal rules seem to be suspended." The words tasted bitter on his tongue.

"If it makes you feel better we'll leave the door open and I can get one of the other girls out here too." Oceana conceded.

"That won't be necessary. Leave the door open by all means but Mia will suffice." He laid his cheek against the top of her head. "You and she have become quite close."

"She's nice." Oceana smiled. "We've saved each other from the loneliness. I know she loves the other girls but they don't have as much in common as we do."

"Do you want me to move her up to the house to be closer to you?" He offered and she shrugged.

"I'll ask her if she wants to but the decision can be hers. It'd be nice if she could come and eat with me every now and then so you guys don't have to sit and watch me out of politeness. I can make her a piece of jewellery so she doesn't get snared all the time."

"As you wish. Let me know what she decides." He sighed. "I have much to be getting on with. I'll send Will across next."

"Okay." She waited for him to release her and accepted his kiss with enthusiasm. "See you later."

When Will arrived his eyes were downcast.

"I guess you just got read the Riot Act too?" Oceana tried to cheer him up.

"Something like that." She had barely seen him for the last two weeks since that morning and she was horrified at how dull he sounded.

"Will, are you okay?" She reached up and tipped his chin so he would look at her.

"Hopes apace Were changed to long despairs, till God's own grace Could scarcely lift above the world forlorn My heavy heart." He quoted, his voice full of pain.

"Elizabeth Browning again." She recognised the quote and took his hand gently, mindful of Mia's presence and the open door which left them in full view of the house. *"Lest these enclaspèd hands should never hold, This mutual kiss drop down between us both As an unowned thing, once the lips being cold, And Love be false! If he, to keep one oath, Must lose one joy, by his life's star foretold."* She whispered. With her other hand she brushed a curl from his forehead, sweeping it back into his hair with tenderness.

"You know her works?" Even his eyes were full of pain, hollow and bleak. She wondered what on earth Tristan had said to him to hurt him so deeply.

"I do." She squeezed his hand gently and he squeezed back.

"Then as you speak her words aloud in your thoughts, imagine them in my voice so that you may come to know the depth of my regard for you." The oddly formal words made it that much harder to bear and Oceana's throat ached with unshed tears.

"I will." She promised quietly, her voice hoarse.

"Come Master Will." Mia's voice was gentle as she broke in. "It's time to fit your armour."

"Of course." Blinking, he released Oceana's hand and heaved a great breath to try and release the moment. "What do you need me to do?"

"Just take your shirt off and hold your arms out." Mia continued when Oceana still couldn't speak. "We'll do the rest."

He stripped without hesitation and raised his arms, his haunted eyes following Oceana like a hawk as she moved around him. He flinched when she laid her hands gentle upon his waist and sucked in a breath, trying to contain himself. It didn't help. She was so close and he leaned down and breathed in the fragrance of her hair. It smelled of summer, of tropical fruits and sunshine, and it stung all the way down with bitterness.

He left as soon as they were done and Oceana stared after him, weighted down with sadness.

"It's so Shakespearean." Mia murmured, touching Oceana's shoulder gently. "Like Romeo and Juliet."

"Well hopefully in this version no-one dies." Realising she sounded melodramatic, she tried to shake off the melancholy. "Tristan has asked if you want to move up to the house. I think he's worried I'm getting lonely with everyone so busy planning. I said I'd ask but please don't feel-"

"I'd like that." She responded shyly. "I haven't been spending much time with the other girls lately and I like it in here. I'd like to learn how to do it properly."

"You want to learn to make jewellery?" She wasn't really surprised. Mia had been great at helping out. "Well I'd love to teach you. Any style in particular you'd like to try?"

"I'd like to learn all of it eventually." She was blushing now and Oceana smiled.

"I tell you what, we'll start off making you a necklace. Have a flick through some of my books and do some image searches online and when you see something you like the look of make a note of it. When we've got several pictures we'll sit down and draw a design and make it and then if there's any one aspect you enjoy most we'll start there first."

"That sounds great." Mia was about to add more but Charlie arrived at the workshop door.

"I was sent down for some sort of fitting?" He sounded confused and both girls burst out laughing.

"Come right on in Charlie." Oceana beckoned him through the door. "We'll get you kitted out in no time..."

CHAPTER FOURTEEN

That night Mia and Oceana ate their dinner in the study in front of the computer. Mia was still a little uncomfortable being around so many vamps after Oceana had given her one of her bracelets so she didn't get snared all the time and they stayed out of the way.

"Is there a particular stone you like?" Oceana asked, clicking through bead displays on the website of her favourite supplier. "Or a favourite colour?"

"I like pearls but they're too plain on their own."

"Well that's a start. If you mix them up with gemstones they offset beautifully. I like to make mine with sea glass but it depends on the lustre you choose. Some of them go with amethyst or blue lace agate and some look gorgeous with garnets or rubies. The other option is to mix pearl colours – have plain white with the odd black or pink thrown in or vice versa. What's your favourite colour pearl? You can get dyed ones too in just about every colour of the rainbow."

"I like the black ones." Mia seemed a little overwhelmed by the choice on display.

"Excellent choice. I like black ones too." Oceana grinned at her. "So the next choice is whether you want freshwater or cultured, how dark you want them because some of the paler greys are gorgeous and whether you want a red or blue lustre."

Mia was about to answer when the sound of angry voices erupted from somewhere else in the house. For a few moments they sat in silence as the rowing continued and then Oceana sighed.

"I'd best go see what's happening. Here." She opened up a search page for black pearls. "You have a look at all these and I'll be back in a minute." She set her plate on the desk and went to see what all the fuss was about.

She found them all in the dining room which they had converted into an impromptu headquarters for planning. There were blue prints and charts tacked up all over the walls and the table was full of pieces of paper and the odd stray pencil.

"No." Tristan was as angry as she'd ever heard him sound. "I won't allow it."

"Won't allow what?" She asked, walking in, and abrupt silence fell as everyone looked guiltily away except Wulfric.

"Tristan cannot find a hacker." He told her bluntly. "He wants to go in blind instead of using this Oliver chap."

Oh. That would explain the shouting for sure. Carefully keeping her face neutral she turned to Tristan. "Be reasonable Tris." She told him. "It's not worth risking your lives over your pride. The armour I have made you will only go so far and you said you would consider it if you couldn't find someone else."

"I have considered it. The answer is still no." They stared at each other across the expanse of table for a long moment.

"Can you all please give us a moment alone?" Oceana said eventually, not taking her eyes from Tristan's, and there was a rushed rustling as everyone else filed out of the room ahead of the fireworks. She waited until the door was closed and then spoke. "Tristan, you need to let it go and be rational about this. It's not worth losing any of your men over. *I'm* not worth losing any of your men over. It's my body Tristan and I will bargain with it as I see fit but not with Oliver, with you."

"What do you mean?" His gaze narrowed and she took a shaky breath.

"I care about these guys Tristan. Xav, Charlie, Jo, Will...even Wulfric. If you will let us try and strike a deal with Oliver I will do whatever you want me to do to prove that I am loyal to you alone."

"Whatever I want?" That had definitely given him pause but Oceana didn't look away.

"I won't let you turn me Tristan. I'm not ready to die just yet and I still want kids but that's about where the boundaries lie. Do you want to bite me? Tattoo me? Do you want me to promise to stop arguing when you want to sleep with me? Promise to stay here forever? What do you want?"

"I want to own you, body and soul." He moved towards her around the table. "We'll work around the kids issue but you are mine. If I allow you to strike a deal with Oliver then I want you to sign the paperwork that declares you as my mate."

"You need to explain the mate concept to me. I don't really understand it." She admitted. "What exactly does it entail?"

"You will be mine to do with as I please. No more arguing about sleeping in your own room. No more not letting me in. If I give you an order in public I expect you to follow it, whatever it is. You will wear what I tell you to wear. You will eat what I tell you to eat. I'll allow you to keep your house for weekend breaks but this will be your permanent residence. There is no breaking this contract. I will be your absolute Lord and Master for as long as you live. You sign that piece of paper and you are mine for life to deal with as I see fit."

"And that's what you want in return for protecting the lives of your family?" She was shaking although she didn't know if it was from anger or fear.

"That's what I want." He confirmed resolutely.

"How long do I have to think about it?"

"You have until morning." He sounded entirely too smug as though he knew she wouldn't agree to his conditions.

"Then tonight I will sleep alone." She replied stiffly, turning to leave.

"Oh and one more thing..." He sounded amused and she stopped at the door.

"What?"

"If you sign those papers the first thing I'm going to do is bite you. Just so you know." His satisfaction followed her out of the room and even on her way up the stairs she could still hear it echoing in her thoughts. Bastard. She was trying to help him and that was the price he demanded? Bastard!

"What happened?" Wulfric was standing on the landing outside his room.

"He asked me to bargain my life for yours and become his mate." She couldn't even look at him. "I have until morning to decide. Can you please tell Mia she's on her own for tonight? I can't concentrate right now."

"I'll tell her." He replied gravely, stepping aside so she could pass. "But I will tell you this now – don't sacrifice yourself for us. We have lived many times your lifespan and in all probability will continue to live many more times your lifespan. The value of the help of this Oliver man cannot be worth the sum total value of your freedom."

"It's not the value of his help, it's the value of the lives we'll lose without him." She swayed on her feet and he steadied her gently.

"Going in blind is not the end of the world." He reminded her. "These are battle-hardened warriors. Tristan maintains a fit and deadly house and he is the deadliest of them all. I'm sure they'll be fine."

"And what happens afterwards if the council is alerted too early?" She continued, feeling a headache start behind her left eye. "Even Tristan is wary of going up against them as a unified force."

"We will deal with that when it happens." He told her. "It is not your concern."

"And the data?" She persisted. "What about the information that could be transmitted and stored anywhere else in the world that will allow them to just start up again exactly where they left off? What is the price of my freedom against the price of hundreds of thousands of human lives that could be snuffed out if we fail in this?"

He looked troubled. "I can't answer that except to say that it is not your burden to bear. You shouldn't have to be in this position. Tristan should never have asked it of you. I will try and intercede on your behalf."

"He wants me Wulfric. He always has." She took a shaky breath. "This isn't even really about Oliver or Venogen. It's about him manipulating me into giving him something he wants."

He glanced down the stairs and stepped backwards slightly, drawing her into him. "There are other options." He murmured so softly she could barely hear it. "I cannot help you...I have too much at stake also. But you could go to another House...offer your services in return for protection. When this is all over I would shelter you."

"Do you really think that would stop him?" She asked bitterly.

Seeing the fight was lost he conceded defeat. "I doubt it. Even if we could get you through this he would challenge me for you and I don't know that I would win. Please, I beg of you, do not agree to his terms. It is not your burden."

"I have to think about it." She hung her head and the conversation was over.

"As you wish." He watched her walk into her room and then went to plead with Tristan on her behalf.

***

When Oceana emerged the next morning the house was strangely silent. Mrs Wells was bustling round the kitchen making her pancakes but the vampires were all out and Mia had taken herself off to the workshop already.

"Where's Tristan?" She asked Mrs Wells as she received her plate of food and Mrs Wells smiled.

"The master went out for a run. He won't be long. Are you okay dear? You look like you're coming down with a cold."

"No I'm fine. I just had a rough night." She'd been up most of the night crying and her throat felt scratchy and dry and her eyes were puffy and red.

"I'll make you a soothing drink. It's a little cooler today so it'll be all right." She made her up a honey and lemon warm drink with a healthy dash of whisky. "It's a little early in the day for drinking but it'll be our secret, yes?" She winked and Oceana had to smile.

"Thank you."

She accepted the mug laced with whisky and sat quietly until she heard the front door go and Tristan's feet bouncing lightly up the stairs as he took them two at a time on his way to the shower. She took her time to finish the drink and then went to wait for him in the study, knowing he wouldn't be much longer. Within moments of her arrival he stepped through the door behind her and she turned from where she had been standing at the window.

"You have a decision?" He seemed calm but under the surface something was churning.

"You knew what my decision would be when you made me the offer." She replied bluntly. It was the one thing that had cycled through her thoughts again and again overnight. The dash to save him when she thought Will was hurting him, the crazy stand-off in front of the council to protect him...it was in her nature to put everyone else before herself.

"I didn't think you'd actually take it." His voice was so carefully calm, so cautiously neutral that she knew it was an act.

"You knew I would otherwise you would never have asked it of me." She abruptly looked away. "I'll sign your papers Tristan but you had better make damn sure that you bring every one of your and Wulfric's men back alive from this and that Venogen is utterly destroyed."

"You have my word. And if I do not bring them all back alive you may petition me to annul the contract." He moved across to the desk and unlocked the top drawer, removing a thin sheaf of papers. "Here. You need to sign the bottom of each page where it says."

With shaking hands she signed the bottom of each page before she could chicken out and laid the pen down gently on the desk. "There. What happens now?"

"You go to our room and await me. I have to go to the kitchen."

"Okay." Numbly she turned and walked out of the study, each step towards the bedroom seeming like an infinite distance. She couldn't believe she'd been so roundly played, even though he was a master of manipulation. What had she been thinking, even making that crazy offer? But then he'd probably known she would try to intervene the minute Oliver ever became an issue. With hindsight she should have fought harder to make Oliver accept a different method of payment the first time round and then this would never have happened but she hadn't had the time to make the wards. Tristan had needed the answer immediately. Tristan...always Tristan. There was nothing she could do about it now except hope that being bound to slavery was not as bad as she was expecting. Forever was a very long time.

That said, she was sure she had heard him correctly when he had offered to allow her to petition for annulment if someone died. She hadn't been expecting that and wondered if it was a measure of how shaken he was by her determination to protect the members of his House. It was a small concession but a significant one nonetheless. She also strongly suspected that he would never treat her as he had threatened. He wouldn't tell her what to wear or what to eat and she couldn't envisage him asking her to do anything too awful in front of others. Just because he could behave like that as the dominant partner didn't mean that he would. She knew that Tristan had never taken a mate before so this was new ground for both of them.

He was gone for almost ten minutes and when he came to her she was sat on the bed flicking absently through the poetry book he had left on the bedside table after their talk a few nights previously. She closed it when he walked in and looked up at him nervously.

"I went to milk my venom." He explained. "Don't need you out of action for 3 days right in the middle of this."

The bottom dropped out of her stomach. "You're going to do it now?"

"No time like the present." Something in his body language changed and he flowed towards her darkly. If it wasn't so beautiful it would have been terrifying. Oceana could well understand how animals sometimes got mesmerised by their predators. She tore her gaze away and began to turn her bracelet, looking for the clasp to take it off. "No, leave it on." He commanded.

She swallowed, nerveless fingers dropping the chunks of sea glass. "Won't that hurt?" She hated that her voice was shaky.

"A little. But I'll make it worth it. I promise." He purred. Taking her chin in his strong fingers, he tilted her face up to him and leaned down to kiss it, gently at first and then with measured intensity. Scooping his hands under her thighs he moved her back onto the bed and she allowed herself to be laid flat as they kissed. "Relax." He whispered, fluttering kisses at the corners of her mouth. "You're so tense."

"I'm scared." She replied bluntly.

"Don't be." He stopped what he was doing and looked her right in the eye. "It won't hurt anywhere near as much as you think it will." Deft fingers unsnapped the button on her jeans and roamed beneath them, teasing and flickering gently as he captured her mouth again, and she arched against him, a soft moan escaping from her. For a few glorious moments she became mindless with pleasure and then his lips left her mouth, travelling south down her throat. The reality of what they were doing crashed in almost immediately and she went instantly cold and still. He chuckled lightly against her skin and raised his head to look at her. "Look, if it freaks you out this much I won't do it, okay?"

"Really?" She was so relieved she wanted to cry.

"Really. Now stop stressing and relax." He rubbed the tip of his nose against hers and smiled. "Abandon yourself to me Oceana."

And so she did. They started slowly and teasingly, exploring each other with hands and tongues and want. He pushed her almost to the edge before lifting her into his lap and entering her slowly, building up to a steady, thrumming rhythm that drove her almost crazy with need. When she couldn't take any more he brushed over her with gentle fingers and she came apart in his arms, free-falling into bliss without even noticing the sharp sting at her neck. By the time she returned slowly to herself her fingers were twined in his black curls and she had fallen into him and the pain was gone, there was only the sensation of sucking and the soft satisfied noises he was making. It felt wrong and yet it was the most poignantly intimate thing she'd ever done in her life.

When he was done he ran his tongue gently over the mark. There wasn't enough venom left over to heal it completely but there was enough to stop it bleeding. "Are you okay?" He asked, laying gentle kisses over the bite.

"It didn't hurt as much as I was expecting." She was so overwhelmed by the enormity of what had just happened that she couldn't help but sound subdued. "It's actually a lot like getting blood taken at the doctors...a sharp scratch and then you don't feel the needle in your arm."

He sat back slightly and gathered her hair away from her face, running his fingers through the curls, untangling them gently from each other. "Did you enjoy it?"

Her face flamed at the memory of his lips caressing her throat. It had been both erotic and sensual, the way his tongue flickered softly against her skin as he moaned with pleasure. "It was intense." She answered honestly. "I've never abandoned myself to anyone so completely before. You could have killed me and I trusted you not to."

A twisted smile turned up the corner of his mouth. "Considering I fibbed about doing it, it's still probably the most honest thing that's ever passed between us."

Her eyes widened. "You totally lied to me!" She slapped his shoulder and he burst out laughing.

"Technically I didn't." He ducked another swipe and caught her wrist, pressing a kiss to the underside of it. "I said if it freaked you out that much I wouldn't do it but right then you weren't capable of freaking out."

"You bastard!" She leaned back, bracing her hands against his thighs and then immediately wished she hadn't as his eyes took a long steady cruise down the length of her body. "Stop looking at me like that." She murmured, blushing again. "We just finished. Surely you don't want to start again?" He was still inside her and she felt him twitch but he shook his head.

"We can't spend all day in bed. There's too much to do." His tone spoke volumes about the regret he was feeling over that statement. "Come here." He reached around to the small of her back and drew her against him in an embrace. "Will you let me do that again?" He asked, his voice muffled into her shoulder.

"Do I have a choice?" She didn't mean it to sound bitter but the contract of binding was never far from her thoughts.

"Okay, let me rephrase." He sounded amused. "Do you *want* me to do it again?"

She wanted to say yes. Oh god, did she want to say yes. "Let me see what a mess you've made of my neck and then I'll decide." She said instead.

"Your body says you want me to do it again." He sounded satisfied and smug and she wanted to slap him.

"Luckily my brain takes precedence. Let me up Tris, I need to go shower. Again."

"I could order you not to." He teased lightly, running his fingers lightly up and down the spine in the small of her back.

"Not to what? Shower?" Confused she leaned back as far as she could in his arms and looked at him. "Why would you do that?"

"So that I'm on your mind all day." He grinned. "So that every time you move you can smell me on your skin and whenever you feel sticky and uncomfortable it's because you know I'm dripping in your pants."

"That's gross." She screwed her face up and he laughed, planting a kiss on the tip of her nose.

"Give me a good reason not to and I'll think about it." He teased.

"I've got bite marks on my neck and I've just signed my life over to you." She said flatly. "Trust me Tristan, you're going to be on my mind all day whether I smell of you or not."

"Good answer." He slapped her lightly on the ass. "Go get in the shower then princess. I'll call down for Mrs Wells to have tea ready." She opened her mouth and he pressed a finger to her lips. "You'll be dehydrated. You need to drink."

"Fine." She sighed and climbed off him. "I won't be long."

***

By the time he was satisfied with the amount of fluids she had ingested, Jo had returned from her visit with Mr Applemac. They met in the dining room to look at the pictures and even Oceana had to admit they were eerily good. Wulfric actually shuddered all over looking at them. They were in Polaroid format so Tristan photocopied them, slipped the coded note in the Wulfric had designed in between them and dropped them in an envelope.

"When are we going to do this?" Wulfric asked and Tristan shrugged.

"Charles and Xavier should be back from their surveillance activities tomorrow. The council meeting is four days from now. I think we should go ahead tomorrow afternoon. Once the Masquerade Ball is announced we will only have a small window of time to plan so the more we can get out of the way now the better."

"And how go the plans for the assault on Venogen?"

"All is in place except the security issue but we'll be speaking to Oliver this morning." Ignoring the sudden silence that fell, Tristan turned to the blue prints pinned up on the wall. "Near as the men can make out, the captives are being held here and here." He gestured towards the areas they had identified. "We need to have the support structure in place to make the smash and grab the day of the ball. Oceana was right...we need to sneak it in under the radar."

"Did I hear that right, you're bringing Oliver back into this?" Jo asked the question that was on everyone's mind and Tristan gave her a level look.

"Yes." Will got up without a word to anyone and left the room, obviously knowing what that meant for Oceana and she stared after him sorrowfully. "He'll get over it." Tristan said quietly to her and she swung to him, lit up with a sudden anger.

"Would you? If it was the other way around?" Without waiting for an answer she left too, taking herself to the library for some time alone. It was all too much too soon.

When Tristan came to find her a couple of hours later she was sat in the window seat flicking through a Book of Shadows from his collection. "Anything interesting?" He asked and she shrugged.

"It's hard to tell. I can't read much of the writing so I'm mostly just looking at the diagrams."

"It's a start." He took the book from her hands and closed it, setting it on one of the chairs behind him. "Come with me." He took her hand. "There's something I want to show you."

"I'm still mad at you." She told him as he led her out through the house and into the walkway. "I hate that you're managing my life this way."

"I know."

"I hate what you've done to Will as well."

"I know."

"And you totally suck at arguments. You're not supposed to agree with me. You're supposed to defend yourself so I can shout at you and feel better for letting off some of my pent-up frustration."

"I know." He snickered and despite herself she laughed.

"It's not funny Tris. One of these days I might wind up hating you for being so controlling."

"We'll cross that bridge when we come to it." He unlocked the room containing his artefacts and led her in. She was instantly comforted by the soft hum of the generators and the golden lights displaying cases of history. It was an extraordinary treasure trove. "Here." He led her to the trays she had been looking through all those days before but this time there were a couple pulled out and open. "It's traditional for mated vampires to give each other gifts upon mating as a mark of respect and affection. I'd like you to choose one to wear as a mark of my affection for you."

Oceana looked into trays full of rings from almost every era of history, some plain, some intricate, many studded with priceless gemstones, and her jaw dropped. "I can't accept any of these Tristan." With shaking hands she touched the surface of the glass topped drawer in front of her. "They're priceless. Too priceless to be worn."

"They were designed and made to be worn." He disagreed. "We're not leaving this room until you choose one, even if it's just a stone you like and want set in a ring of your own design."

"Really, I don't need a gift." She tried again. "I'm not a vampire. This is not a traditional mating."

"Nevertheless, you will choose one."

"Does it have to be a ring?" She asked plaintively, realising she was going to lose this battle, and he nodded resolutely.

"I want you to have a ring. What's wrong with a ring?" He demanded and she blushed, unsure how to explain it.

"You must know that rings between humans are given for proposals and marriage." She tried. "You and I aren't married and not engaged. Whatever this mating thing is it's not...that." She tailed off lamely.

"It's exactly like that." He insisted. "We're tied for life. It's not just a contract and the sooner you get your head around that the better."

Her eyes filled with tears. "I don't want to be married to you Tristan. That's not how I planned my life to be."

"I know. And I'm sorry, but that's the way it is. That's the way it has to be."

She studied the tray of rings, wanting to choose something totally unacceptable as a petty revenge but at the same time knowing he would make her wear it every day. There were stones of every cut and colour sparkling under the lights, rings of gold, silver and platinum.

"Do you want a diamond?" He asked her tentatively, seemingly aware that she had given in.

"No." She'd never been fond of diamonds. They'd always seemed so cold. "Tristan, I have not the heart for this." She backed away from the trays. "You decide."

"Are you sure?" She nodded so he turned to the trays and without any hesitation lifted the glass top of the tray to the left and selected a ring. "Here." He lifted her left hand and slid it onto her ring finger.

"Why that one?" She asked and he smiled.

"Doesn't the stone remind you of anything?" He sounded both sad and amused somehow and Oceana met his eyes. The blue emerald-cut stone twinkling on her finger matched the shade of them exactly.

"That's uncanny." She held her hand up next to his face to look between the two and it was true – the stone was the exact same cornflower blue of Tristan's eyes. "What is it? A sapphire?"

"I have no idea. I take it to get it examined every now and then but no-one knows what stone it is. I believe it was created by magic. It belonged to your predecessor."

"My predecessor?"

"Mary." He looked down at the ring, a wistful smile touching the corners of his lips. "She was a witch too and my companion for many years."

"What happened to her?" Oceana couldn't help the question.

"She was burned in the witch trials."

Wow. She hadn't seen that one coming. "I'm so sorry."

"It was a long time ago." He turned away and began slotting the trays back into their cabinets but not before she had seen the flash of pain in his eyes. Whoever this Mary was, she was someone he had cared for deeply.

"Could she not save herself? Was there nothing she could do?" Oceana knew that she would use any power within her control to save herself in that situation.

"That was not where her gifts lay. She was a seer. Her other powers were limited." He took her hand and kissed the knuckle above the ring. "It suits you."

"The ring or the slavery it represents?" Her smile was twisted with a touch of bitterness.

"The possession." He drew her to him and gentled the frown on her face with kisses. "I wish I could mark you all over. Possession suits you."

Her traitorous libido was ready to grovel at his feet but her pride and self possession stopped her knees from wobbling. "I have no desire to be marked Tristan."

"Now that you are mine your desires are irrelevant." He whispered. "I own you Oceana. You are mine to do with as I please."

"But you will take my desires into account anyway." She shivered involuntarily as his breath caressed her neck.

"If you please me." She gasped as his fangs snicked out and he grazed them lightly over her skin.

"You bit me even though I pleased you." She pointed out breathlessly.

"That's because I know your desires better than you do."

The sheer arrogance of him took her breath away. "I have no desire to be marked." She repeated absently as he scooped strong hands behind her thighs and lifted her jean-clad legs around him.

"You lie." He pressed her back against a glass-fronted cabinet that displayed a staggeringly valuable piece of art. "I want to mark you and it turns you on."

"Not in here Tristan, please." The cold glass against her neck had shocked her out of the haze he induced. "Something could get damaged."

"If I ordered you never to wear jeans again how many times would I have to punish you before you acceded?" He ignored her plea and wrestled frustratedly with the button of her jeans.

"Tristan stop, we can do this at the house." *Please don't allow this to interfere with the calm of my last sanctuary* she thought inwardly. She loved her time in here, marvelling at the antiquities, and didn't want it marred with memories of their intimacies.

"I want you here. Now." His voice was rough with need and she sighed. She knew he'd been alone for a long time but they weren't long out of bed.

"Tristan I can't keep up with you." She curled her hands in his lustrous hair and tugged his head back so she could look at him. "I'm a human. We're fragile. I don't heal instantly. If you want me again I'm going to be sore afterwards."

"I could fix that." With a filthy grin he caught her wrist and brought her hand around to his face so he could suck her finger between his lips.

"Oh." She gasped as his tongue swirled around the pad of her finger and her eyes fluttered closed, briefly losing herself to the moment.

"Bargain with me." He murmured, letting her finger slide from his mouth as he rocked his hips slightly in a way that tipped her off the edge into the abyss.

"I can't think straight." She whispered back, eyes still closed.

"You have five seconds to come up with something I want enough to let you go for now." He was amused. The bastard. "Five...four...three...two..."

"Let me go and I'll never wear jeans around the house again." She blurted out.

"Ooh! Good call!" He considered it for a moment and then released her, steadying her until she had her balance back. "Go and get changed Princess. You win this round. I'll put these trays away."

They met again in the hallway as she was halfway down the stairs and Tristan eyed her corduroys unimpressed. "Uh uh uh." She tutted before he could say anything. "I said I wouldn't wear jeans around the house. There was no mention of any other form of trousers."

"I am burning every pair of trousers you own." His voice was low and dangerous but she just shook her head.

"They're all in my room Tristan." She pointed out gleefully. "You can't get in there. And before you go throwing your weight around with the girls, I've added another ward to my room so humans can't get in there either."

"I am burning every pair. Starting with those." He stepped towards her but Jo appeared in the doorway to the kitchen.

"Uh...master?"

"What?" Tristan snapped without taking his eyes off Oceana.

"Oliver is refusing to deal with me. He says he'll only bargain with Ana." The temperature in the room dropped to subzero and Oceana wrapped her arms around herself.

"Call him and tell him we will be visiting this afternoon." He waited until Jo left and then pointed at Oceana's trousers. "This conversation is a long way from being over, Princess." He warned. "Right now you are going to eat whatever I damn well tell you to eat for lunch and then we're going to go and hand this jumped-up geek his balls on a platter. Do I make myself clear?"

"I'm allergic to red food colouring."

"What?" Whatever he had been expecting her to say that wasn't it.

"Well, you know." She rolled her eyes like he was being stupid. "If you're going to try and tell me what to eat you should at least know to avoid what makes me sick."

"There's no try about it." Exasperated he ruffled his curls until they stood up at odd angles.

"I don't like olives either." She continued blithely. "They make me throw up. It's not a pretty sight. And anything with anise or aniseed makes me extremely nauseous."

"So no glace cherries, no olives and no aniseed. Anything else Miss Fussypants?" He demanded sarcastically.

"I'm not a big fan of offal. You know, no livers or kidneys." She made a face. "Oh...and I don't like-"

"Oceana will you shut up and get into the kitchen!" He roared.

"Well there's no need to get so testy." Her eyes were twinklingly mocking him. "I'm only trying to help."

"Fine. You pick, I'll approve." He held his hand out and when she got to the bottom of the stairs she took it, letting him lead her towards the kitchen. He frowned as she stepped into the sunny room and laid a gentle hand against her forehead.

"What's wrong?" She asked, trying to duck away from his hand.

"You feel like you've got a temperature." He pushed her into sitting on the table. "Jo fetch me the first aid kit."

"Of course." She dashed from the room and Oceana sighed.

"I feel fine Tristan." She told him irritably. "It's a warm day."

Ignoring her he pulled the neck of her T-shirt aside and studied the bite mark he had put there earlier, swearing as he saw it was almost healed but the whole area was slightly inflamed. "We took too long before I bit you." He muttered. "There was too much venom."

"Then you know I'm fine."

He pushed her back down in the chair and growled at her as Jo reappeared with the first aid box. "Sit still damn it or so help me I will tie you to that goddamn chair!" He roared, snatching the box from a startled Jo and rummaging through it. Finding the digital thermometer he snapped a new tip on it with practised precision and pressed it into her ear. A few seconds later it beeped and he read the display, his face darkening with anger. "You have a temperature!" He accused. "Why didn't you say anything?"

"Because I genuinely feel fine." She responded, a little bewildered. Sure, she was tired and a little grouchy but it had been a trying day and she'd donated some of the red stuff that morning.

"This is not good enough Oceana." He swung to Jo. "Find Mrs Wells and tell her I want a steak sandwich delivered to my room, soon as. Medium rare. With salad. And 2 paracetamol tablets. And call that man and tell him we'll go tomorrow instead. Oceana is resting today." Discarding the thermometer on the table, he scooped Oceana up despite her protests and started for the stairs.

"Is everything all right?" Will was on the landing and Tristan nodded curtly to him.

"Oceana is not well. She is going to bed for the afternoon." Will caught her gaze and something in it let her know he knew what was wrong and was thinking of the time he had tasted her in the workshop. She brushed her fingers lightly across her cheekbone in acknowledgement and was glad when his eyes widened. However Tristan had hurt him, he still had that. He was still the first she had willingly allowed to taste her.

CHAPTER FIFTEEN

After a whole afternoon and night confined to bed rest Oceana was just about climbing the walls with boredom and could have cried with relief when Tristan took her temperature again after breakfast the next day and declared her back to normal. He still insisted she took another 2 Paracetamol before he'd let her get up but by 9am they were in the car on the way to visit Oliver.

He opened his front door and the initial joy on his face at seeing Oceana flattened slightly when he saw Tristan standing behind her and Xavier behind them, waiting by the car.

"Oliver." Oceana greeted neutrally, trying to calm the churning in her stomach.

"Ana. It's good to see you again. Are you better? Jo said you were ill." He stepped aside to let them in and closed the door behind them.

"I'm fine." She led the way through to his living room and took a seat by the door. Tristan moved to stand at the window and Oliver looked at him uncomfortably.

"Who's tall, dark and grumpy?" He muttered to Oceana and her jaw tightened.

"My security. My owner will not allow another bargain such as the last one to be struck."

"Your owner?" He gaped at her in disbelief and Oceana nodded.

"Yes, my owner." She gave him a level look. "He is a powerful and very dangerous man Oliver. I suggest you don't upset him."

"I'm not so sure you have anything I want enough to bargain with if I can't have you." The hacker said dismissively and Oceana prayed for Tristan to rein in his temper.

"I have something of immense value." She disagreed. "I can give you the ultimate in impenetrable firewalls. That coupled with the fact that you will be helping us to do the right thing for humanity should be profit enough for you."

"You'll give me the secret to your employer's firewalls?" He tried to say it nonchalantly but there was no mistaking the spark of interest in his eyes.

"Yes I will. I assume you have been trying to hack our network."

"Around the clock since it came on my radar." He admitted. "I'm impressed. I've never seen anything like it. Even the government doesn't have tech that solid. Here or in the States."

"Agree to work with us for this one project and I'll hook you up." She looked back at Tristan to disguise her nervousness as Oliver thought it over. His jaw was twitching in barely suppressed rage which, for Tristan, meant he was really on the edge. She hoped he could keep it together.

Finally the hacker sighed. "Okay I'll do it. I have most of the codes anyway, you just need to give me a time and date and an hour or so to set it up and I'll get you into Venogen."

"We also need you to destroy all their data sources and caches." She insisted. "They're planning mass destruction with incomprehensible loss of life here Oliver. They cannot be allowed to start up elsewhere with barely a hitch."

"Agreed." He leaned forward, his eyes glinting greedily. "Now give me the software."

A small smile flirted around the edge of her lips. "Do you have some sort of mobile device you can hack easily?"

"Sure." He pulled a smartphone from his pocket.

"Give it to me." She held her hand out and waited. "Now go and hack it." She ordered, accepting the phone.

"No need to. I've done it before."

"Humour me."

"Fine." He went to his computer and within a few keystrokes a message flashed up on the screen of the smartphone – *happy now?*

"Of course. Now come out of the phone." As the screen went black she took out a tiny mobius design in micromaille and pressed it to the back of the phone, focusing on it until the rings rippled beneath her fingers and adhered to the surface of the phone. "Now try hacking it again." She set it on the coffee table so he could see she was in no way interfering with it and sat back to watch as he attempted to break into the phone's programming.

After ten minutes or so he conceded defeat and returned to the chairs, snatching up the phone to study it. "What is this?" He demanded curiously, running his fingers over the tiny rings. "Some sort of nanotechnology?"

Oceana snorted. "Not even close. I have enough with me to firewall five more objects of your choosing. I suggest you select wisely."

"You're not going to tell me how the program works?" His face went red. "That's not in the spirit of the deal."

"There is no programming to explain Oliver." She let him feel the truth of her words. "It's more like a..." she struggled for the words.

"It's a jamming device." Tristan helped her from where he was glaring out of the window.

"Exactly." Relieved, Oceana smiled at Oliver. "It's like a jamming device. It blocks all unwanted intrusions."

"Even jamming devices have programming." He insisted and Oceana shrugged.

"If you can find it then I will be more than surprised." She checked her watch in a not so subtle manner. "Bring me what you want protecting and then we have to go. We have stuff to do."

"I'll figure out how it works." He said stubbornly, placing three laptops and another phone in front of her. "You can do the main computer tower too."

"Of course." Oceana warded the items requested as Oliver watched closely, searching for some clue as to how she was doing it, but she knew that from his perspective it just looked as though she was pressing the rings onto the surface of the objects.

When the main tower was done they stood up to leave and Oliver walked them to the door. "If you change your mind about telling me how it works then call me." He pleaded one more time and Oceana shook her head.

"If I told you that I'd have to kill you." It came out a little more seriously than intended and Oliver blinked.

"Oookaaay." He held his hands up in deference and let them pass but Tristan paused a second on the doorstep before turning back.

"You ever lay another finger on my woman again and I will rip your head from your body and stuff your balls down the gaping cavern of your throat. Do you understand me?" He hissed. Without waiting for an answer he turned and flowed, panther-like to the car. Oliver barely registered the spreading wetness in his pants.

***

That afternoon they faked Wulfric's death. Oceana and Jo were walking around the walls of the property as though they were enjoying the sunshine, feeling like actresses in an action movie. They were just about at the front gates when the shouting started and they both paused, looking back towards the house.

"Do you think we should go see what's wrong?" Jo was playing her part well. It sounded totally natural.

"No. Tris and Will are probably throwing down on each others' ass again." Oceana sighed. "The sooner Will gets it through his head I'm mated to Tris the easier this'll be for all of us." She took Jo's arm and they continued to walk.

They had barely gone five paces when the front door of the house crashed open and a brawl spilled out onto the driveway. "Oh my god!" Squeaked Jo. "That's Wulfric!"

"Fuck!" Picking up her skirt, Oceana started running towards the house but she could see that the blond vampire was up and running towards her. Tristan was faster though. He pounced on Wulfric from behind in a flying leap that arced through the air like a meteorite. A split second later Will was with him and they hauled Wulfric back into the house, the big vampire fighting them every inch of the way.

"What's happening?" Oceana called to Xav who had appeared around the side of the house and he caught her before she could go through the door.

"You don't want to go in Ana." He told her grimly. "Wulfric was scheduled for execution."

"What?" She shrieked just as Jo arrived. "Wulfric? No!" She tried to push him out of the way, fighting to get through the door but he pinned her arms to her sides and bodily hauled her away from the door.

"A little help here?" He snapped at Jo and she picked Oceana's feet up.

"Stop it!" Oceana screamed. "Put me down this instant! What did he do?" She suddenly went limp and burst into tears. "What did he do?" She repeated miserably. "What did he do? I liked him."

"We all did sweetie." Xav nodded at Jo warily and she let Oceana's feet touch the floor. "We all liked him. But sometimes the master's job is hard and he still has to do it. I'm sorry." He turned her in his arms and let her cry into his shirt.

They waited in the sunshine until Tristan appeared in the doorway of the house. He was splattered in blood and it was dripping from the tip of the short sword he was carrying, pooling on the floor in a viscous mirror that reflected the face of death. "It's safe to come in." He called out and Oceana started shaking.

"I don't want to see it." She murmured to Xav. "I don't want to see Wulfric. I liked him. I don't want to see him dead."

"It's okay, you don't have to." He promised her. "Jo, go tell them to clear it up. I'm taking Ana to my room in the guest annexe. We'll wait there until it's all over."

***

Two days later they headed to London for their audience with the council. Tristan had requested a private session but as expected they had made it an open audience and the buzz on the grapevine was that the big smoke was once again full of vampires, all come to see Tristan humbled. Wulfric had to stay home under strict orders to remain out of sight and away from the windows. Jo had remained behind with him to keep him company but mostly because she was still uncomfortable with the whole scene. They had heard rumours that word of Wulfric's death had spread in the city which only served to confirm that the house was being watched. Their ruse had obviously been believable and the photographs Tristan held were just the icing on the cake.

"Are you okay?" Charlie whispered quietly to Oceana as she nervously smoothed the velvet on the corset she was wearing over a full velvet skirt. They were standing in the hall outside the council chamber waiting to go in.

"I'm fine." She couldn't quite muster up a smile and her eyes kept flicking to the boxes they were each carrying. She had hidden tiny micromaille trackers under the surface of each lid that would detach and stick themselves to the council members somewhere unobtrusive and hopefully entirely unnoticed. Tristan shot her a concerned look at the sound of Charlie's voice but before he could say anything the doors in front of them swung open. *I'm fine* she mouthed at him and he nodded once, turning and striding across the amphitheatre floor towards the seated council members.

"Tristan." It wasn't the woman that greeted them this time as they formed up behind him. Instead an athletic looking man stood up. He must have been in his forties when he was turned but it was definitely in the prime of his life.

"Councillor Marcellus." Tristan nodded back respectfully. "Thank you for granting me an audience."

"State your business." The councillor sat down again without breaking eye contact.

"I have two matters to bring before you." Tristan stepped forward and handed across an envelope to the councilwoman sitting nearest him. "Wulfric is dead. He was, however, my long-time friend and I have chosen to retain his body privately until his House can come and claim him."

"We will make the arrangements." The council members passed the envelope between them, flicking quick glances across the gruesome photographs. "And the second matter?"

"Next week I will be hosting a celebratory masquerade ball. As a mark of respect and deference I have commanded my witch to make you masquerade masks. Please accept the gifts I humbly offer." Will, Charlie and Xav all dropped to one knee, offering up the boxes they held with their eyes on the floor. The council members stirred uneasily.

"Are they enchanted?" Marcellus asked and Tristan nodded, gesturing to Oceana to explain.

"If I may, Councillor Marcellus." She kept her eyes lowered as Tristan had requested. "Do you have a favoured pet to hand? I believe it would be easier to demonstrate."

"Tell me what it does and then I will decide if a demonstration is necessary." He was curious but keeping it under control.

"The mask will allow a human to resist being snared by your gaze." As if to prove a point she raised her eyes to his and gave him a look heavy with meaning. "When was the last time you took a woman that was not blindfolded who writhed and squirmed beneath you?"

Marcellus pursed his lips but was beaten to responding by another councillor who cleared his throat. "Never mind Marcellus, I wish to see this for myself." He crooked a finger to one of the vampires standing behind him deferentially. "Fetch Christa."

"Of course master." The vampire rushed away so fast he was almost a blur.

"Bring me the mask." The councillor demanded imperiously and Tristan didn't move so Oceana turned to the kneeling vampires. Will gestured with the one he was holding in his right hand which was obviously the one designed for the councillor they were speaking to. She brushed his fingers as she accepted the box and his lip twitched slightly. Stepping around Tristan, she approached the councillor and stopped directly before him. "Open the box." He commanded. She raised the lid and held the box out to him so he could examine its contents. "This is fine work." He congratulated as he reached forward and lifted the red and black chequered mask out of the ripples of satin to examine it.

"Thank you." Curtseying gracefully she set the box by his feet and stepped back just as the vampire he had sent away returned with a startlingly beautiful brunette.

"Kneel." The councillor commanded and the woman dropped instantly to her knees, her skin slapping on the stone floor. Oceana winced but didn't look away. "Close your eyes and raise your face." The woman did as she was told and the vampire leaned down and tied the mask on her. "Now open your eyes and behold my face." It was obvious the woman was confused but she did as she was bid and then her eyes widened as her mouth pursed in an O of wonder.

"Master!" She breathed. Oceana relaxed inwardly, grateful the mask had worked as intended. The vampire stared down impassively at the beauty kneeling before him.

"Pleasure me." He commanded.

"Yes master." She reached for his trousers and Oceana managed to tear her gaze away. She had no desire to watch this. Thankfully it seemed the other council members did not either and she heard a rustle of expensive clothing as Marcellus stood up.

"A further demonstration is not necessary Octavius." He said sharply before turning to Tristan. "These are worthy gifts Executioner. We accept. Are we to assume that we are invited to the ball?"

"Of course Councillor Marcellus." Tristan stepped aside as the others got to their feet and moved forward to place the masks by the councillors they were intended for. Oceana watched them in the periphery of her vision but did not see even the slightest flash of movement as the trackers leapt to their new hosts like magnets drawn to each other. "We only arrived in the city this morning. Your invitations are in the boxes with the masks. We were remiss in not sending them out earlier."

"It is of no concern." Smiling now, the councillor retrieved his own box and studied the green and gold mask within. "These are exquisite. May I enquire what it is we are to be celebrating at this ball?"

"I have taken the witch to Mate." Tristan's words rippled through the hundreds of silent watching faces like a sandstorm and there was a flurry of murmuring before Marcellus' hand cut the air in a demand for silence.

"Congratulations Tristan." He said mildly. "I assume you will be turning her in the near future?"

Will touched Oceana's back briefly as she fought to remain still and she drew strength from the silent support even as Tristan shook his head. "She has expressed a desire to procreate, Councillor Marcellus." He sounded almost apologetic. "She is the last female of her line. It seemed wise to grant the request so that future generations of witches could serve my House."

"Wise indeed." Marcellus congratulated drily. "One hopes you will allow your council to employ the services of your witches, both current and future."

"Of course." Absolutely nothing in his demeanour suggested he was anything other than calm but Oceana knew he had to be raging inside.

There was a moment of silence and then Marcellus returned to his seat. "Thank you Tristan. We will see to it that Wulfric's house is informed of his new status." And just like that they were dismissed. Oceana was immeasurably grateful that Tristan took her arm as they walked back across the expanse of gleaming black marble. The weight of hundreds of stares was threatening to bring her to her knees. It had gone better than expected but she had been more nervous than she had realised.

"How are you holding up?" Tristan asked under his breath as soon as the doors swung closed behind them and they were out of earshot of the guards.

"I'm okay." She gathered herself enough to smile. "Being angry at you helps."

"What have I done now?" He sounded amused.

"Geez I don't know..." She snarled sarcastically. "How about promising all the future generations of my family to slavery? Or maybe not telling me that I would have to be turned when I signed the papers declaring me your mate? Either or...you pick. Both are pretty damn good reasons in my humble opinion."

He sighed but it wasn't really an offended sound. "We'll discuss this at the flat."

"We're not going to the hotel?" She was startled enough to stop and he pulled her back into motion.

"The others are but you and I are going to the flat. We need some alone time."

"We do?" He didn't answer and her heart sank. She'd known him long enough to understand there was something else going on here, something that was probably going to upset her, but she had no idea what it was.

There were cars waiting outside and after briefly hugging Charlie, Xav and Will Oceana allowed Tristan to settle her in the back seat and waited as he settled in next to her. They sat in silence all the way back to the flat and she waited again as he opened her car door. There was no point arguing with him when he was in this sort of mood.

"Will you be okay for a couple of hours on your own?" He asked her as they closed the door of the flat and moved into the living room. "I have some work to do."

"I'm not a four year old Tristan." She smiled to soften the sting of her words. "I'm sure I can managed a couple of hours by myself."

"I should have booked you into a spa or something." He seemed chagrined and she laughed.

"I don't need to visit a spa. If it makes you feel better I'll take a long hot bath with a cup of tea and a good book."

"Excellent idea. I'll put the kettle on and run the bath. Did you bring a book with you?"

"Yeah. There's a couple in my overnight bag." He shooed her out of the room to go and fetch a book from her bag and made her a cup of tea while the bath ran.

"I like doing this." He said as she settled into the bubbles. He sounded bewildered by the realisation. "Taking care of you I mean."

She burst out laughing. "You sound so offended about it."

"Well it is something of an alien concept." He chuckled. "I'd better leave before I give up on work and climb in there with you."

"Will you light the candles for me before you go?" She pointed at the row of scented candles on the ledge at the end of the bath.

"Sure." He lit them quickly and then pressed a kiss to the top of her head. "They don't smell as good as you."

"Yeah yeah, I know. I smell good enough to eat..." She made a face at him but he looked hurt.

"That's not what I meant!" He protested. "Not everything I say is a joke. I do genuinely care about you."

"I know." She examined the ring on her finger. "I know you care. We just have...different frames of reference."

"We are lifetimes apart in experience. We're bound to have different frames of reference." His voice seemed full of nostalgic melancholia. "Enjoy your bath princess. I'll come find you when I'm done." He left, leaving her wondering what the hell had just happened.

***

She soaked in the bath until her fingers were like raisins and then made her way through to the bedroom, where she dried her hair and pinned it up out of the way. Sitting before the mirror she plugged her iPod into the dock and let the music flow over her softly as she cleansed and toned her face, cooling her freshly steamed skin with cucumber, aloe and rose.

She was just shimmying into a summer dress when Tristan appeared in the doorway and swept her into a dance. "What is this song?" He asked as they waltzed around the bed, swaying gently as the soft music wrapped around them.

"It's A Thousand Years by Christina Perri."

"The words are so apt." He twirled her and they moved smoothly on.

"It was recorded for a vampire movie I think." She smiled, resting her head against his chest. "One of those with the limpid teenagers."

"That does detract slightly from its charm." He joked. "No really, it is a beautiful song."

"It's one of my favourites." They moved on in silence, dancing until the music ended and he released her. "Did you get your work done?" She asked quietly. It was so hard to stay mad at him when he was like this, so charming and attentive.

"Just about. I've got a bit more to do in the morning but I missed you."

"You missed me?" She blushed. "You saw me just over an hour ago."

"I know. But I knew you were in here and you smell like the spring and then I heard you singing and I didn't want to be at my desk any more."

"You can be very sweet sometimes."

"It's you." He kissed the tip of her nose. "You make me less and yet more at the same time. I'm so sorry Oceana."

"For what?" She let him pull her back into a hug, leaning against the smooth planes of his chest.

"For everything. For crashing into your life like a wrecking ball. For taking you away from everything that's familiar. For taking away your choices and manipulating you into signing the contract. I wish I could make it right but I wasn't lying to you. I don't know how to let you be anything other than mine."

"What's done is done." She said philosophically, her bath and the gentle waltzing having lulled her into a state of zen-like calm. "Just don't make those mistakes in the future. You can still let me have choices Tris. I can still have a family and my own home. You just have to be prepared to compromise. Not controlling every moment of my life doesn't make me any less yours."

"I'll try." He cupped the back of her head, his fingers twining into her hair. "Will you let me love you 'Cean? Now?"

She had never heard him sound so lost or fragile and it made her undone. "Yes."

"Good." He tilted her face back and kissed her gently, moving them back towards the bed where he laid her down and proceeded to worship every inch of her body with a tender reverence, filling her so completely and deeply that it felt as though he was connecting to her soul with each breath and moan. When she came it was so intense that she felt as though the blood in her veins had vaporised, sending her floating weightless into a blinding light. She never noticed the pain at her neck or the whispered apology that sent her free-falling from the light into a numbing, soothing night. In the end, she knew only darkness.

CHAPTER SIXTEEN

Oceana slept fitfully and awoke feeling achy and thirsty. She blinked blearily at the curtains which were dappled with bright morning sunlight and pushed the covers off, registering that there was music playing somewhere in the flat. Tristan must have been up already. Feeling a little woozy she got to her feet and went to the bathroom intending to have a shower but got as far as cleaning her teeth before she had to sit down.

"Hey, are you okay?" Tristan appeared in the doorway wearing just his jeans. "I didn't hear you get up."

"I feel terrible." She hung her head between her knees as she sat on the edge of the bath. "I think I'm coming down with something."

"You're coming back from something." He knelt in front of her. "I'm so sorry. I got carried away...it was the music and the dancing and it was just so incredible...I bit you by accident."

"You bit me?" She jerked her head up and felt her neck. There was no mark. "How long have I been out for?"

"Just over two and a half days. You must be hungry. And thirsty."

"Two and a half days?" She was totally bewildered. How did you just lose two and a half days of your life?

"I'm really sorry. It won't happen again."

"No it's okay." He looked so worried that she forgave him. She'd let him bite her once before and had agreed to maybe doing it again so it wasn't as though he'd done something she abhorred.

"Let's get you a drink." He scooped her up and carried her down to the kitchen, sitting her at the breakfast bar and pouring a tall glass full of apple juice. "Drink that and I'll fill the next one with ice." He ordered, grabbing a packet of paracetamol and setting it on the counter next to the glass. "You still feel a little warm."

"How are the plans coming along?" She asked, her voice a little gravelly with the delicious chill sliding down her throat from the glass. She'd been out for almost 3 days right in the middle of all the planning?

"Good." He watched her carefully as though she might shatter at any moment. "The caterers and music have all been organised. I've booked a photographer. Wulfric's family are arriving at the estate tomorrow. The flowers have been chosen and the ice sculptures ordered. The rest of my House are already gathering at the estate. Oliver is on standby. We're ready to roll."

"When are we going in?" She swallowed the rest of the apple juice and he took the glass to refill it.

"We're going in the morning of the ball. You are staying here."

"You should take me with you!" She protested. "No-one else is gifted like me."

"But you are also untrained. I couldn't bear for anything to happen to you." He filled her glass with crushed ice. "We know what we're doing princess. We'll be fine. I need you here in case there are any slip-ups with the plans for the ball. We've got to maintain the image until it's too late."

"Are you sure breaking into a secure facility in broad daylight is the wisest option?" She asked dubiously, knowing when the battle was lost.

"It's when they'll be least expecting it. Security is also lower during the day." He set her refilled glass down on the counter in front of her and put his arms around her. "In three days time this will all be over."

"What will happen afterwards?" She leaned against him and breathed in deeply. "With the council gone who will lead?"

"That's not our problem." He shrugged easily. "My hope is that my people will embrace democracy and elect new leaders."

"Would they elect you to lead?"

"I don't think so." He gave a self-deprecating smile. "I've been doing my job for so long that most of them are terrified of me. To my own kind I will always be the stuff nightmares are made of."

"That doesn't mean you aren't clever or wise or capable of leading." She pointed out and he laughed.

"I have no desire to lead. If they elected me in a moment of madness I would turn it down. I don't even know that I would remain Executioner."

"What would you do instead?" She asked curiously and his arms tightened around her.

"Stay home with you. Learn to be a better man. I've had enough of death and destruction. I don't want to become like the council members…losing my humanity to the point where it's okay to play war on a global scale just for the hell of it. I'm not far off but I'm not there yet."

"You'll never be like them Tris." She squeezed his forearms reassuringly. "Even when I met you I knew you still had an understanding of right and wrong." She shuddered. "I guess I never realised how twisted the council are until that Octavius dude was ready to get his rocks off in front of everyone else. That poor girl." She shook her head slightly. "I know that under the terms of our agreement you could order me to do that but you wouldn't because it's wrong. That's the difference."

"No." He disagreed. "The difference there is that Christa was just a pet. I love you. I would never shame you in front of others."

She smiled softly. "Right or wrong, it's love that makes the difference."

He chuckled with her. "I've been listening to that damn song on repeat since you went under."

"Which song?"

"The one we were dancing to. The one about loving you for a thousand years and loving you for a thousand more."

"I love that song. Maybe we can dance again later." Her stomach growled loudly, startling them both. "Did I eat at all while I was down?"

"No. But I had the fridge restocked for when you woke up." He released her. "I don't know how to cook or I'd have made you something."

"It's okay." Her legs were feeling a lot less wobbly after the sweet juice so she slid off the stool and went to rummage in the fridge. It was full of food but she just fancied scrambled eggs and smoked salmon and before long she had a pan on the hob and bread in the toaster. "Are we returning to the Estate today?" She asked as he set out a plate and cutlery for her.

"No. We're staying here until the ball. You have a dress fitting tomorrow." He sliced a lemon into wedges and set two on the edge of the plate. "I just wanted us to get some alone time before it all kicked off."

"Oh okay." The thought made her feel warm inside. For all he was a domineering jerk most of the time, when he was like this, all vulnerable and loving, she couldn't help but care about him.

"I ordered a load of DVDs." He smiled proudly and she hid a grin, realising he'd probably never ordered a DVD in his life before, whatever the collection of classic films in his library looked like. "I thought we could watch them together."

"Sounds lovely." She gave him a genuine smile in return. "You'll have to teach me the basics of dancing too. I'm okay when I'm with you but if I have to dance with anyone else at the ball they might not be such a good lead and then I'll embarrass myself."

"I just won't let you dance with anyone else." He shrugged easily. "It's not like we'll have much time for dancing before all hell breaks loose anyway."

"That's true." A cold stab of fear slid through her belly and she shivered.

"You'll be fine." He covered her hand with his own and squeezed it. "I won't let anything happen to you."

"I know." She raised his hand to her lips and kissed it. "I know."

***

They spent the next three days cocooned in the flat, watching DVDs and laughing while she ate too much ice cream and they had popcorn fights. Tristan was so relaxed for the first time that he seemed almost human. They danced and made love, took baths together and watched the sun rise and set. He sat in the kitchen watching with fascination as she cooked and tasted a little bit of everything from her tongue. It was a magical time.

The morning of the ball he rose with the sun at 4am and took a shower while she dragged herself sleepily through to the kitchen to make him coffee for the road. "When I'm gone you should go back to bed for a few hours." He told her when he emerged, kissing the top of her head as he held her close. "It's going to be a long day and you don't have to be at the hotel until midday."

"I will." She promised. She handed him the flask of coffee and abruptly her eyes filled with tears. "Be careful today, okay?" She swiped at her face. "You bring everyone back to me in one piece, you hear?"

"Will do." He set the flask down and hugged her with both arms. "We'll be fine. Don't worry about us. Jo will be on her way down this morning to keep you company. And don't forget your dress is being delivered this morning. You'll have to sign for it."

"I know." She didn't want to let him go but she knew if she didn't he would be late so she reluctantly released him. "*The widest land Doom takes to part us, leaves thy heart in mine With pulses that beat double.*" She quoted softly and his face lit up in a dazzling smile.

"Are you quoting me love poetry?" She blushed and tried to look away but he tilted her face towards him. "Did you just quote me love poetry?"

"Yes I think I did." She snatched her chin back and meticulously studied the floor. "It just seemed appropriate at the time."

He laughed and gathered her up all over again, swinging her round with joyous abandon. "That's made my day." He crowed triumphantly. "I knew you would come to love me."

"I don't know that I love you." She said crossly. "It was more that I don't want to lose you and I'm afraid."

"You're so cute when you're cross." He planted a kiss on her nose as he set her back on the floor and she glowered at him.

"And you're so annoying when you're gloating." She shot back. "Go get in the car. You're going to be late."

"I know." He checked his watch and then cupped her cheek in his palm. "I love you." He told her seriously. "I'll be back this afternoon."

"Be safe." She rose up on tiptoes and kissed him tenderly. "I'll be waiting." And with that he was gone.

***

As promised, she went back to bed and slept until the postman arrived just after 9am. She was eating breakfast when Jo arrived and they sat in worried silence together as Oceana finished eating.

"Do you love him?" Jo asked suddenly when Oceana was done eating and they had moved to the bedroom. She was sat on Oceana's bed while Oceana got dressed.

"Who? Tristan?" Oceana smoothed down the maxi dress she had slipped on. It was too hot in the city for jeans.

"Yes Tristan. I don't understand why you signed that contract. Will is devastated."

"He didn't leave me a choice." Oceana didn't want to talk about it. She sat at her dressing table and tried to tease her curls into some sort of order. "I can't regret the things I've done for the good of others. Just leave it at that."

"Will you ever be free of him?" Jo got up and stood behind her, taking the comb from Oceana and starting to work on her hair.

"Probably not." Oceana's shoulders slumped. "But then he would never let me go, whether I signed his contract or not."

"You have to find a way, when this is all over." Jo couldn't meet her eyes in the mirror. "It's starting to sink in you know...all the things I've lost by becoming this...by becoming vampire. It's against every law of nature. The inability to have children is just so...crushing. I guess I never realised how much I wanted it until I couldn't have it any more. Same with my job. I loved it and I had to give it up. The idea that you will grow old and die and I'll remain forever this way...without you." She shuddered. "It doesn't bear thinking about. I don't know how to reconcile myself with it. You have to get out before it's too late."

"It's already too late." Oceana touched the pearls dangling on her masquerade mask where Tristan had left it sat on the glass top. "I'm something more than human, less than vampire. I was already on the fringes of this world. I was just too ignorant to know it."

"You could still go back!" Jo insisted but Oceana was shaking her head sadly.

"How do you go back? After this? How do you pretend that everything is normal when you've had your eyes opened to what's really out there?"

"You pretend it never happened!" Jo said fiercely and Oceana sighed.

"I pretend *you* never happened? My best friend for the last eight years? I just pretend you never happened because you're something else now?"

"Sometimes when you love someone you have to set them free." Jo's hands were shaking and Oceana turned around on the stool to face her.

"You and I both know that's not Tristan's mentality Jo. As far as he's concerned if you love someone and they don't come back within 20 seconds, you hunt them down and make them sign a damn contract." She smiled to show the humour behind her words. "It's too late. I'm here and I'll make the most of the hand I've been dealt. Some day it will get easier."

"I'm scared for you." Jo sounded lost and Oceana took her hands, squeezing them gently.

"I'm scared for all of us. But we'll be okay. I promise."

***

Her dress arrived shortly after 11 and they had one last fitting before leaving the flat for the hotel. Oceana had been expecting to catch the tube but Tristan had arranged for a car to pick them up and they were driven to the hotel in air-conditioned luxury. It was a stark reminder of the things she'd have to give up if she ever did manage to leave him.

When they arrived the ballroom was coming along well. Candles were being installed in sconces and candelabras on the tables. Flower arrangements were appearing here and there. The ceiling was draped in diaphanous blue and green fabrics the colour of sea foam and Oceana smiled looking up at them. Tristan had done his best to show it was in her honour.

"I don't understand why you need caterers at a party for vampires." Jo was frowning at the tables where silver platters were being laid out for a cold buffet. "It's not like we eat anything."

"Not everyone that's coming is a vampire." Oceana pointed out. "I eat. I gather the councillors have some humans amongst their entourages. They'll need to eat too. The hotel is putting on the food for you guys."

"For 'food' read 'people'." Jo muttered under her breath. "I still think it's fucked up." Oceana agreed with her silently but didn't say anything, moving instead to examine the gift bags that had been laid out in the antechamber to the ballroom. The hotel manager was there overseeing proceedings and he bowed low to her.

"Welcome, Mistress, welcome." He straightened. "I hope everything is meeting your expectations?"

"You've done an excellent job." Feeling uncomfortable at being in charge Oceana tried to smile at him. "Is there anything I can do? The master sent me here to oversee proceedings but it seems you have it all in hand."

"The Executioner did suggest you would like to approve the catering for this evening." He offered. "If you'd like to come with me I can take you to the kitchens where you can speak to the chefs directly."

"Thank you." She followed him obediently and spent an enjoyable hour in the kitchen with the chefs going over the menus for the evening. The food was spectacular and her taste buds were tingling when she left the kitchens. When she emerged the flowers were all done and the room was almost ready apart from a small stage being set up at the far end for the musicians. The ice sculptures Tristan had requested would be delivered at the last minute.

"I don't think there's anything else we can do." Jo had checked everything off against the list Tristan had left her. "We just need to get you home and fed and then even more impossibly beautiful than you are already."

"It's only half past one." Oceana grumbled. "It doesn't take that many hours to get ready. The party doesn't start until eight."

"You have an appointment at the salon for a facial and a haircut." Jo had the grace to look embarrassed. "Tristan arranged them while you were ill. By the time we've made it back across town and you've had lunch it'll be time to head out again."

Oceana had to smile as they headed across the lobby towards the reception desk. "That man..." She shook her head. "Managing me again. He thinks if he keeps me busy I won't worry about them." They said goodbye to the manager at the desk, reassuring him that everything was coming along nicely and then waited out the front for the car to pull round.

"How do you suppose they're getting on?" Jo glanced sideways at her and Oceana shrugged.

"I don't know." She checked her phone again for the millionth time. "There's no word yet. I'm sure if something had gone wrong one of them would have let me know. It'll have taken them a while to get there and back anyway. It's an hour and a half from the house to Cambridge and we have no idea what state the captives will be in. They may have detoured to seek medical assistance."

"I can't believe you're so calm about all this." Jo sounded almost accusing as they climbed in the car and Oceana slumped against the cool leather of the seat gratefully.

"I'm not calm. I'm just trusting them to know what they're doing." She allowed herself a small smile. "He promised he would love me for a thousand more."

"Huh?" Jo blinked and Oceana laughed.

"Never mind. It's a private joke. Let's just get back to the flat. I'm starving."

***

If Tristan had a heart beat it would have stopped when Wulfric tried to lead the escape from the captives' quarters and rebounded from some invisible barrier. This was bad, *bad* news.

"Is it a ward?" Will was just as shocked as he stepped up to the door and examined the frame, pushing his hand futilely against the opening.

"What the fuck are you doing?" Oliver sounded tinny in Tristan's ears. "Why are you just standing there?"

"Oliver have you got eyes on the other side of this door?" Tristan barked, his mind skimming through the possibilities.

"Yes." He could hear the clacking of keys. "There's a camera at the far end of the corridor."

"Study the doorframe. I need to know if there's anything there."

"Stand by."

"This is bad." Wulfric turned to Tristan as they waited. "If the council has a witch they probably already know we're here."

"It was always a possibility, my brother." Tristan clasped Wulfric's arm and gripped his shoulder. "If we go down at the ball, we'll still go down fighting." His grin was full of fierce joy and Wulfric let it rise through him, grinning back.

"Yes we will, brother."

Tristan's ear peace crackled as Oliver came back on the line. "There's something above the door. I can't focus clearly enough to see what it is though."

Tristan grinned. There was no chance the witch was as good as his Oceana. "We can't use the doors boys." He winked at a vampire hefting a war axe. "So we'll go through the walls. We're leaving this place as the crow flies."

"Yes master." With a buoyant smile, the vampire charged the wall and they began to break their way out.

***

Tristan had still not returned by the time the two girls had emerged from the salon, primped and glamorous, and Oceana was really starting to worry. She checked her phone when they got in and there was nothing. It was almost seven o'clock and he had never intended to be this late.

"I think you should call him." Jo watched her pacing up and down the living room. "They must be out by now."

"You're right. Something must have happened." Oceana stopped pacing and pulled her phone out of her pocket but just as she was dialling they heard a key in the lock and she rushed to the front hall. "Tristan!" She hurled herself into his arms, knocking the breath out of him.

"Steady princess." He laughed. "Why aren't you in your dress yet? The car will be here soon. You look beautiful."

"You were late and I was so worried and I thought something had happened and I didn't know-" He cut off her garbled concerns with a kiss.

"I'm fine. We're all fine. We got all the captives out safely and Wulfric and his House are taking them to where they can get help." He brushed away a smear of lipstick with his thumb and gently set her back on the floor. "Go get your dress on. I need to shower."

"Why were you so late?" She didn't move and his eyes clouded with concern tinged with anger.

"There were wards at the facility. It took us some time to get past them and the human captives were in a much worse state than expected. We had to find somewhere safe to leave them."

"Wards?" Oceana's eyes widened. "The council has a witch working for them?"

"Not a very good one." He chucked her under the chin. "Whoever it is had nothing on you. They might even have bought the wards from an independent."

"What if the wards notified the council that the facility was broken into?" Jo asked and Tristan shrugged philosophically.

"They have no way of knowing it was us that did it. As far as they know I've been here organising a party all week and they think Wulfric's House is an enemy of mine for the death of their sire. We'll just have to brazen it out."

"I don't like it." Oceana murmured and he kissed her again.

"We'll be fine. Go get your dress on, quickly. We haven't got long." He propelled her along the corridor. "You too Jo. Get your dress on. Quickly."

***

They dressed in a flurry of activity and by the time the car pulled up outside at twenty past they were just about ready. Tristan's hair was still wet as he laced up the back of Oceana's ball gown but it wouldn't take long to dry. It was a warm evening and they wouldn't be greeting guests for another forty minutes.

"You look incredible." Jo's jaw dropped when Oceana appeared at the top of the stairs clutching her mask in hand.

"Thanks. You're looking pretty extraordinary yourself." Oceana blushed as she headed down and straightened Tristan's tie before he opened the door. "We're all looking pretty spiffy tonight."

"Spiffy." Tristan's lips twitched as he ushered them out into the street. "That's not something I've ever been called before."

"Add it to my list of words for you." Oceana grinned and he burst out laughing.

"Yeah, along with 'mothersucker' and 'fangboy'. At least spiffy is a compliment."

"Don't you forget anything?" She demanded, going a little red under her make-up and he shook his head playfully.

"No, those ones I specifically noted in my journal for future reference. I still laugh every time I remember you standing there bold as brass saying 'Bite me mothersucker'. Funniest. Thing. *Ever.*"

"You said that?" Even Jo was amused and Oceana climbed into the car, ignoring the laughter. It was her attitude that had landed her in this mess. Had she been a sweet and docile thing she probably would have got out eventually, like the mysterious Mary. She must have been out of Tristan's control if she'd managed to get herself burnt at the stake. He'd never have let that happen. Instead she'd opened her big mouth and laid down some attitude and ended up contracted into the nearest thing to an infinite marriage the vampires had. Who knew they'd find it irresistible?

Tristan's men were waiting at the hotel when they arrived and Will's jaw dropped when he saw Oceana. "You look amazing!" He breathed. Charlie, Xav, Robbie and the others swung round.

"It's a beautiful dress." Oceana blushed and Tristan squeezed her hand. The bodice was pale blue lace that matched exactly the colour of Tristan's eyes, hand stitched with pearls and crystals that sparkled in the light. The skirt was full and layered with lace and silk and satin in a way that caught and shimmered in the light. It was a spectacular dress and she didn't want to know how much it had cost. She knew that she and Tristan together were dazzling – he all shades of ice and night, she all sunshine and golden hair, tied together by the cornflower blue.

"You are beautiful." He smiled down at her, raising their joined hands to his lips. "There's not a dress on earth that could compare to what's within."

"Can we stop with the love please?" She shifted, embarrassed. "Has anyone arrived yet?"

"No." Robbie was the first to stop staring. "Reception called through to say that cars were starting to arrive but no-one has appeared as yet."

"Then, my mated companion, may I have the first dance?" Tristan grinned and pulled her through to the ballroom. It was even more spectacular than it had been that morning and Oceana caught her breath. The ice sculptures shone, bathed in blue lights, and everywhere the facets of crystals caught the candlelight, scattering prismatic rays all around.

"Oh Tris!" She gasped. "It's beautiful!"

"I'm only ever going to mate once." He pulled her into his arms. "I may as well do it properly." He nodded to the musicians who struck up a new melody and they whirled around the empty floor, spinning and flowing with the music, letting it carry them away from the events of the day until there was only the two of them in the whole world, wrapped in each other's arms and moving to each other's beat.

When the music finally tailed away there was a small scattering of applause from the guests who had started to arrive and Tristan bowed to Oceana. "I do love you." He whispered. "I know I may not show it in the most human of ways but whatever happens, I beg of you – do not doubt it."

"I won't." She held his gaze for a moment before he kissed her and then they left the floor to begin greeting the guests.

***

At 10 o'clock Oceana stiffened slightly. "What is it?" Xav was standing with her by the doors watching the whirling mass of masked dancers on the floor. Tristan was away speaking to other Masters of Houses and had left the blond vampire to watch over her.

"The councillors are on their way." Her eyes were slightly unfocused as she struggled to maintain her grasp on the resonance with the wards she had placed on them. "They'll be here in the next ten minutes."

"Charlie, Will." Xav snapped and they turned from where they were standing about 20 feet away. He gestured and they excused themselves and rushed over. "The councillors are coming." He told them quietly but urgently. "Guard Oceana. I will fetch the master."

"Of course." They stood to either side of her and Oceana turned slightly.

"Can you guys relax slightly?" She murmured. "You look like sentinels. The council sees you behaving like this, they'll know something is up."

"Sorry." Will shifted his feet and Charlie cleared his throat.

"It's been a long day." Charlie admitted and Oceana touched his arm.

"I know. But I'm so proud of you guys. You saved a lot of people today."

"It'll be over soon." Tristan murmured from behind her and she resisted the urge to lean back into him for comfort. They were all on edge.

"Some wedding party this is." She joked as they waited and some of the tension eased slightly.

"We'll make it up to you." Will promised, his light voice disguising the hurt in his eyes.

"Too right you will." She swatted his arm playfully and then turned to Tristan. "They're here."

"Okay." She saw it, the moment he steeled himself, and then he flowed into his most charming mode and turned to the door to greet their latest guests. The council members swept in as one unit and she was pleased to see that they were all wearing the masks she had made. They stopped just within the door and looked around, cowing the room under the weight of those ancient gazes. The music stopped instantly and everyone hushed, dropping into bows or curtseys. Oceana followed everyone else's lead as Tristan stepped forward. "Councillors." He greeted warmly. "Welcome to the masquerade. We are honoured to have you here."

"Your invite was most gracious." A tiny oriental woman inclined her head slightly. "Please continue."

"Yes, Councillor Ling." Tristan nodded to the string octet who struck up again with the music and slowly couples began dancing again. Oceana didn't realise she'd been holding her breath until she rose to her full height and moved to Tristan's side to greet the councillors individually. He had told her their names but right then she couldn't remember any of them and just smiled and nodded as they complimented her dress and the room, returning the compliments as best she could in the flowery language they were accustomed to.

Most of them moved off to greet other Masters of Houses in the room but Octavius lingered in front of them. "May I have this dance?" He murmured politely to Tristan who nodded.

"Of course." He stepped aside and, trying to ignore the way her skin was crawling, Oceana accepted the councillor's arm and allowed him to draw her out onto the dance floor. Other dancers respectfully made space for them and he took her into his arms.

"So, you've mated with the Executioner." It wasn't really a question but he looked at her expectantly.

"Yes. He's a masterful being." She managed to restrain herself from snorting at the compliment but it was the only really appropriate thing she could say.

"You are the first mate he has ever taken." He continued, ignorant of her internal amusement. "I am curious as to what is so special about you."

"I challenge him." She caught a stumble as he abruptly changed direction. "I was never the meek and docile type. I suspect he finds it refreshing."

"You underestimate your charm." He gave her a smile that felt like slime dripping down her neck. "You are power and charisma in a most exquisite package." He changed direction again. "Should there come a time when you wish to leave the Executioner I would be most glad to have you as an addition to my House."

"You are most kind." She forced a grin and prayed silently that the music would be over soon. She felt like she needed a shower. "But I love Tristan. I cannot envisage leaving him any time in the foreseeable future."

"Love?" He let out a long peal of laughter that startled everyone close to them. "I see you are amusing as well as charming. Think on my offer witch."

"Of course Councillor." The music drew to a close and Oceana fought the urge to dry-scrub her arms when he released her but, before she could find Tristan, Marcellus stepped up.

"May I have the honour?"

Cursing inside, Oceana gave him a dazzling smile. "The honour is all mine Councillor Marcellus." Octavius stepped aside and Marcellus took his place as the music started again. He was a much better dancer than Octavius had been but neither matched up to Tristan and Oceana was struggling to concentrate on the movement as well as maintaining her distance.

"Congratulations." He smiled down at her. "The Executioner...quite a catch."

"He pursued me." She responded truthfully. "Lucky for us both that I am more than passing fond of him."

"It seems the members of his house have fallen under your spell also." It was a throwaway comment but something in it set Oceana's nerves jangling.

"It is just the fascination one feels towards creatures that are other than oneself." She dismissed. "Our mortality makes us see life differently. I am the first real human interaction they have encountered for centuries."

"We all find you fascinating." His smiled was glittering and cold below his mask. "Should anything befall the Executioner you would be more than welcome as a member of my House."

"As his mate I assume I would be the property of whoever challenged him." She smiled sweetly. "Not that anyone would win of course. The Master is a warrior without compare and where he is otherwise engaged I am more than capable of defending our bond."

"Yes, your display did not go unnoticed." He was about to say something else when the music faltered and then died altogether in a cacophony of discordant sound.

"What's happened to the music?" Oceana turned to look but then the screaming started and Marcellus grabbed her arm in a vice-like grip.

"You will come with me, Witch." He snarled, all pretence of charm gone.

"Let me go!" She struggled uselessly against him. "Tristan! Tristan!"

"Silence!" He roared, slapping her hard across the face. She slumped, dazed, to her knees, the coppery tang of blood filling her mouth.

"Oceana!" She heard Tristan calling her name somewhere in the room and then Will was there, sword in hand looking fearsome. Vampires were screaming and scattering everywhere but Oceana could see bodies on the floor as Marcellus tried to drag her away.

"Marcellus!" Challenged Will. "Let her go!"

"She will be mine." Marcellus flung her behind him and she slid across the polished floor until she crashed in a tangle of flailing limbs into the body of one of the waiters. Rising to all fours she tried to stop her head spinning but the floor felt like it was tilting. She dragged her mask off and discarded it where it fell, splattered with the blood she spat out.

"Oceana!" Tristan sounded furious and she raised up on wobbly knees to try and see him. Marcellus and Will were still battling it out near her and she staggered sideways to look around them. There was a huge cluster of people by the doors and she could hear sounds of fierce fighting in between the guests trying to flee.

Finally she spotted his dark curls whirling about in the section where the fighting was thickest and began to crawl towards him until the ground stopped moving enough for her to get up. Her ears were ringing but her balance was improving. The last of the guests had left and Tristan and his House were battling furiously with the councillors. Xav was already down, pinned to the floor with a sword through his chest. Charlie had been skewered to the wall but the others were still standing and Will looked to be getting the better of Marcellus.

And then she saw her. Out of the corner of her eye Oceana saw a tiny figure in a silver dress hold her hand up and point to Tristan. The dots all connected in her head in a bright flash of fiery agony...the wards at Venogen...the council's suspicion...of course they had brought their witch to bring him to heel. "No!" She screamed. "Tristan, no!"

The girl in silver screamed *"Extinguo!"* and Tristan just dropped to his knees as though his strings had been cut.

"Tristan!" Oceana screamed and ran for him but before she could get there Octavius had swung his sword in a massive sweep and taken Tristan's head clean off at the shoulders. *"Tristan!"* Oceana screamed and screamed until the sound drowned out all the air in the room. Her rage and grief lit within her like a swelling ocean and she lashed out, the masks the councillors were wearing instantly pulverising their heads as they dropped like flies around the room.

Still screaming, Oceana called all the metal in the room to her and wrapped it around the girl in silver until she too had been pulverised in amidst agonised screams and the gurgles and pops of snapping bones and flesh.

She screamed until her voice was gone and then she crawled across the floor to where her beautiful master lay and rested her head on his chest, sobbing helplessly and ignoring the blood that soaked into a dress the colour of eyes that would never behold her again.

CHAPTER SEVENTEEN

A week later they were at the Estate when the chimes started outside. "Oceana, my love." Will spoke quietly from the doorway of Tristan's bedroom where Oceana was lying in bed, holding on to the last few things that smelled like him. "The Lore maker is here with Tristan's will and testament. You have to get up."

She ignored him, gazing listlessly at the play of light on the drapes from the window. "I'll get her dressed." Jo sounded hushed as she came in beside Will.

"Make it quick." Will sounded sympathetic. "I'll try and stall him for a few minutes."

"I'll do what I can." Jo physically hauled her out of bed, patiently unfolding her every time she tried to curl in on herself to nurse the grief that was clawing her hollow. She wrestled her into a plum-coloured dress and pinned her hair back in a quick French twist, slipping ballet shoes onto her feet. "Come on Ana." She muttered, scrubbing her face with a wet wipe. "Snap out of it. This is important."

"He's gone. How can it be important?" Oceana tried to curl up again and this time Jo actually slapped her.

"Get a grip!" She snapped, colour rising high in her cheeks. "You think this is going to bring him back? Well do you?"

Oceana stared at her in stunned silence for a moment and then her face crumpled. "I miss him Jo."

"I know sweetie." Grateful for the most lucidity she'd seen in a week, Jo gathered her up in a hug. "We all do. But the others need you. I need you. Come back to us." She let her sob for a few moments and then she pulled back, handing her some tissues. "Come on. We'll go listen to the reading and then we can celebrate his extraordinary life. The others are waiting for you."

"Okay. Just give me a moment, please. I'll be down in a sec."

Jo gave her a measuring look and seemed happy with what she saw. "Fine. I'll wait with the others downstairs."

When Oceana emerged her eyes were dry and although she was pale she walked with her back straight and her gaze clear. "Sorry to keep you waiting." Her voice was gravelly with grief but she managed to maintain a serene posture as they gathered in the dining room.

The lore maker was the first old vampire she had seen. He must have been turned in his late 60s but he still looked hale and hearty, even with his white hair and wrinkles. "Is that it?" He asked as they filed into the room. "Are we all here?" Mia slipped through the door and knelt at Oceana's feet, wrapping a comforting hand around her ankle as she stared around defying anyone to comment. Oceana touched her hair briefly in thanks and the lore maker cleared his throat. "Yes. Well. Then I shall begin. The Executioner had a most unusual will. Although I have the official documents with me, it was his express request that the contents of this letter and parcel be delivered to one Lady Oceana of this House to be read by her and her alone before the remainder of the will is read to the House as a whole."

Everyone shifted uncomfortably as he passed a parcel and an envelope down the table to her and she lifted them with shaking hands. The parcel was tied loosely with string and she untied it, letting the paper fall away unnoticed to the floor. Inside was an iPod, a thick golden band made to fit a man's finger and an ancient book. It took her three attempts to get the ear plugs in, her hands were shaking so badly, but eventually she managed it and pressed play. Instantly the sound of Christina Perri singing A Thousand Years filled her head and she closed her eyes and wept. It was a reminder of such a happy time, the two of them dancing in the flat, throwing popcorn at each other and laughing until they hurt. As the music played on she managed to gather herself, wiped her eyes and studied the book. Opening the front cover, she flicked through the first few pages and realised that it was a Book of Shadows but it wasn't like any she had seen before.

"That's Mary's." Will spoke just loud enough for her to hear over the music. "I recognise her writing."

So this was the Book of Shadows belonging to his dead companion? Oceana had no idea why he had entrusted it to her unless there was something she needed to learn from it. Setting the book down she reached for the envelope. It was addressed to her in Tristan's bold script and she took a moment to trace the letters before opening it up and starting to read.

Princess,

If you are reading this then I am dead and you are about to learn that everything you know is untrue. Everything, that is, except my love for you which is as honest and deep as the ocean for which you are named. Please bear that in mind as you read on.

The first thing you leave behind when you become a vampire is your sense of morality. All life becomes a game, a twisted masquerade where everyone is a pawn to be used to suit your own ends. I used you mercilessly and I will confess all but you should know that it is the hardest thing I have ever done. The remorse I feel is the only thing keeping me upright and loving you and I hope that one day you will forgive me.

I knew I was going to die. If you have already opened the parcel you will know that the book is a Book of Shadows belonging to Mary. I mentioned her to you once. It is her ring that you wear. The last prophecy that she made before she left me concerned my death. It is written on the last page. She foretold that when my heart started beating again and I abandoned all that I was to make a stand in this world, I would be at peace with the gods and it would be my time to die. My stand was against Venogen. I couldn't bring myself to let them unleash such a pointless war, but I never thought I'd have a reason for my heart to beat again. And then I met you.

You told me once that love was something that took time. You are right. Will and I had been watching you for many months before I ever approached you, not the couple of weeks that I once stated. I think I fell for you long before we ever spoke. You were so bright and vibrant, like an hibiscus flower in a bed full of daisies. I did not know that you were a witch but I knew there was something about you that I needed to discover. And as I watched and waited for the right moment to approach you, you stole my heart right out from underneath me. I am sorry that I did not tell you sooner.

There never was a rival family. I staged the attack on your house after I had watched you ward it because I knew it would drive you into my safe-keeping. Likewise, I was behind the attack on Jo. It was never intended as a warning for you my love. It was just another reason to make you stay. You ask why I went to all the trouble of making you come to me when I knew I was going to die? The prophecy concerns you too.

Will is a fine man and he would make a great leader but he is not strong enough to hold my House against the turbulence of the coming days. The prophecy speaks of a strong-willed woman, capable of withstanding any storm. I thought it might be you but I tested it and tested it, almost beyond your endurance. I needed to understand the lengths you would go to, the fears that you would face to protect my family and you never failed me once. The fight with Will, the willingness to submit to me over the issue of Jo, the challenges, the contract...even after I had warned you I would bite you. You are as steadfast and enduring as the ocean my love. You will make a fine leader for my house. A fearsome leader. People will think twice about challenging you after you so easily destroy those that would harm you.

As for how that will happen, I also have a confession to make about the contract. You were never mated to me. After you signed the papers I filled them in with Will's name and made you the dominant partner before I registered them. I knew he loved you but for the few, short months I had left I was too selfish to let you be with anyone other than me. I wanted my last days on this earth to be with you. I hope now you will go to him with my blessing. The ring in the parcel is for sealing the contract. I hope he too will forgive me in time.

Finally, I have one last thing to confess and it is the hardest of all. The Lore makers will insist that to lead my House you must become vampire. To avoid any fighting over levels and succession I have had enough of my venom frozen at a special storage facility in London. The details are written on the back of this letter. If you inject it straight into your heart it will turn you. I know that this is something that you never wanted and ultimately it is your choice. You can choose to walk away and return to your old life and my will has left instructions that no-one is to stop you, but I beg you to please reconsider if that is your immediate wish. I know that you have dreams that becoming a vampire will take away so this was my last gift to you in the days before I died.

When I bit you it wasn't an accident. I knew exactly what I was doing. When you signed the contract I stole your diary and calculated when I thought you would be ovulating. It happened to fall while we were in London and so I bit you and while you were unconscious I had a doctor artificially inseminate you over the course of those three days. It is my hope that as you are reading this you are pregnant. If you are, they cannot force you to change until the child is of an age where it is no longer nursing. There is nothing to stop you conceiving again in that time, unless of course Will has other opinions. It was the only way I knew to protect you. Once again, I am sorry and I hope that you will one day forgive me. Know that for the precious last few days I had you I considered that child to be not just yours but ours. I hope that you look at him or her and remember me and know that I loved you.

I am sure there are many other transgressions I should confess but none as major as those above and right now I can hear you singing along to something on the radio and it's making me smile. I'm going to go and kiss you until you are giggling helplessly in my arms because it's all I have left to live for. There is nothing left to say except this...

Darling, don't be afraid I have loved you for a thousand years. I'll love you for a thousand more.

Tris.

She read the letter end to end twice and then covered her face with her hands, dropping it to the table and pulling the ear plugs out.

"What does it say?" Will asked but she just shook her head, hearing rustling as he scooped the papers up and began to read them. "Oh." He swore softly under his breath as he read Tristan's words and when he was done his hands were shaking as much as Oceana's had been. "Oceana, look at me. Please." She shook her head again so he pushed everyone out of the way and gathered her up in his arms. "Please Oceana, look at me. Tell me. What are you thinking?"

"What am I thinking?" She raised her white face to his and fought the urge to break into hysterical laughter. "Right now what I'm thinking is what the hell am I going to do?"

THE END

If you have enjoyed this then watch out for further books coming in Summer 2012.

Follow me on Twitter: @Alylonna

Read my blog at Wordpress: www.alylonna.wordpress.com

Cover art by Mathew Ward: Follow him on Twitter: @nedling

Editing by KWB